The Trolltooth Wars

It started with an ambush.

When Balthus Dire's bloodlusting Hill Goblins mount their raid on the Strongarm caravan, they little realize what dramatic consequences their actions will have. For that caravan carries cunnelwort, a mystical herb from Eastern Allansia, destined for the evil sorcerer, Zharradan Marr! *War* – between two forces well matched for evil – is soon to ensue . . .

As the war escalates, the Kingdom of Salamonis comes under threat. A champion of the court, Chadda Darkmane, is summoned to undertake a perilous mission. Somehow he must turn the war to the advantage of Salamonis. Somehow he must prevent the bloodshed and chaos a victorious army's invasion of the Vale of Willow would bring about.

The Trolltooth Wars follows Darkmane's journey from Salamonis to the mysterious desert city of Shazâar, to Yaztromo's Tower, south of Darkwood Forest, and finally to Kay-Pong to seek out Zagor, the Warlock of Firetop Mountain.

Will Darkmane succeed in his quest? And will Balthus Dire's chaotics or Zharradan Marr's undead prove victorious? The answers are here, in *The Trolltooth Wars*.

Steve Jackson is a well-known figure in the fantasy gaming world. With Ian Livingstone he co-founded Games Workshop Ltd. In 1982 their first book, *The Warlock of Firetop Mountain*, was published – it was to be the first in the now hugely successful Fighting Fantasy adventure gamebook series. Now, at last, the first Fighting Fantasy novel is here – the start of a new and exciting development that will thrill Fighting Fantasy fans and new readers alike!

Steve Jackson

A Fighting Fantasy Novel

The Trolltooth Wars

Illustrated by Russ Nicholson

PUFFIN BOOKS

PUFFIN BOOKS

Published by the Penguin Group
Penguin Books Ltd, 27 Wrights Lane, London W8 5TZ, England
Viking Penguin, a division of Penguin Books USA Inc.
375 Hudson Street, New York, New York 10014, USA
Penguin Books Australia Ltd, Ringwood, Victoria, Australia
Penguin Books Canada Ltd, 2801 John Street, Markham, Ontario, Canada L3R 1B4
Penguin Books (NZ) Ltd, 182–190 Wairau Road, Auckland 10, New Zealand

Penguin Books Ltd, Registered Offices: Harmondsworth, Middlesex, England

First published 1989
5 7 9 10 8 6 4

Text copyright © Steve Jackson, 1989
Illustrations copyright © Russ Nicholson, 1989
Map copyright © Leo Hartas, 1989
All rights reserved

Printed in England by Clays Ltd, St Ives plc
Filmset in 10/12pt Palatino

Dedicated to J. S.
May his Amonour flourish

Contents

1
THE RAIN OF DEATH   11
2
THE STORM GATHERS   16
3
THE BLACK TOWER   27
4
KING SALAMON'S COURT   35
5
THE CHERVAII   43
6
THUGRUFF'S PLAN   57
7
THE FOREST OF YORE   69
8
THE RAID ON COVEN   87
9
BATTLE PLANS   101
10
SHAZÂAR   109
11
A WARNING FROM LISSAMINA   138
12
A SPIRITUAL JOURNEY   152

The Trolltooth Wars

13
YAZTROMO'S TOWER *160*
14
THE COMING OF THE SORQ *180*
15
INTO THE MOUNTAIN *190*
16
THE BATTLE OF THE PASS *203*
17
ZAGOR'S DOMAIN *219*
18
THE BATTLE IS WON *241*
19
A DARK SECRET *249*
20
INTO THE *GALLEYKEEP* *264*
21
THE FINAL STRUGGLE *273*
22
THE JUDGEMENT *289*

1

The Rain of Death

'Goblins! Goblins!' A voice rang out through the darkness like an alarm bell, shattering the stillness of the night. 'We are under attack! Take guard! Goblins! Ambush!'

But the Strongarm captain's cry of warning came too late. An instant later his screams were silenced when a necklace of blood appeared on his throat; the rabid Hill Goblin chief, wielding a dripping knife, shoved him off his horse and took his place in the saddle. The berserk attacker was foaming at the mouth and cackling with savage joy as he grabbed the horse's reins and yanked them brutally to one side. The frenzied beast resisted, whinnying and bucking, and for an instant its eyes met those of the Goblin. Then the terrified horse turned, as its new master had commanded, to face the terrible scene of carnage lit up in the flickering torchlight.

The caravan had been caught unawares. Thirty-eight Strongarms were no match for the horde of hysterical Hill Goblins dropping on to them from the rocky crags above Trolltooth Pass. Shrieking and whooping, the filthy creatures bowled the Strongarms

11

The Trolltooth Wars

from their mounts and grappled with them on the ground. Blades flashed; screams from both sides rang out, and for a full hour the battle raged.

'Taste blood! Taste blood!' yelled Foulblade from the dead captain's mount. The Goblin chief drew his scimitar, dug his heels into the horse's flanks and galloped into the mêlée. His first slash caught a dismounted Strongarm just below the elbow. The human screamed and watched in horror as his left forearm dropped to the ground, the sword still clutched in his hand. With a maniacal laugh, Foulblade rode on towards his goal: the wagon at the centre of the caravan.

Fighting desperately to keep control of the two drawhorses, Donnag Kannu was on his feet, gripping their bridles to steady them as they tried to break free. His hired Strongarms were making a valiant stand, keeping the Hill Goblins from the wagon, but one by one they were falling to the demented creatures. It was Foulblade's charge which eventually caused their ranks to break, as his scimitar, dark with blood, cut down two more of the Strongarms.

Donnag Kannu reacted instantly. He swung himself up on to one of the drawhorses and, grabbing his mane, he urged it into a head-on gallop towards the charging Goblin chief. The frantic beast bolted, dragging the other drawhorse with it. But the second horse, once given a lead to follow, immediately took up the pace, and the wagon lurched forward, picking up speed. Foulblade was forced to swerve to one side to avoid the collision, and pulled his horse up short as the wagon thundered past him. He ground his sharp teeth and snarled angrily as he turned to take

The Rain of Death

up the pursuit. He would not be denied his victory prize!

His scimitar bit once more; but this time it was the flanks of his own horse which felt its bite. The terrified steed, though exhausted, gave a high-pitched squeal and leapt forward with renewed vigour, through the Goblins and Strongarms locked in battle, to pursue the wagon. Again the scimitar slashed, and bloodied the beast's other flank. He was closing rapidly on the wagon!

Seconds later the two were alongside each other. The Goblin steadied himself. Then, with a daring leap, he jumped from his horse on to the wagon. Donnag Kannu looked round in despair to see the bulky creature crawling awkwardly over the jostling wagon to its seat, where the reins were tied. Its gnarled fingers grasped the reins and tugged on them. The confused horses reacted hesitantly but their pace began to slow. An evil grin spread across Foulblade's mouth as he sensed success.

Kannu thought quickly. With a shortsword he was no match for a fully armoured Goblin chief. Cargo or no cargo, he must escape! Instinctively he drew his sword and, with a swift chop, slashed through the horse's traces and dug in his heels. The leather parted instantly and his mount broke free of the harness that bound it to the wagon. As he galloped off into the night, Kannu turned to see the Goblin chief standing, cursing, on the wagon behind him. The creature may have won its prize, but his orders had been to leave no survivors: his master would not be pleased. And little did he know of the consequences of his failure. How could he guess the events that were to follow?

*

13

The Trolltooth Wars

When Foulblade arrived back at the scene of the ambush, the battle was over. His Goblin pack had been reduced in numbers, but they had still overwhelmed the Strongarms. Mutilated bodies from both sides littered the area. The surviving Goblins were recovering. In the cool night air their panting breath steamed from their snub noses and wide mouths. They snarled ineffectually at their lifeless foes and one or two were feasting on the still-warm horseflesh. The younger members of the party were taking delight in tormenting a couple of badly wounded Strongarms whom they had found. Their swords would eventually silence their prisoners' whimperings, but not until they had had their fun.

The Goblin chief climbed down from the wagon and stepped over to his battle-sergeant, Orcleaver.

'Foulblade take ca'van,' he announced proudly, pounding the exhausted sergeant on the back.

Orcleaver grunted in reply, and the two of them surveyed the scene of battle. Orcleaver did not particularly admire his superior – but he knew that he was next in line for the chief's position, so he remained loyal. For the time being, it suited his purpose.

'Wagon here. We look. *Gold!*'

Together they climbed on to the wagon and rummaged among the boxes and sacks which the caravan had been transporting to its destination in Western Allansia. Several more Goblins came over to join them but were ordered away by Foulblade. If there was gold in the cargo, he wanted as few sharing it as possible.

'Fou'blade! HERE!' The stocky sergeant stepped back to let his chief look into a sack he had opened. At first Foulblade was angry: this sack did not contain gold! But then, as the aroma of its contents reached his nostrils, his expression turned to one of curiosity. The sack contained some sort of ground-up herb, dried and flaky; its rich, sweet odour hung heavily in the air above the opened sack. A contented expression had spread across Orcleaver's face and his eyes were fixed on some imaginary point far beyond the sack. Foulblade felt his own head swimming and the noises round him faded, not to silence, but to an indistinct background hum. His mouth dropped open and his unfocused eyes gazed vacantly at the sack . . .

'Chief! Master! See! *Look this!*' A young Goblin came running up to the wagon, grunting excitedly and clutching something in his hand. The clanking of his scimitar against his armour startled the drawhorse, and the wagon lurched forward, sending Foulblade and his sergeant sprawling. Both Goblins were awakened by the sudden jolt. They picked themselves up and scowled at the youngster.

The panting Goblin stopped beside the wagon and held out his hand. 'Find this!' he spluttered. 'Round neck human! More on others! See!' Hanging from his clenched fist was a leather thong. As his fingers slowly uncurled, the two Goblins gasped as with a single voice.

'No! Not pos'ble!' stammered Orcleaver. 'Gods' eyes, NO!' But the evidence was there before them. They fell silent as they realized what they had done. And they shuddered at the possible consequences. For, lying in the Goblin's dirty palm, was a medallion of dull metal with two figures – the number '85' – cast into it.

15

2

The Storm Gathers

Beads of sweat rolled down Donnag Kannu's forehead, making him squint as they trickled into his eyes. He shifted nervously on his seat, his grubby fingers fidgeted and his fists clenched and unclenched.

'My lord,' he stammered, 'we were hopelessly outnumbered. They . . . they caught us by surprise. Dozens of them there were . . . We should have camped on the edge of the Flatlands and taken the Pass by day. Damn! I knew it. I blame myself, sire. I will accept my punishment . . .'

'SILENCE!'

The word was spoken not loudly but in a tone of such overwhelming power as to halt a Hell Demon in its tracks. The steely voice went on to command Kannu to stop his snivelling and relate the events in detail. The caravan leader shuddered; he was disgusted with himself for his cowardly manner. He fought desperately to overcome his own fear. But he had failed his master and he knew perfectly well what the consequences of failure would be. Slowly he composed himself. He took a deep breath and began to retell the events which led up to the ambush.

The Storm Gathers

'The long journey back from the mouth of the Sardath River was welcome after our months of searching through the Fenlands. Several of our party were slain in the Forest of Night when we were set upon by Dark Elves, but this was merely a minor skirmish – battle practice for our swordsmen. As we left the forest, we came across a Strongarm camp, and here we picked up replacements for the party.

'For three whole days we travelled across the Flatlands until we reached the Moonstone Hills. It was late afternoon when we arrived at the Pass. Some wished to camp there; others, eager to return to their homes, wanted to hurry on and insisted that we press on through Trolltooth Pass. The Strongarms decided among themselves. They had served me well and I was willing to allow them the final say. But now my lesson has been learnt. Those brutes are all muscle and no sense. Their recklessness has cost them their lives and me my cargo – *your* cargo, my lord – and my mission has been in vain.'

'Now tell me of your attackers,' ordered the voice. 'And your life is forfeit if a single word veers from the perfect truth.'

'O-of course, my lord,' coughed Kannu. 'L-let me see. We must have been halfway through the Pass when the foul creatures dropped on us. The torches we carried gave us no warning until they had already set to, knocking my Strongarms from their horses and butchering them with their weapons. I was thrown from the wagon when my drawhorses panicked. I tried to control them, but in the end I was forced to mount one of them because their chief was almost upon me, yelling his battle-cry, waving his scimitar and – '

He was stopped mid-sentence: 'His *what*?'

'Er, his *scimitar*, my lord.'

'I see. Describe this creature to me.'

Kannu searched his memory. The image of the Goblin chief riding alongside his wagon was stamped indelibly in his memory.

'He, ah, was dark-skinned. Ugly as a crone. Worse. Sharp teeth, broken at the front. Wore mail armour of chain. Carried, as I said, a scimitar. And he seemed to be missing one ear – I couldn't be sure – but his helmet was cut round his ears. The one on this side was large and I remember thinking his head looked lop-sided. Yes, that's what it was. He was missing an ear.'

'Did any of the others address him?'

'*Address* him, my lord?'

'Yes, fool, *address* him! Address him by name!'

'Er, no. I don't think so. Wait! As he broke through the line towards me, I do remember one of his troops calling after him, egging him on. His name was – '

Again he was cut off mid-sentence. '*Foulblade!*' The voice deepened to a growl, then rose to explode with such force that Kannu trembled visibly in his seat. 'FOULBLADE! That stinking runt dares to plunder my caravan. He cannot know. He would not dare. He will roast slowly. He . . .'

Anger mounted as the significance of the event became more clear. This had been no mere Goblin prank.

The voice spoke again, but this time more quietly and with considerable self-restraint: 'No. Of course. This plot comes from a higher authority. Otherwise I would have foreseen this ambush. Foulblade takes orders from his master . . .'

The Storm Gathers

There was silence in the room – a threatening silence. It seemed to resound in Kannu's ears, louder than a thunderclap. His heart was thumping in his chest as he waited anxiously for his master to speak. Though desperate to break the silence, he knew he must not speak lest he disturb his master's concentration.

The dark eyelids slowly opened. Two glowing red eyes burned into Kannu's mind. Unable to hold his master's gaze, his eyes dropped down to fix on his restless fingers, still fidgeting in his lap.

'I understand,' growled the voice, the lips moving strangely as if Kannu were hearing the sounds through some sort of translation device. 'The significance is clear. I must abandon my search and turn all my attention to this event. And I must act quickly.'

'Master, if I can be of any assistance . . .'

'GO!' The eyes widened to emphasize the command.

Shaking visibly, Donnag Kannu obeyed. He rose clumsily from his chair and stumbled backwards, bowing awkwardly on his way out. He was frightened but relieved. His master, wrapped in thought, had not pronounced his fate. He must leave quickly before the matter of his punishment should occur to the ghostly creature before him. Behind his back, his hand touched the doorknob. He grasped and twisted it, opening the heavy wooden door and stepping out into the corridor beyond.

He breathed a long sigh. But his relief was short-lived. Before he could pull the door to, four rough hands grasped him firmly by his elbows and shoulders. The shock startled him and he turned to face his molesters. Piggish eyes stared at him stolidly out of two long-nosed faces of grey hide. Each sported a cruel horn at the end of its snout. *Rhino-Man guards*, he thought. *The master has not forgotten my punishment at all*. He turned back towards the red-eyed figure with a pitiful pleading look before being marched away along the corridor.

His fate had been decided before he even entered the dark dungeon room. Decided by an unforgiving master who allowed no such acts of incompetence to go unpunished.

Zharradan Marr.

'*There!*' A welcome sneer spread across the Goblin's face as he turned to face his companions. 'Black Finger! Up there! Soon there!'

All eight weary faces followed Foulblade's gesture. They stopped in their tracks and squinted; in the evening half-light it was difficult enough to follow the path, let alone make out any meaningful shapes in the surrounding mountainside. All they could see were more jagged outcrops of the Craggen Heights reaching upwards like the teeth of some gigantic snaretrap. They snorted their disbelief.

'No. *There*. Look there.'

They strained their eyes to see what Foulblade had spotted. In the far distance, one towering rock seemed more regular than the others: a smooth shaft reached upwards and ended in a shape that, from this distance, resembled a witch's pointed hat.

One by one they recognized the dark tower.

'See? There. Black Finger!'

The Hill Goblins held the fortress in awe. Though they knew little about it, they felt it somehow represented a force of order and strength well beyond the comprehension of their own simple minds. In the local Goblin legends it was referred to as 'The Black Finger' as to them it indicated some sort of gesture of crude defiance directed at the heavenly deities themselves. The Goblins admired such bold audacity: a true statement of chaos.

The guttural chucklings of the party signalled a suitable time for a break in the journey. After their long hours of endless climbing through the Craggen Heights, the sight of their goal was sorely welcome. As a chief, Foulblade knew the uplifting effect this moment would have on their morale. He signalled for them to set up camp for the night.

Half an hour later, darkness had descended on the party. The Goblins were huddled round a flickering fire, tearing ravenously at their uncooked meat. Orc-leaver swatted away one of the younger Goblins as he tried to rip a tasty sliver of flesh from the thighbone that the battle-sergeant had laid to one side. Two of the others were gesturing and making jokes about each other's battle prowess, and the sound of their gasping snorts of laughter rang through the still night air.

Foulblade was deep in thought, fiddling absent-mindedly with what was left of his right ear and staring into the dancing flames. The two Goblins keeping watch were sitting on the sacks and boxes looted from the caravan. Every so often a distant noise caught their attention and they peered out into the gloomy darkness, hands poised on their weapons. But the air was still and, one by one, the Goblins fell asleep.

*

The Trolltooth Wars

'Graaauuughh! Eeeeyaaargh!'

The agonized shrieks woke the party with a start. Foulblade was already on his feet, scimitar at the ready, prepared for battle.

The excited night-watch guards gestured towards an area of undergrowth off the path. 'There! Orc-leaver! Go latrine. Bushes! Come!'

Led by their chief, the Goblins sprang towards the cries. A rustling bush attracted their attention. They stopped dead, eyes wide.

In the dim light they could just make out the struggling figure on the ground behind the bush. Their battle-sergeant was locked in a furious battle with . . . *something.*

It seemed as if a deep black *shadow* was wrapped round his body. Although Orcleaver was struggling to free himself, he could not break loose from the shadow creature. The frantic battle-sergeant was trapped in a living net of blackness and, the more he struggled, the more he appeared to entangle himself in the formless shape. He fought hopelessly against it.

The Hill Goblins had never encountered a Night Shadow before. If they had, they would have realized how hopeless their sergeant's struggles were. They would also have realized that their best course of action would be to abandon their companion and leave the area. However, their instincts told them otherwise – especially since Orcleaver was now making choking sounds as the creature wrapped him in its deadly embrace.

The Goblins sprang to his aid. They grasped and pulled at the flimsy black shadow, but to no avail. The ghost-like spirit was half solid, and it remained

wrapped round the sergeant. Its substance flowed through their fingers like thick, oily liquid.

'Fire!' yelled Foulblade. 'Get fire.'

One of the Goblins dashed over to the fire and rushed back with a flaming branch. But in his eagerness he stumbled over a rock, sending the branch rolling across the roadside, where it went out. Picking himself up, he ran back to the fire to fetch another branch.

'*Aaaggh! Aaaaakk!*' Orcleaver's chokings were becoming weaker. '*Oooommphh!*' His stomach heaved up its contents into the shadow creature's dark form. Just then the young Goblin arrived with the flaming branch.

Foulblade snatched the branch and held it out at the creature. At first there was no reaction, but then something stirred. As if taken by a fisherman's hook, the shadow suddenly slipped over Orcleaver's chest and head and made off along the ground into the night. In an instant it was indistinguishable from the rest of the night's blackness.

'What that? Where gone? Orcleaver dead?' The Goblins chattered nervously, terrified by the unknown creature.

Foulblade bent over the sergeant's limp body. 'Not dead. Carry there.' He barked the order, trying to bring a semblance of order to his party. The tone of his voice showed only a hint of the fear he was feeling inside.

The Goblins carried their companion over to the fire and laid him down beside it. Foulblade ordered more wood, for safety dispatching two Goblins to fetch it. They returned and the fire was stoked up. For some time the party discussed the incident, keeping an eye on Orcleaver for any signs of improvement. Eventually they settled down to sleep again but first Foulblade made sure that the night-watch was increased to three.

They awoke at dawn and packed in preparation for their journey to continue. Orcleaver awoke with the rest, complaining of 'sore head' but otherwise none the worse for wear. However, when the Goblins asked him about his encounter with the black shadow, he simply looked at them vacantly. He had just fallen asleep with the others and woken up with them. He had no recollection of any incidents during the night. What *were* they talking about?

The others did notice a slight change in their sergeant, however. He was much quieter than normal and seemed a little detached. When they pressed him further, he became quiet. They let the matter drop and continued on their way. They arrived at the Black Tower late in the afternoon.

3

The Black Tower

The Black Tower.

Built two generations earlier from the very Craggen Rock on which it stood, the Citadel of Chaos struck both fear and respect into the hearts of the creatures of the Craggen Heights. Its black stones had been laid in place by an army of creatures enlisted by the sorcerer Gandor Dire – some say with a little help from the netherworld deities.

The wealthy but hermit-like sorcerer was not himself an evil man, but his unhealthy fascination with demonic matters worried the inhabitants of his home town of Warpstone, who branded him a black magician. Eventually their continued harassment forced him to leave. He, his lady wife and their young son journeyed northwards through the Craggen Heights and it was here, on Craggen Rock, that he decided to build his sanctuary.

The building was completed remarkably quickly, but Gandor had ignored the warnings of others concerning his new choice of home. Not only did all manner of dangerous and mysterious creatures live out their wretched existences in the Craggen Heights

27

– the very essence of chaos festered in the rocks of the mountains themselves. Like a sinister disease, this spirit of evil seemed to infect all who dwelt in the area. Little did Gandor Dire know that the very stones with which he built his sanctuary would eventually warp his mind. Slowly and surely, like the vile creatures who were his neighbours, Gandor Dire began to change.

At first he became tolerant towards the creatures of chaos; later he even became sympathetic. He invited them inside his tower, where they performed unspeakable duties and were rewarded with food, shelter and the occasional copper piece. But the longer he lived in the Black Tower, the more he became like them.

When Gandor died, his son Craggen Dire inherited the citadel. Having lived all his life in the Black Tower, Craggen was an evil-hearted rogue through and through. During his lifetime he spent most of his father's fortune on indulgences, of which he had two: his magic arts and his only son, Balthus.

Craggen Dire was never a particularly successful sorcerer; he would perhaps have been better suited to a military vocation. But he did spend many a long hour with the young Balthus, who became obsessed with the mystic arts. Balthus Dire was an exceedingly bright child who quickly took in all that Craggen could teach him. By the beginning of his fourteenth year, his ability had surpassed that of his father and he had come to despise the older man's shortcomings. Eventually Balthus persuaded – or rather *bullied* – his father into sending him to a more learned master who could teach him the skills he wished to acquire. Fearing his own child's wrath, Craggen Dire secured a place for Balthus with Volgera Darkstorm in his school of magicianship in the Flatlands, and here, in time, Balthus Dire's knowledge of the black arts became formidable.

On returning from Darkstorm's school, he was greeted by his father with open arms. By then, however, mere family loyalty had no place in Balthus's black heart; he had resolved to dedicate his life to the pursuit of *power* – at any cost – and nothing would stand in his way. At the very moment of his homecoming embrace, the tears from his father's eyes froze on his cheeks as Balthus returned his greeting with a knifeblade – pushed quickly through Craggen Dire's ribs.

The first requirement of his newly chosen pursuit was a power base. The Black Tower was now his.

The minions of the citadel at first greeted their new master with suspicion and even contempt: how could one so young consider himself master of such a place? Within a very short time their contempt had turned to abject fear as the young Balthus took command with a ruthlessness that struck terror into the heart even of a Flatlands Barbarian.

But Balthus Dire was also a great military strategist. His father's troops had comprised no more than a small band of citadel guards. Balthus quickly realized that without troops he could be no conqueror, and from the outset he began to build up his forces. To the warlike tribes and clans of Goblins and the other chaotic creatures which scratched their living in the Craggen Heights, he became a living legend. Some joined his forces out of fear of the consequences of refusal, but most joined because they wished to be a part of this growing force of chaos, savouring both

the atrocities and the riches that were the spoils of conquest.

His initial attacks were confined to small communities of creatures near the Craggen Heights. Balthus Dire concentrated on developing his magical powers for warmongering. He became curious about a little-known type of warmagic that had sprung from the court at Royal Lendle in Gallantaria; it was carried across to Allansia by the spirit-like Ganjees, who had little interest in its application but were fascinated by its mysterious origins. This battle-magic could be cast on to an enemy in battle, with devastating effects. So far, however, the Ganjees had not been forthcoming with information about the secrets of their art.

Stories of Lord Balthus Dire's growing power spread, and soon the more warlike creatures of chaos were streaming to the Black Tower. Snub-nosed Orcs, black-hearted Kobolds, wandering Ogres and the like joined his forces, as did tribe after tribe of Hill Goblins, anxious to serve their new, all-powerful master.

One such tribe was led by Foulblade, who served his master well and became commander of Dire's troops. But Dire himself remained contemptuous of the Hill Goblins, whom he regarded as stupid but nevertheless essential to his plans for conquest.

A discordant fanfare announced the arrival of the Hill Goblin chief.

Foulblade pulled the heavy helmet off his head and placed it carefully under his arm. Motioning to Orcleaver, he stepped proudly through the wide doorway, his battle-sergeant following three paces behind. They

entered a large wood-panelled room that was adorned
with exotic weapons and portraits of long-dead ances-
tors. Seated behind a sturdy desk at the far end of the
room was Balthus Dire.

The Goblin felt his confidence ebb away. As he
stepped forward, he could feel his heart fluttering
nervously in the presence of his lord. This reaction
was understandable: the figure seated behind
the desk was grand in appearance. A tall, wide-
shouldered, powerful man turned towards him. The
expression on his stony face remained fixed, but beneath the heavy lines of Balthus Dire's dark eyebrows
two glaring eyes burned deep into Foulblade's brain.
The otherwise bald sorcerer wore a topknot of
long, jet-black hair which fell straight back to end at
his high collar. His mouth was shut in a tight line.
Nothing in his expression gave away anything of
his mood.

One mistake, one discourteous remark, thought the
Goblin, though in a somewhat simpler Goblin
language, *and he will take my life as punishment.*

Balthus Dire knew well the effect his presence had
on his minions. At an early age he had realized that
both humans and non-human creatures were almost
instinctively aware of their positions in the pecking
order of life. Intrigued by this discovery, he set about
finding out just what it was that made one man lower
his eyes to another. He watched and he read. And by
now he was a master of the art of imposing his will
on others.

Foulblade bowed low before his master, then gestured to the other Goblins to bring in the sacks and
crates plundered during the ambush in Trolltooth
Pass.

'Your mission was successful? You have the cunnel-wort?'

Dire's words echoed in Foulblade's ears. He struggled to come up with a reply, but his dim brain choked and would not provide him with a single sentence. He nodded quickly, then stepped over to one of the sacks and opened its neck wide, turning his snout away from the sweet-smelling herb's fragrance.

Balthus Dire reached into his desk drawer, drew out a small vial of liquid, and took three careful sips. He waited a few moments for the potion to take effect, then pushed himself to his feet. He stepped over to the sack and plunged his hands into the dried herb, rubbing it between his palms. He sniffed deeply and his eyes closed slowly.

'You have done well, Foulblade. You have done well,' he said, his lips turning upwards almost into a smile. 'Casualties?'

'Few. Not many,' shrugged the Goblin chief.

Dire understood this could mean anything from ten to forty. Goblins were unable to count. He nodded. 'Survivors?'

Foulblade coughed and shifted his feet nervously. 'Kill all. Except . . .'

'EXCEPT?' Dire's anger exploded, and the Goblin's mouth dropped open in silence. He was transfixed, riveted, powerless, by his master's icy glare.

Eventually he stammered out the story of the ambush and the chase, begging pitifully for forgiveness as he explained how the wagon rider had escaped into the night. But there could be no forgiveness, for Dire had one rule of command. Those who served him well survived; those who failed him perished. When his excuses came to an end, Foulblade was seized by two guards and marched out of the room.

Orcleaver had been listening to this and watching with the same strange indifference that had been his manner since his encounter with the Night Shadow. When Dire's eyes fell upon him, he pulled his hand out from his tunic. 'See this.' He held out the dull medallion which the young Goblin had given to him. 'On humans. Round neck.'

Balthus Dire grabbed the medallion and stared, wide-eyed, at it. Quickly he looked up at Orcleaver. 'Go, Orcleaver,' he commanded. 'Leave now.'

Orcleaver turned casually to leave the room.

Balthus Dire added: 'And you take your chief's place with your creatures. You will be commander of the Goblins. I have ordered it.'

Orcleaver allowed himself a secret smile of satisfaction.

As the Goblin sergeant turned, loose-limbed, and departed, Dire pondered for a moment the Goblin's attitude: he had known Orcleaver for some time, but now he had none of the crisp, precise movements that betrayed his military background. He seemed almost *casual* in his manner . . . But Dire quickly dismissed all thoughts of Goblins – the matter in hand was far more serious. He looked down at the medallion and ground his teeth in concentration. Had he known about this, he would never have ordered an ambush. The caravan raid would be avenged . . . There was a survivor . . . That survivor would be reporting back to his lord . . . A lord whose troops wore numbered medallions.

The legionaries of Zharradan Marr.

The war had begun.

4

King Salamon's Court

'Arise, Darkmane.' The king looked down at the figure kneeling before him. *Hmm*, he thought, *promise. This young officer is certainly built for the part. Perhaps a little inexperienced at the moment but, given the right opportunities, the right training . . . If his mind is as sharp as his shoulders are broad . . . Hmm. But he will have to do something about his appearance. More like a Flatlands barbarian than a knight of the court . . .*

He watched as the tousled mop of jet-black hair was flicked back to reveal Chadda Darkmane's stern face. His unblinking eyes held King Salamon's gaze with an expression of almost irreverent self-confidence. Whatever mission the king had summoned him for, he was determined to succeed. This was his chance to prove himself, to build his Amonour, his reputation in Salamonis.

Darkmane put his hands on his knees and pushed himself up into a standing position, his polished military armour creaking at the joints. He stood tall before Salamon. *Like an eagle*, the king thought. Broad shoulders accentuated by wide armour, narrow waist, solemn expression, intelligent eyes. He held his

helmet under his left arm, his right hand resting casually on his sword-hilt. *A born leader of men.* But there was something about him that the king felt uncomfortable about. Was he just a little too cocky? Was he too young to be trusted with a mission of such vital importance? Could he be trusted at all? Or was it only his untidy appearance that Salamon found distasteful?

The Allseeing Three had never failed him in their judgement before. They had selected him themselves for the king's mission, from half a score of candidates. Though to date his service in the Salamonian army had been short, he had advanced rapidly through the ranks and on training missions he had excelled. When his troops had been brought in on occasion to deal with civil disturbances, they had always handled the problem quickly and forcefully, but never thuggishly.

'You have been summoned here on the advice of my loyal sages, the Allseeing Three,' the king began. 'They are of the opinion that this mission is best left to a single unknown member of the Salamonis court: one who may cross Allansia without arousing suspicions; one with the vigour to accomplish the task he is set, and one whose Amonour stands to gain much from a successful outcome.'

At these last words, Darkmane raised an eyebrow. For the aristocracy of Salamonis was founded not so much on family ties or even on wealth and riches. These were all secondary to a man's reputation – his Amonour. The people of Salamonis loved to hear stories of great adventurers slaying ferocious creatures, discovering a wealth of jewels or challenging the forces of evil. Thus a person's rank in society was determined largely by the reputation he had managed to build up for himself. If a man worked hard all his life in the fields, or at his craft, or even within the court circles and never left his family to seek adventures, then his Amonour – and his status – would be poor. On the other hand, if wandering minstrels sang songs relating his courageous exploits, then he was virtually guaranteed a place at King Salamon's High Table of Knights. Darkmane relished the opportunity to feed his Amonour.

The king continued: 'Word has reached me of a gathering storm. The storm itself is of little concern. Though thousands will die as it ravages the hills of chaos, Salamonis may feel little effect until after it is over. It is the calm after the storm that worries me.

'This land is cursed with two incarnations of evil, both spawned by that foul Flatlands necromancer, Volgera Darkstorm. He received his just deserts for passing on his arcane knowledge to the next generation, when his pupils assassinated their teacher but not before they themselves had acquired this knowledge. Their names will be familiar to you: Balthus Dire and Zharradan Marr.'

Darkmane nodded. These names were well known and well despised in Salamonis.

King Salamon continued: 'These two are cursed, and they revel in their dark ways. For years they have been building their power bases, Dire to the south in the Cragrocks and Marr to the north in the lands round Coven. For years they have been content to avoid confronting each other. Until now. The clouds have gathered and the storm must break.

'To apportion blame is irrelevant – this conflict was

38

bound to come. Like it or not, however, we are caught in the middle. We must be forewarned as to the outcome of this war. For, when one side wins the battle and his opponent is slain, *all* the territory lying between Craggen Rock and the Deedle Water will be claimed by the victor. Our presence in Salamonis will at first be a nuisance, then it will become a thorn in the flesh of whoever is triumphant; it will simply be a matter of time before Salamonis is at war. And I cannot say for certain that our brave troops will be able to defend us against such an all-powerful sorcerer, aided by his battle-lusting armies of chaos.

'So we come to your role, young Chadda Darkmane.' The king looked him over again. 'Your mission is this: you must find a way to enable us to benefit from this war – to avert the inevitable attack on Salamonis.'

There was silence as the two men looked at each other. They stared into each other's eyes. The silence continued. Around the grand hall, the king's entourage of nobles began to look at one another nervously. Now was the moment for Darkmane to speak, accepting his mission and thanking the king. This behaviour was outrageous! All eyes focused on the young, shaggy-haired figure. His granite jaws opened slowly.

'Your majesty . . .' The deep voice echoed round the room. 'I accept your mission. It will be my honour to serve you. And to serve the people of Salamonis. I will leave in two days' time. Meanwhile I shall be making preparations here. I will require a bedroom and personal quarters fitting for a member of the nobility which I am to join. And I shall require a manservant, one who will do as he is told and need never be told twice.'

Gasps came from the audience. Who was this young upstart to talk in such a way to the king of Salamonis? Such arrogance could not go unpunished. But for the moment he was locked once more eye to eye with the king. This time it was Salamon who spoke.

'Young man,' he began in a calm, almost fatherly manner. 'You have a great deal to learn about the ways of court etiquette before you will rise to that nobility to which you aspire. But you have courage and determination. And you do not waste words. You shall have from me what you request. But you must pay me back with success. Are we agreed?'

Darkmane nodded. He would not fail. He regretted his brusque manner towards his sovereign, but both his upbringing and his pride prevented him modifying his approach. He knew little and cared less for 'court etiquette'. He had been asked to undertake a mission. He had agreed. What more was there to discuss?

He turned from the king and strode towards the door. More gasps came from the crowd. The king had not given him leave to go. Such impudence! How would Salamon react to this insult?

But the king was wrapped in thought as he watched the solemn figure striding away from him. Had the Allseeing Three made the right choice? Did this Chadda Darkmane have the qualities necessary to complete a mission of such importance?

Salamon slumped back in his seat. As the door closed behind Darkmane, his fingers absent-mindedly stroked the neatly trimmed beard which adorned his square chin.

Eventually his thoughts returned to the subject at hand. 'Next!' he commanded.

King Salomon's Court

A gaily dressed herald stepped forward. 'Your high-ness, may I present Vignor, a merchant of Harabnab in faraway Ruddlestone. He would speak with you on the subject of the shaggle harvest.'

Another one, groaned Salamon to himself. At this time of year there were always numbers of hopeful merchants from the Old World and Khul who came to Salamonis, trying desperately to persuade the king to part with some of his shaggle – a medicinal herb which promoted the rapid healing of wounds – in exchange for Skunkbear skins, or something equally useless. He granted audience to these merchants out of courtesy only. Not one had ever managed to per-suade him to part with any of the shaggle.

The herald bowed low and the door opened to admit a plump and dubious-looking man dressed in silky blue robes. He was laden down with jewellery – a habit that Salamon found objectionable in men – in order to give the king an indication of his wealth and prestige. The fat man was sweating; he forced a smile from between his teeth as he bowed before Salamon's seat.

'Your highness. Your *majesty* . . .' he began, red-cheeked from the effort of bending over. 'I have come to offer you a proposition. Indeed, a proposition so generous that I cannot myself understand how my fellow traders have managed to put it together. Er, may I rise now, your majesty? I regret having to ask this of you, but my health is poor these days. Overwork, according to my physician – but then, what do physicians know, eh? Thank you. Now, where was I? Ah yes, my proposition. I know how bitter it gets in Northern Allansia in the cold season. I have seen your people huddled round their fires, shivering, unable to leave their hovels. I have just the thing to ease their suffering, and I assure your majesty that I will give you a fair rate of barter for your shaggle. You will never be so warm as when you are wrapped in a Skunkbear skin . . .'

After his final petitioner had departed, Salamon breathed a heavy sigh. Alone in his chamber, his thoughts returned to the strange, unmannered man whom he had sent on what was undoubtedly the most important mission of his lifetime. Could he safely rely on this enigmatic character? Or were this Darkmane's ambitions motivated in other directions? If only Salamon were thirty years younger, he would undertake the mission himself. But no, it must be an unknown Salamonian. And he trusted the wisdom of the Allseeing Three. Now, what could he do to ensure Darkmane's continuing loyalty?

His eyes narrowed and he nodded slowly to himself. King Salamon had a plan.

5

The Chervah

There was a knock at the door.

Darkmane was lost in thought, staring out of the window at the Forest of Yore in the distance.

'Enter!' he snapped at last.

The door opened to reveal a slim figure, perhaps a metre and a half tall. Although dressed in colourful court robes, this creature was certainly not human. An Elf? No, the skin was much too dark and the face was a little too large. But definitely Elf-like, with wide-apart eyes and large ears which had pointed tops and lobes. A Black Elf? No, the head was bald and the face almost baby-like, though the nose was perhaps a little smaller than suited the rest of his features.

Darkmane had never come across a Chervah before. He watched as the Chervah entered the room. His steps had a spring to them and his eyes darted from side to side. There was something almost comical about the little creature as he took each step on thin legs, his round head bobbing about like a child's ball floating in the sea.

'You requested a manservant, my lord. I am he.

My name is Sroonagh Monnow Pirrashatha. I suggest you will find it easier to call me "Chervah", as that is my race. I will not take offence if you are to call me this, though you probably would, were I to call you "human". This custom is common with our people when in strange lands. We are proud of our race, you see.' His voice was high-pitched, but it had a certain musical ring to it which Darkmane found curious.

The little creature continued: 'I see that my appearance is puzzling to you. I am from the town of Rimon in Arantis. All our people are similar to myself – or, rather, I am similar to them. I was aboard a sailing vessel bound for the Old World, not two days' journey out of Rimon, when a demon wind caught our ship.' The Chervah's expression saddened as he recollected the event. 'For

The Chervah

a day and a night we wrestled with the wind as that demon took the ship and tossed it about as one might throw a small ball from one hand to the other. When he finished with us, there were few survivors. I was one. We limped back towards Allansia and encountered the coast at Oyster Bay. My travels took me inland to Salamonis, where I have remained ever since. I am happy in my new home – and my new position in life. It was suggested that I would be a suitable choice as your manservant during your stay in Salamonis.'

Darkmane gave a non-committal grunt. He was not particularly interested in hearing the little creature's life-story. But since his train of thought had already been disturbed, perhaps now would be a suitable time to eat.

'Very well, manservant

– *Chervah*. It is time for me to take my meal. Will you bring me –'

'Forgive me, sire,' the little creature interrupted. 'I have anticipated your hunger. Here is my own selection of nourishment, especially chosen to build up your stamina and prepare you for the journey ahead.'

He pushed in a serving-cart upon which was a selection of cold dishes, mostly vegetables. Darkmane looked at the food with disdain.

Sensing his disapproval, the Chervah quickly explained: 'Sire, if you will allow me to explain. You should start with a plate of tigerplant leaves, here. You will find them quite chewy and not unpleasant to the taste. Tigerplant leaves contain plenty of wholesome goodness to build up strength and stamina. There is a saying where I come from:

> *"If tomorrow you must fight,*
> *Eat three tiger leaves tonight."'*

Darkmane looked at the three thick, orange-coloured leaves lying limply on the plate and scowled.

The Chervah continued: 'I urge you, sire, to try these tasty leaves. Then you should sip this Valeherb tea. With all due modesty, I pride myself on my ability to prepare a fine tea. In fact, when I was first washed ashore in Allansia, one of my prime sorrows was being unable to brew my teas, as I was unfamiliar with the local herbs. Eventually, however, I came to know the herbs of this region. The finest herbs grow in the Vale of Willow. This tea is prepared from them. Please – see how you like it.

'Then you should sample my Salamon Stew – I named this after the king himself, for I feel it is my finest creation. But the ingredients are quite simple, really; any vegetables can go in. Its secret is the specially seasoned broth which – '

'ENOUGH!' The Chervah was cut off mid-sentence by an angry outburst from Darkmane. 'Manservant, save your rabbit food for the peasants. I will have none of it. Go. Bring me bread, ale and a roasted joint of mutton.'

The Chervah's skinny jaw dropped and his tiny eyebrows jumped high up his forehead in a pained, sorrowful expression. His new master was displeased with his cooking! He stammered an apology: 'B-b-but of course, sire. A thousand pardons, sire. R-right, er . . . right away.' He bowed quickly and left the room, looking unnerved and disheartened at his new master's outburst of temper.

Idiot! thought Darkmane. *Stupid, prattling idiot. Do I look like the sort who has been nurtured on nuts and berries?* He glanced at the serving-cart. The tigerplant leaves. That – what was it – willow tea? Then he noticed how the food had been laid out delicately and deliberately, with garnishes and tiny coloured fruits arranged here and there to make the food look pleasant. Darkmane frowned. The little creature had gone to some effort here. Had he perhaps been somewhat harsh on him?

He stepped over to the serving-cart and took a tigerplant leaf from the plate. Grasping it by the stalk, he turned it in his hand. The heavy leaf flopped over. He raised it to his nose and sniffed at it. The smell was curious – something like ground nuts, but with a faintly sweet smell too. He remembered the creature's rhyme. *If you battle tomorrow, eat three leaves today*, or something like that – Darkmane had never had the patience for poetry.

He nibbled at the tip of the leaf. The texture was chewy and spongy, and the sweet nutty taste was not unpleasant. He took a larger bite and finally popped the whole thing into his mouth. He sat down on the bed to savour the taste.

Tomorrow, he thought, he must wake early and visit his friend Calorne Manitus, the census-taker. For the journey he planned to undertake, he would need companions; a party of four should suffice. However, being a solitary character, Darkmane had had little contact with others in Salamonis; he hoped his friend could help. He stood up from the bed, absent-mindedly picked another tigerplant leaf and bit into it, deep in thought.

At that moment there was a knock at the door. He snapped out of his reverie, dropped the leaf back on to the plate and opened the door. The scrawny manservant had arrived again, this time with a hearty meal. His head bowed, the Chervah pushed this new serving-cart into the room.

'Shall I leave the other food, sire? Perhaps you may feel inclined towards it later?' he asked hopefully.

'No,' Darkmane answered firmly. 'Take it away.'

The little creature sighed and took hold of the first serving-cart. He had worked hard preparing the herbal food, and all he had succeeded in doing was angering his master. And his dishes would be far more nourishing than the roast joint and bread which Darkmane had ordered. He pushed the cart towards the door. Then he noticed the missing tigerplant leaves.

A small private smile spread across the Chervah's face. One bite would have sufficed to taste the leaves;

only someone who enjoyed that taste would eat a leaf and a half.

Darkmane awoke the next day shortly after dawn. At the end of his bed he found fresh clothing for the new day neatly set out for him. His manservant had been in during the night. He had even anticipated Darkmane's somewhat unusual preferences for dark-coloured clothes, having laid out a heavy pair of black riding breeches and a black padded overshirt.

After dressing, Darkmane left his room, descended the stairs and stepped out into the courtyard. The water pump by the well was on the far side.

A squeaky voice caught his attention as he made his way towards it to wash: 'Sire! Please, allow me.' It was the Chervah, panting heavily as he trotted after Darkmane. 'You have merely to ask and I will bring a basin of water to your room. Those sleep demons must have held on to my soul for an extra moment, since I did not hear you awaken. My apologies, sire. Please. I will bring your wash-water. Return to your room.'

'Do not fuss yourself, Chervah.' Darkmane forced a smile. The little creature, having been caught unawares, was now in a flustered state and still pulling his coloured tunic on. What is more, he had not noticed that one of the sleeves was turned inside out, and his right arm was making comical motions – like a dog with a tick – as he tried hopelessly to find the hole for the sleeve. 'You return to the room. Fix me my morning breakfast. I prefer to wash myself in cold, fresh pumpwater in the crisp morning air. Calm yourself down, put on your tunic and bring my food to my room. But none of your vegetables. More bread. And three eggs.'

The Chervah turned and rushed off eagerly towards the kitchens. Darkmane turned to the pump and cranked the handle until the water began to flow; he splashed some over his face. The cold water was a welcome shock. He cupped his hands to take more water, splashed again and rubbed the sleep from his eyes.

When he opened his eyes and looked up, he found himself staring into the face of a fair-skinned woman dressed in colourful robes. Taken aback by the woman's silent approach, Darkmane spluttered. He opened his mouth to speak, but the woman held up her finger and placed it upon her lips. She smiled at him, then bent to gather water from the gushing pump. Darkmane took the handle and cranked it for her. He watched as her long fingers formed a delicate cup under the flowing water. She swung her head to left and right so that her long, fair hair was off her face. Her clothes were light and colourful; she may have been an entertainer – maybe a dancer. Or perhaps a lady-in-waiting to the queen herself.

The water splashed on her face and she opened her eyelids slowly, staring straight up into Darkmane's own eyes. For an instant, time stood still as they remained held in each other's gaze. Then she turned and left.

Darkmane watched her go. Her nimble feet, in delicate slippers, seemed to carry her, floating, across the courtyard. He was transfixed by the sway of her hips and by the way the breeze tugged gently at her hair. He took in a breath to call to her, but then decided against it and returned to his chamber.

The Chervah

Who was that beautiful creature? he asked himself.

As ordered, the Chervah brought Darkmane his bread and eggs. But he did also bring in some herbal tea. He watched contentedly as Darkmane, his mind on other things, drank the tea. *That will be better for him than any other drink*, thought the Chervah as he fussed about, tidying the room.

'And now we go,' announced Darkmane finally. 'We must find Calorne Manitus, census-taker for this area of Allansia. For my plans I shall need extra hands – and extra minds. Manitus knows much of the goings on of the people who live around Trolltooth Pass. His advice will be second to none in helping me to pick my travelling companions.'

In the courtyard outside they found two horses saddled and ready for their departure. Darkmane could not fathom how they had appeared.

'If you will forgive me, sire,' explained the Chervah, 'I made arrangements for our horses to be ready at all times. I would not wish your mission to be delayed while the stableboys were saddling up your mount.'

'Good. Let us depart.' Darkmane was impressed by the little creature's attention to detail.

They rode out through the palace gates into the town of Salamonis. Market stalls lined the path that led into the centre of the town. As Darkmane passed by on his proud, black horse, whispers spread among the peasants. A few beggars shuffled into the road in front of him, holding up their begging bowls, but the horseman ignored them and continued onwards.

The Chervah gave a constant commentary as they rode: 'Now, see him? There, Caddentras, the fat one with the striped hat. No, not him. Yes, that one. Well,

51

he sells the most exquisite tongos. You know, it's important to eat tongos at just the right time. When they are just ripe, and the skin is dark. Well, that Caddentras seems to have a knack for picking them. But don't trust his smile. Count your change carefully in front of him. And count your fingers, too!' The Chervah's laugh was more of a squeal. He continued: 'And see there that Smoking-Weed vendor? The king will not allow them to set up stalls along the palace approach, so instead they have to tout for business in the street. Now – see the monkey-man? He has his monkey well trained to dance to his pipe. But chances are he has another monkey trained in a much more profitable craft: picking the pockets of the onlookers! I may be unkind – not all monkey-men are rogues. But I'd be wary if I were down there watching . . .'

Salamonis was generally considered a pleasant place to live in. Under King Salamon's civilizing influence, tribal squabbles had been all but eradicated. The town itself was prosperous. Standing at the gateway to the Trolltooth Pass, traders of all kinds would meet in Salamonis, to barter and to organize their cross-country caravans. Strongarms arrived at Salamonis knowing that it would always be easy for them to get employment on a caravan going east, as hired protection was essential for the journey across the Flatlands. And Strongarms leaving their westbound caravans at Salamonis arrived flush with silver pieces. Being the sort who loved nothing more than a mug of ale, a hearty meal, a good story, a flirtatious serving-wench and maybe even a good brawl, Strongarms naturally gravitated towards the town centre of Salamonis, where there was a growing num-

The Chervah

ber of rowdy taverns, though these were not the sort of places that the locals frequented.

Outside the town, the Vale of Willow stretched out to the Whitewater River, through the Forest of Yore to the north-west. The Forest of Yore was the residence of Vermithrax Moonchaser, the Grand Wizard of Yore, a solitary character about whom not a great deal was known. He shared the forest with his friends the Yorefolk – a race of Half-Elves – and because of his advanced years he never ventured out of the forest. His magical abilities were notorious, and over the years he had shared much of his knowledge with apprentice magic-users, specially selected by the Grand Wizard. His most famous pupils included Arakor Nicodemus of Port Blacksand, Gereth Yaztromo of Darkwood Forest and Pen Ty Kora of Arantis. Non-magical folk simply did not venture into the Forest of Yore unless they sought audience with Grand Wizard Moonchaser. Visitors were spied straight away by the Yorefolk, challenged and asked to leave. If they ignored these warnings, the Yorefolk would have them blowpiped. Death was instantaneous.

The Vale of Willow was a rich valley, kept fertile by the Whitewater River which ran across its western reaches. It was here that the farmers of Salamonis tended their crops. Wheat, pygmy corn and shaggle were the staple crops, the latter being peculiar to the area and much sought after round the world, as its use had truly astonishing effects on the speed with which wounds were healed. Cattle and other grazing animals were also raised, particularly bearsheep, whose coats were much warmer than those of mountain sheep and whose wool was much easier to spin.

The Trolltooth Wars

There were many small villages in the Vale and some of these specialized in more esoteric herbs and spices, used for both medicinal and magical purposes.

The inhabitants of the Vale of Willow were a very insular people, however. They disliked strangers intensely, always suspicious that newcomers were trying to steal their secrets. They traded only reluctantly with the rest of Allansia through the markets of Salamonis town. Their dress, their customs and their language were all peculiar to them, and most outsiders simply left them to it. But they were well respected by the town-dwellers of Salamonis, who understood that their farming brought great riches to the markets.

Further on down the road, the market stalls gave way to ramshackle huts. Darkmane and the Chervah rode on into the centre of town, turned left into Chillwind Street and then right down Coldwater Lane, before stopping outside a fair-sized wooden hut with a thickly thatched roof. Pretty flowers bordered the path up to the front door. Two tall moonweed plants grew on either side of the doorway, their round, white flowers swaying gently in the breeze. A shy bristlebeast – perhaps a neighbour's pet – poked its nose round the corner to watch Darkmane walk up to the door and rap on it with the knocker.

After a few moments shuffling feet approached the door and it swung slowly open. Inside stood an old man, bent almost double. His wrinkled face reminded the Chervah of a dried lemonberry.

'Well?' the withered voice rasped. 'What's your business? What d'you want?' The bristlebeast came scurrying round the corner and ran between the old man's legs into the house.

The Chervah

'I seek Calorne Manitus, the census-taker,' Darkmane began. 'You are not he, yet this is his home.'

'Calorne is not here. Hasn't been here for weeks. Who wants to meet him?' The old man squinted up into Darkmane's face.

'I am Chadda Darkmane, an old friend. I would seek his advice on a matter of some urgency, old man. Please tell me where I can find him.'

The old man rubbed his stubbly chin. 'Darkmane. Chadda Darkmane. Hmmm. Yes. I've heard my son speak that name before. Was it not you, Chadda Darkmane, who outwitted the Volee Hanu?'

Darkmane nodded. His clever manipulation of the scheming sorceress had added much to his Amonour in Salamonis.

'Well, then, I'm honoured to make your acquaintance. And I shall be happy to tell you how to reach my son. He is working at present in Shazâar, on matters of the census. You will find him there. He stays at an inn called the Fatted Pig.'

Darkmane thanked the man and turned away from the house. Shazâar was several days' ride west of Salamonis, across the Whitewater River. He had not counted on having to make a long journey and was now forced to reconsider his options. If there was any alternative to this journey, it would be preferable, but Darkmane knew that only the census-taker had a wide knowledge of the various peoples of the area. Only he would be able to suggest suitable additions to Darkmane's party. However, he did not relish the thought of a visit to Shazâar. Standing alone in the northern reaches of the great Southern Plain like an oasis in the desert, Shazâar was a haven for brigands, sandtrackers and shamans. The latter group held control over the city, and as a result the customs of Shazâar were strange and difficult for outsiders to comprehend. Visitors witnessed things in the streets of Shazâar which they found meaningless (like a man walking round in a circle, backwards, for an entire morning) or idiotic (some Shazâarians were employed to dig small holes in the streets while others were also paid to follow them round filling in these holes). And during a stay in the city it was not uncommon to witness a seemingly horrific act of cruelty – say, a group of youths forcing another youngster to eat a glowing hot coal. However, if an onlooker sprang valiantly to the defence of the poor fellow, the victim himself would defend his torturers against any rescue attempts. Visitors minded their own business in Shazâar!

The Chervah looked up at his master as if to inquire what their next move was to be. Darkmane had decided: first of all, they must return to the palace to make their final preparations. Then they would have to set off on their way to this mysterious city of Shazâar.

6

Thugruff's Plan

In a room deep in the underground labyrinth tunnelled beneath the small village of Coven, a conversation was taking place. Flickering torchlight cast eerie shadows round the room, which was lined with bookshelves, straining under the weight of the heavy volumes they bore. A wide desk stood in the centre of the chamber, covered in books, charts and peculiar trinkets which gave the impression that, however sparsely furnished the room might otherwise be, it was undoubtedly occupied by a person of great importance. Standing before the desk was an ugly Half-Troll and behind the desk was a heavy wooden carved chair. But the chair was empty. Instead, the Half-Troll was facing an ornate full-length mirror that hung on one wall. In the dancing torchlight, it may have looked as if he was holding a conversation with his own reflection, but the second voice was unmistakable to those acquainted with Zharradan Marr. For here, burrowed deep beneath the peaceful village and its simple peasants, the necromancer made his abode.

Marr looked down at his sergeant-at-arms, and a slow smile spread across his thin lips. His eyes shone

with wicked excitement and he raised his bony arms in appreciation. 'Yes,' he hissed. 'An *excellent* plan. And you will lead this raid personally, Thugruff?'

The Half-Troll's pride showed as he shuffled on his feet and nodded back at the ghostly figure shimmering in the full-length mirror before him.

Marr's deathly image quivered in the glass; the mirror was the portal between his own world and the material plane outside. He preferred to remain inside his mirror whenever possible – he felt more comfortable there. But whenever he had to hold audience with a stranger or with someone whom he could not trust completely, he had to force himself to enter the physical world.

He could trust Thugruff, however. As one of Marr's most trusted aides, Thugruff had served him well. When Marr had made clear his wish for retaliation against Balthus Dire, the burly Half-Troll immediately busied himself in preparing plans for his master's consideration. Thugruff revelled in the prospect of battle. He was an ugly creature, with rough, pitted skin, but his square-hewn features and heavy muscles commanded respect. His strength and weapon skills were considerable. And he knew it.

'Of course, master. We shall of course need someone with the authority to offer terms. I suggest that I take two units of Soulless Ones – four-score troops in all should be sufficient. I will also need a handful of Droomies to enter the Black Tower, and a few Craggeracks to lead us through the mountains and infiltrate the Goblins. I thought I would also take a cage of Mutes and let them loose around the tower, just to frighten any of Dire's minions who have never heard of marrangha.'

The Trolltooth Wars

Zharradan Marr smiled again as Thugruff mentioned the Mutes. His sergeant had made his plan well; this was a stroke of genius. Marr's experiments in the witching art of marrangha left many unfortunate creatures hideously deformed as limbs and organs were magically transplanted from one body to another. Because very few experiments were ever successful, the results were pitiful creatures living with the agonies of unhealed wounds and permanently broken bones; those who could screamed constantly for their lives to be ended. Usually their wishes were granted, since their incessant howls disturbed Marr's concentration. But Thugruff had come up with a perfect use for these mutated wretches: they would be displayed to the enemy as a terrible warning of Marr's power. *Excellent!*

Marr dismissed Thugruff and summoned Vallaska Roue. A burly, unshaven human came bustling into the room, his leather tunic straining to retain Roue's considerable bulk. Vallaska Roue was another of Marr's most loyal henchmen. He had travelled throughout Western Allansia on his master's behalf, searching out suitable recruits for Marr's forces. While Marr avoided having to mix with the common rabble of Allansia, Vallaska Roue revelled in the low life, drinking and brawling in taverns. He also enjoyed learning all the world's news and gossip, and retelling it to his master, who always listened to his stories with great interest. Vallaska Roue was Marr's intermediary with the despicable creatures of the world as yet outside his power.

But Roue was an eminently dislikeable man, brash and aggressive. His bulbous head squatted on a fat bull-neck, and he sweated profusely. This, coupled with the fact that he washed only infrequently, resulted in a musty body-odour which made people turn their heads away from him as he entered a room. But anyone commenting on his unpleasant smell would soon regret their words: his temper was short and his strong arms could lift two men – one in each hand – high into the air or send them flying across the room. Brawls were sport to Vallaska Roue and the scars of his sporting activities could be seen on his face. A deep scar – a memento of a bar-fight in Zengis – running from his left ear to his nose showed where a blade had cut him deeply before its owner's body had been crushed in a vice-like bear hug. And the black patch over his right eye covered an empty socket, following a drunken brawl with a wily cutthroat in Port Blacksand. The fellow had dared to refer to Roue as a 'walking heap of Skunkbear dung' and had paid the price painfully – but not before his knife had pierced Roue's eye.

Zharradan Marr outlined Thugruff's plans to Vallaska Roue. Thugruff would lead a band of Soulless Ones – his undead troops – through the Cragrocks to the Black Tower under cover of night. Any settlements of Balthus Dire's Hill Goblin allies they might encounter would be destroyed. When they reached the Black Tower, two Droomies would be dispatched to enter the tower to seek out Dire's Ganjees and cajole them into switching their allegiance to Marr's war army. If the Ganjee battle-magic could be used to aid Zharradan Marr, victory in this struggle would be certain. Even if the Ganjees refused to help Zharradan Marr, at least he would be preventing them from fighting on the side of his enemy.

Roue listened intently and nodded his approval.

'Yah,' he grunted. 'But what makes you think them Droomies'll convince baskin' Dire's Ganjees to join us?'

This was a problem and Marr knew it. But he also knew that Ganjees had one weakness: they were insatiable scholars of the magic arts. They would be intrigued by Marr's marrangha experiments and would be eager to learn more; and in his turn, he wished to find out about their battle-magic. Here was the basis for a deal. Nor did loyalty enter into any discussion with Ganjees. These mysterious creatures from the spirit plane cared nothing for the affairs of men. The impending war was to them no more than a mere curiosity; its outcome could have no effect on their own existence. Most probably they cared only to side with the victor, since a powerful lord would attract powerful allies; and no doubt many of these allies would also have interesting magical secrets for them to steal. A loser would be able to offer them nothing.

Marr spelled all this out to Roue, who thought it over and finally concurred. Then he stood up to leave. He must help in the preparation of the troops.

'*Wait!*' Zharradan Marr's icy command halted him in his tracks. He turned to the mirror to face the spirit-like image. Its lips moved, pronouncing strange words, but the effect of the dimensional mirror was to translate them into his own language: 'Vallaska Roue, I have a further mission for you. Sit down.'

The bulky figure scratched his flabby chest and sat down again.

'This battle will escalate,' said his ghostly master. 'We shall need recruits. And quickly, before Dire does the same. Help Thugruff get his troops together for the raid, then make plans to leave. I need soldiers, sergeants and war sorcerers. Fetch me muscle and minds from the Plains.'

'Aye, master,' he replied, nodding his agreement. 'You're right. I'll find you the best villain baskers in Allansia.'

Zharradan Marr watched him go. Roue had served him well and, unpleasant creature though he was, he had always managed to discover fine recruits: the fiendish Darramouss, master of his dungeons and his mine; the Festering Kantie, slaver of the undead; even Thugruff himself – all had been introduced into his service following Vallaska Roue's travels. Disgusting he might be, but he seemed to have the knack of choosing perfect recruits. And if there was to be a war with Balthus Dire, Roue would need to be particularly successful . . .

The two lumbering Rhino-Men drew back the gates to let Thugruff's undead regiment through.

The Half-Troll wheeled his nighthorse around and urged it forward, to strut proudly through the gates at the head of the fearsome troop. His gleaming armour, festooned with deadly piercer spikes, clanked rhythmically to the steps of his mount. Behind him rode his two sergeants-at-arms: Krravaak, a burly Rhino-Man, to his left and Tankasun, a one-armed Gorian, to his right.

The furtive glances of the four brown-skinned Crag-geracks riding behind the sergeants darted about them. These Kobold-like creatures disliked Rhino-Men intensely; they were convinced that the two holding the gates open were planning to close them quickly and thereby crush the wily guides. Their sharp teeth flashed. One of the Rhino-Men guards stamped his foot down just as they were passing, to torment them. All four jumped in their saddles, then started jabbering excitedly, and one of them spat at the Rhino-Man. But the heavily armoured beast was in no danger. He merely guffawed and watched them pass. The Craggeracks were no fighters. Their role on this mission was simply to guide the troop safely through the Cragrocks at night.

Following their commanders and the Craggeracks came Thugruff's foot-soldiers. Four-score wretched Soulless Ones shuffled from the Testing Grounds along the path into Knotoak Wood. All wore the sign of their allegiance to Zharradan Marr: a numbered medallion hung round their neck.

The Soulless Ones were Marr's proud creations – mindless, death-dealing zombies whose undead sunken eyes stared lifelessly upwards as they shambled along, dragging their rotting limbs. These seemingly pitiful creatures were deadly in battle. Soulless, mindless and emotionless, they knew nothing of fear or danger. They simply carried out their orders to kill. Injuries might maim them, but they could not be destroyed. An opponent's only hope was to hack off their putrid limbs so that they could no longer advance. But they came in such numbers that they overwhelmed their opponents. And any wound caused by their sharp nails or bony fingers almost certainly meant a slow, painful death, for their rotting bodies were covered in a foul slime which would immediately infect any clean flesh it could enter.

Four horsemen at the rear of the troop pulled a cart on which sat a large square box, the height of

Thugruff's Plan

Thugruff's nighthorse. Although covered with coarse sheeting, the squealing and moaning sounds coming from inside identified its contents: Mutes. These hideously deformed creatures would be released outside Dire's Black Tower.

The remaining members of Thugruff's regiment of death would join the others at their destination. The ghostly Droomies would follow at their leisure. These spirit-like creatures could make the long journey into the Cragrocks in less than an hour, whereas Thugruff's troops would take several days and nights on foot.

As this legion of horror passed through the gates, the marching pace quickened until the Soulless Ones had reached their limit. A swift journey was of the essence, so a good speed of march had to be maintained. Soulless Ones were not ideal foot-soldiers because they could not match the pace of an Orc or Goblin infantry unit. But what they lacked in marching speed they made up for when it came to battle. These fearless creatures struck abject terror into the hearts of any opponents. And they were totally dispensable. The witch-cursed graveyard behind the Testing Grounds could generate as many Soulless Ones as Thugruff could use. All Vallaska Roue needed to do was provide the bodies that had to be buried there for the three-day incubation period. During the third night following burial, a Soulless One would emerge from each fresh grave, ready to follow a master and do his bidding.

Even now, Roue was arranging with a throat-slitter to bring fresh corpses.

'That's the best offer you'll get from me!' Roue

announced to the weasel-faced little man whose beady eyes peered up at him expectantly. 'Fifteen copper pieces a body. If you're not interested, there's plenty of others who'll not turn their noses up at easy cash. What's it t' be, throat-slitter?'

The grubby little rogue looked about him nervously, considering the offer. Eventually he flashed an angry look at Vallaska Roue and nodded. The pay was poor – but at least there was plenty of work; Roue had offered to take all the corpses he could bring, with no questions asked.

Vallaska Roue gestured to a grey-bearded Dwarf standing beside him to make the necessary arrangements while he strode away, back to his room. He had preparations to make for his journey.

'They WHAT?!' roared Balthus Dire in a tone so ferocious that the tiny scout trembled.

'Oh, sire,' he quivered, 'forgive me. I am just the bearer of bad news, not its perpetrator. And who can tell what goes on in those floating heads of theirs? Not I, that's for sure. Yesterday they were here in the citadel, causing mischief. Now there is no sign of them. They are all gone – unless this is just another Ganjee prank.'

'They would not *dare* to leave the Black Tower. They owe their existence to me. They must be found! They must . . .'

A loud rapping on the door interrupted Dire's rantings.

'ENTER!'

It was the Hill Goblin sergeant, Orcleaver, now commander of Dire's Goblin troops. His armour and his face had the battle-weary look of one who has stepped straight out of a fight. But he related his news calmly enough.

'Fight. In night. Hell-creatures from grave. Goblins kill many. Grave-creatures not die. Many Goblins cut by fingers. Cut Goblins sick. Dying. Die. Rest Goblins run. Village no more. Creatures go north.'

Dire listened intently.

'*Grave-creatures*,' he murmured. He realized where the attack had come from and knew that the raiders would be heading back to Knotoak Wood. Zharradan Marr's legions of the undead. He turned to the Goblin: 'What of the Ganjees? Did you see anything of them? Were they taken captive? Speak!'

The Goblin shivered at the mention of the Ganjees. 'No see spirit faces,' he mumbled. 'Many Goblins dead. Die by grave-creatures. Die at night – '

His report was cut off by the sound of more knocking at the door, and he turned to see who came in when Dire gave the command.

Both Orcleaver and the scout gasped as the door opened. Standing in the doorway was one of the citadel guards, holding one end of a length of rope in his hand. A pitiful moaning sound came from the bulky shape attached to the other end and squirming on the floor. The guard stepped forward, dragging the miserable creature into the room; this caused it to squeal and yelp, as if every inch it moved was merciless agony. All eyes dropped to study the misshapen form.

On the ground before them lay a creature, the likes of which they had never seen before. Its skin was a charred black colour, spattered with red gashes where flesh showed or bone protruded awkwardly. One gnarled leg, broken in several places, stuck out like a tail behind it and jerked weakly. Its head was a monstrosity: dark scales had grown over one side of its human-like face; one ear was missing; its only eye was loose in the socket under a half-closed eyelid. The head was joined to the rest of the body by a long, scrawny neck which also seemed to have been broken in several places.

The Goblin and the scout looked away in disgust.

But Balthus Dire studied the creature for a few moments more. 'Where did you find this?' he demanded of the guard.

'Outside the grounds, by the main gate. And there are more of them. Some are in the courtyard if you wish to see them. There is a crowd gathering.'

'Take it away. Destroy it. Disperse the crowd and destroy the others too before there are any signs of panic. All of you, leave me now. I must have time to think. And plan.'

They trooped out of Dire's study, relieved to be excused and pondering on the gruesome horror they had just seen.

Inside his study, Balthus Dire knew exactly what he had seen, however. He had heard something of Zharradan Marr's magical experiments in the alteration of life, but much of what he had heard was dressed in rumour and speculation. Now he had seen marrangha with his own eyes.

Dire was furious. If Foulblade had left no survivors at the ambush, as had been his orders, then none of this would be happening. Zharradan Marr's raiding party was the inevitable retaliation for the theft of his cunnelwort. In order to prevent the chance of any further raids, Balthus Dire knew that he had to act quickly. If war was to be inevitable, he must strike at the heart of Marr's territory.

7

The Forest of Yore

' . . . And that is how the Lord Thimbeth found himself swindled of all his riches by a scampering cooch!'

The Chervah burst into high-pitched twittering laughter, broken by regular loud gasps as he caught his breath.

A hint of a smile appeared at the corner of Dark-mane's mouth. He had been forced to listen to the Chervah's stories all afternoon. Though by now he did wish for some peace, he couldn't help but be amused; the little creature was a natural storyteller – though he doubted whether any of them held much more than a grain of truth.

The rolling pastures of the Vale of Willow were a colourful sight; the larger farmsteads were sur-rounded by their crop fields while in the smaller ones grew strange-smelling herbs. Needless to say, the Chervah gave a running commentary on everything they saw; he professed to know all there was to know about farming in the Vale of Willow.

The sun had been hiding behind puffy white clouds for most of the afternoon. As it made its slow journey across the sky, it would peek out occasionally to shine on the two riders. The day was warm, but not uncomfortably so. Their route took them past several small groups of peasants working in the fields in their bright-coloured clothes. The Chervah had found that if he gave a wave of greeting as they passed, the field workers would return his gesture and would sometimes smile shyly. At first they had stopped to chat with the peasants, but Darkmane soon realized that the Chervah was incapable of just a short chat. If they wanted to reach the Forest of Yore that evening, they must press on.

The trail ahead wound over a small hillock. They drew their horses to a halt at the top to survey the landscape ahead and caught their first glimpse of the green expanses of the Forest of Yore, cut into two roughly equal halves by the great Whitewater River which rolled on southwards along the nearside of the forest. In an hour or so they would reach their destination for the night.

'Ah, this is indeed a beautiful corner of the world,' the Chervah sighed contentedly as he surveyed the landscape. 'Where I come from the land is much more inhospitable. Colours are duller, and during the months of Locking and Freeze those colour demons steal the previous months' brightness away. Everything is a dull shade of brownish grey.'

Darkmane smiled again. His travelling companion seemed to think that all events that were not to his liking were the work of demons. 'Sleep demons' had held on to him if he overslept one morning. Demons caused pains in the head after nights of over-indulgence (though the Chervah himself swore that he did not touch ale or wine). Demons caused his aim to falter in crossbow tournaments. And if a festival day was spoiled by a torrential downpour – well, of course that was the work of spiteful rain demons.

'Come,' said Darkmane. 'We must reach the Whitewater before nightfall. Tonight we camp in the Forest of Yore. You did remember to instruct the court sorcerer to inform the Wizard Moonchaser of our arrival?'

'I did, sire. Nighthawks took the message to the Grand Wizard shortly after we left Salamonis.'

'What provisions have we?' asked Darkmane.

'I have brought with us, let me see . . .' the Chervah considered what was in his pack. 'Ah yes, we have tuktuk fruit – very tasty and full of goodness. And some tuberbeets – good for the teeth and the digestion, too. Here we have some chopped softwood bark – cleanses the blood and the vitals. Also, look here. I've brought – now I know that you secretly like these – some tigerplant leaves. Remember them? You did – '

'WHAT!' Darkmane's voice rose angrily. 'What sort of provisions are these? I want *food*, not leavings from a compost heap. How do you expect me to make a two-day journey on a handful of – what was it? – chewing beets and fat leaves? Have you brought no meats?'

The Chervah shook his head sadly.

'No bread?'

'We have a little bread*plant*!' he said enthusiastically. 'Much better for you and keeps fresh long – '

Darkmane's icy glare cut him short. 'How about boiled poultry eggs?'

'Ah, hrmph. No. Not as such . . .'

Darkmane was ready to explode. 'You *imbecile*! I ask the king for a manservant and he gives me an incompetent vegetable-lover. You may enjoy living

on nuts and berries, Chervah, but I do not. I take a
man's meal: meat, bread, eggs, cheese. And I *will* eat
my fill tonight. We are heading for Yore, Chervah,
and *you* will hunt my food for me. And if you are not
able to trap me a rabbit, a young buck or even a fenzel,
then *you* will roast on my spit, Chervah or not!'

He wheeled his horse round and dug his heels into
the beast's flanks, galloping off downhill towards the
great Forest of Yore. The Chervah hung his head low
and followed.

Darkness was settling over the land as they made
their camp in the forest. Darkmane tied his horse to
a tree branch and hauled his saddle from its back. His
anger had subsided, but his appetite had grown.

The Chervah was struggling with a tinder box,
trying to light a camp fire. 'Aagh! Curse these fire
demons. Where are they? Stop playing with the tinder! Ooop! Ah, there we are.' He used his hand to
fan the small flame he had succeeded in kindling.
Eventually some dry leaves caught fire, and the flame
grew. He placed some small twigs on top and stood
back.

They had reached the edge of the forest and made
camp not far from the banks of the Whitewater River,
whose gurgling and splashing were constant background noises. Deciding to avoid venturing too far
into the woods, they camped in a clearing by a tall
heavenstip tree. Both were a little nervous – the
Chervah particularly so – aware of the stories they
had heard about the Yorefolk. There was a chance
that their message might not have reached the Grand
Wizard and, if not, their lives would be in danger.

'Well then, Chervah,' Darkmane snapped at the

little creature, who was admiring the fire he had just managed to light. 'Fetch me meat. Take your crossbow and shoot me a young deer. Or a rabbit.'

The Chervah was not looking forward to this one little bit. He disliked the thought of hunting and killing animals. Though he carried a light crossbow with him on his travels, this was for show rather than for effect – he had never used the weapon on a living target. Having seen many a proud beast suffer at the hands of an incompetent huntsman, helplessly writhing on the ground in its death throes or hobbling away, mortally wounded, he had resolved never to be the cause of any creature having to go through that agony. But he could not risk angering Darkmane any further. He took his crossbow and backpack and set off aimlessly into the woods, wondering how he should go about catching Darkmane's dinner.

Night was approaching. The tall warrior picked up a fallen branch that was lying near the horses, and walked over to the fire. The twigs and leaves in the centre of the fire were by now alight; flames were beginning to reach upwards, spreading a flickering orange glow round the clearing. The light was fading fast. He sat down and peered into the burning embers, glad of the peace. His stony face felt the growing heat, a comforting warmth in the darkness. He began to consider the details of his mission.

His plan was ambitious. He would need a small party of able-bodied men. They must be fighters – although he suspected he might also have to enlist the help of a magic-user. This prospect was of the greatest concern to him, as he distrusted the tricks of wily magicians. Fighting men he could buy; their loyalty could always be bought with a purse of gold.

But the men of magic were another breed: any worth their salt had no need of his gold; and those who offered themselves for hire at a price were unworthy allies anyway.

When he had found suitable companions, he would set about his master plan. As he saw it, the danger to Salamonis was minimal while the two sorcerers remained locked in battle. So long as they continued their feud, Salamonis would be ignored. King Salamon was quite right when he pointed to the time of real danger. The war would be fought and eventually won; it was *then* that the victor, inspired by his military successes, would turn his attentions to further conquests. No doubt the first target then would be Salamonis.

But it was undoubtedly also true that the longer the war went on, the better things would be for Salamonis. Not only would prolonged warfare delay the fateful invasion but, the longer Marr and Dire were locked in battle, the greater the number of their troops who would be slain in the struggle. If the war could be continued long enough, the victor would find himself too weak even to contemplate another battle. And if King Salamon took the initiative and chose that moment to attack with his own troops, then the dark threat that hung over his kingdom would be banished for ever.

Darkmane's plan therefore was to keep a watchful eye on the fortunes of the struggle. If one side appeared to gain the upper hand he would find ways to aid their enemies; if the balance swung the other way, his allegiance would shift. His party would remain 'behind the scenes', and for this reason he needed to choose his companions carefully. He would need to gain access to both the warring sorcerers. He must find someone who knew Balthus Dire and someone else acquainted with Zharradan Marr. Calorne Manitus, census-taker of Western Allansia, was the person ideally suited to help him assemble such a party.

The branch in Darkmane's hand snapped, startling him out of his reverie. He tossed it on to the fire and watched it spit and crackle as it caught alight and burned with a dancing flame. The flame grew. As the branch burned, Darkmane became transfixed; he stared into the flame which was now, slowly but perceptibly, changing its colour from yellow to deep orange to a shade of red, until finally it turned the deep scarlet hue of the low sun on a dusty evening.

The flame was growing rapidly. It rose from the branch to dominate the camp fire and then continued climbing upwards until it towered above the small fire. A strange smell reached Darkmane's nostrils, one with a hint of sulphur and saltpetre. And this he knew was the odour of sorcery!

He reacted quickly, springing to his feet. His sword was standing, point down, in the ground by his side and he readied his hand on its pommel. So great was his hatred of magic that his nostrils had developed an ability to detect its faint smell and warned him in good time. He stood his ground and watched the flame grow until it exceeded his own height.

Now something was happening to the mysterious flame. Its red glow was lighting up the clearing as might a fireball, but the heat was modest. Darkmane was standing close to it, yet its heat was not driving him back. His eyes narrowed and he gazed into its centre; fiery shapes were beginning to form.

Suddenly, and without warning, the flame rose into the air – not far, but enough to detach itself from the other flames of the fire. It floated across the ground away from Darkmane, until it was quite separate from the camp fire; then it stopped, shimmering ethereally in the air. The fiery shapes he had seen within the flame were now merging into a single shape of roughly human proportions. Darkmane's knuckles whitened as he gripped his sword-hilt tighter.

'Darkmane! Chadda Darkmane!' A whispery voice, like that of the wind itself, spoke his name. It seemed to come from nowhere, yet from everywhere.

The hairs stood up on the nape of the warrior's neck. This was what he hated most about sorcery: you never truly knew whether you were in danger or not. And if you were, you never knew quite what to expect. He stood his ground.

'Chadda Darkmane! Do not be afraid. Release your weapon. You have no need of it.'

'Show yourself!' barked Darkmane. 'If you are friend, then *you* have no need of this alchemy or this showmanship. Present yourself! Then I may judge for myself whether or not I am in danger. I will not trust my life to the word of one I cannot see.'

His anger was aroused. He knew perfectly well that all these cursed magic-users had a liking for the theatrical: such a dramatic entrance was supposed to instil fear in its audience, as well as respect for the power of its wielder. Yet Darkmane was also apprehensive: he remembered only too well that he was in the Forest of Yore. If this apparition was the Grand Wizard, or even one of his envoys, then he must show deference.

But his eyes remained fixed on the flame; the red

glow was dying. The flame itself was shrinking – but shrinking down to a shape . . . a human shape. As he watched, the glow lightened to pink, then to an even paler colour. The shape became more solid; it was a young – and very beautiful – maiden.

She raised her head and let her long, flowing hair fall back over her shoulders. Her arms, crossing her chest, reached back over her shoulders and seemed to grasp what was left of the pale fire; the flames were extinguished immediately and formed a long robe, which she pulled round her shoulders. She stepped forward and her eyes held Darkmane's gaze. She smiled softly with a smile to melt any man's heart. Darkmane relaxed his grip on his sword.

He recognized the face: the woman at the well! Those doleful green eyes, like fine-set emeralds shining through the darkness. And the cascading golden locks that fell halfway down her back.

Her lips parted and she opened her mouth to speak. 'Chadda Darkmane. I see that you recognize me, though you know me not. It is time for me to introduce myself. My name is Lissamina.' Her soft voice flowed into Darkmane's ears. She was speaking to him, but at the same time he was hearing sweet music. He was spellbound by the woman's loveliness. 'I have come not to frighten you, but to help you if I can. I regret that my entrance has caused you some disturbance, but this is the sorcery I have learnt. I know of your mission and I know something of the difficulties you will face. For that is my art.'

Darkmane followed the woman's words. After a momentary loss of composure, his self-control was now returning. And he knew well that, where magic was concerned, things were not necessarily what they seemed to be. Beautiful and charming though she might be, he could not afford to trust this Lissamina.

'I am not one to put my faith in sorcery,' he said. 'My way is the way of the sword, where what is true is true and what is real is real. This is not so with your chosen way. My eyes see a young sorceress whose beauty compares with the finest princesses of Allansia, offering her help. But my mind sounds a warning: *This is sorcery! All is not what it seems.*'

Lissamina smiled and nodded her head slowly. 'Your suspicions are understandable, and I take no offence. Indeed, I thank you for your compliment which is, I am sure, too courteous. My arrival has aroused your distrust. So be it. I can do naught to allay your fears. But allow me to tell you something about myself and about my skill. If you are able to make use of it, then please do so. If you do not, then that is your choice. First of all, I shall reveal to you a purpose which must remain a secret between us. Do you agree?'

Darkmane had nothing to lose. He nodded in agreement.

'My master is your master: King Salamon himself,' she began. 'Following your audience with the king, I was summoned to him. The king was concerned that he had entrusted a mission of great import to an untried stranger – even if one who promised much. My own instructions were to follow you on your travels and to provide him with news of your progress. But not to interfere with your affairs, lest my purpose become known and his apparent lack of trust in you sway your allegiance.'

The tall warrior listened intently. Ever suspicious, he was searching for any flaws in her story which

might give her away. He spread a blanket on the ground by the fire and offered her a seat.

They sat down together and she continued: 'For six years I had been pursuing my studies in Silverton under Gelda Wane. When I returned to Salamonis two weeks ago, I was anxious to use my knowledge to serve my king. And here was my opportunity! My contemporaries in the Orb Guild were spiteful – I put it down to jealousy – but I cared nothing for their resentment. I was anxious to get on with my mission – so anxious, in fact, that I appeared at the well in order to see you for the first time. I have been following your progress ever since.'

Darkmane considered her words. She knew about the well, so she *was* the woman he had seen. And no one else had been present. No one else knew of the encounter. 'What else do you know of me?' he asked.

'Well, I know that you travel with a Chervah.' Here she gave a little laugh. 'I find him most amusing. Don't you?'

He ignored her question.

'And the Chervah is in the woods, gathering meat for you. He will return shortly with a netted hare and a snake.'

Darkmane had forgotten about his hunger; he realized suddenly that the little creature was probably terrified, being alone in a dark wood. He had been gone for some time.

'I also know that you visited Calorne Manitus's father and that Calorne himself was not home. You are now making for the Fatted Pig in Shazâar, to find him.'

Darkmane raised an eyebrow. If she had told the truth about her task, she was certainly doing her job thoroughly.

She saw that he was impressed. 'Oh, and I can tell you more. I can tell you some of the stories the Chervah related as you were crossing the Vale of Willow. I can tell you what you had to eat after you awoke this morning. I can tell you what colour . . . Ah, no. Oh dear.' Her pretty cheeks flushed pink and she held a hand up to cover them. Darkmane laughed loudly. He was more at ease now; she seemed to be telling the truth. 'Well now, young Lissamina,' he chuckled, 'tell me what you are doing here. You have been following me secretly all this time. Why have you chosen this moment to reveal yourself to me? And against the king's wishes, too. What is it that persuades you to disobey a king?'

'The king will never know, if you hold to your side of our bargain and keep our meeting a secret. In any case, I think King Salamon is wrong to keep us apart – I can be of great help to you. Also, now that I have watched you, I am certain that you are a strong enough man to take the king's suspicions in your stride. They are not unreasonable, for you are – as it were – a stranger to him. You yourself are just as distrustful of sorcery. We are all suspicious of that of which we know nothing.' She rubbed her hands and held them to the flames.

Darkmane fetched another blanket and wrapped it round her. For a moment his hand rested on her shoulder. She noticed the gesture and turned her eyes to look up at him.

'Er . . . So tell me of these "powers" of yours,' he said quickly, resuming his seat by the fire. 'How do you think you can help me?'

Darkmane had heard of her teacher, Gelda Wane, in Silverton. She practised and taught a type of magic which concerned itself more with predicting the future than with conjuring and illusions.

'The skills I have learnt are not limited merely to clairvoyance,' she explained. 'Gelda Wane passed on to me her powers of prediction. I am able to see visions of certain *possibilities* that may unfold in the future. These visions will appear to me in my dreams. Seeing into the future is not an exact science, however: there are always many unknowns. But I will aid you if you wish it. At times when you are unsure as to the outcome of your plans – whether to follow one course of action or another – you may call on me to dream for you. My visions will reveal the likely outcome of your proposals.'

Lissamina looked down at her hands, neatly folded in her lap. Her fingers began to fidget. She had not mentioned that her powers of future sight were not without their dangers. She knew that the strain of entering her vision-dreams was severe. When she dreamed of times to come, she grew weak and had to spend some time afterwards recovering her strength. She had no wish to burden the warrior with these problems. For a moment she stared out across the clearing at the shadows of the trees, cast by the flickering firelight, dancing about in the undergrowth beyond.

Darkmane was staring into the fire, considering her offer. At last he spoke. 'How will I summon you,' he asked her, 'should I wish you to predict my future?'

'We shall communicate at night,' she explained. 'Think of me as you are drifting off to sleep.'

That will not be difficult! thought Darkmane.

'We shall communicate through your dreams.'

He nodded thoughtfully. 'Let me also ask you this,'

he said. 'You have clairvoyance and you have powers of future sight. What is your advice to me? Should I seek for adventurers in Shazâar as I plan? Or should I choose another future?'

She paused for a moment's thought, then replied: 'You should know this. Zharradan Marr has succeeded in enticing the Ganjees from Dire's citadel. They have the secret of battle-magic. If he can persuade them to share the secret with him, he will surely be the victor in this war – and in a short time. I know of your plan to prolong the war. If the Ganjees could be persuaded to remain neutral, perhaps this would bode well for your cause. Failing that, Marr must be deprived of his unlimited troops of Soulless Ones. As things stand, however, the battle is definitely weighted in favour of the necromancer.'

Darkmane was shocked. Without the spirit creatures, the balance of power was certainly one-sided.

Suddenly a voice from the depth of the forest startled him. 'Master! Sire! *Help!*'

He swung round in the direction of the voice. The Chervah! And it sounded as if he was in trouble.

The warrior grabbed his sword and leapt up from the fire to the edge of the clearing. He peered into the undergrowth. 'That little fool has . . .' His words petered out as he realized he was talking to no one.

The mysterious sorceress had disappeared.

The Chervah was panting hard as he struggled through the undergrowth, sweeping leaves and branches out of his way with one hand. The other was gripping his crossbow and a net. A crashing noise was coming from behind him. Something was following him . . . something *large*.

He broke through into the clearing. Darkmane grabbed him.

'Sire, please! We must go! It is coming! *Quick!*'

'*What* is coming? Calm down, Chervah! Be still, you idiot! What is following you?'

But before the Chervah could speak, Darkmane's questions were answered. A dark, bulky shape burst out of the bushes into the clearing. The ball of black fur had a distinctive white stripe running the length of its back. It stopped in front of the fire and reared up on its two hind legs to face them. Its eyes glared with a look of fury and its black lips were drawn back to reveal sharp teeth. Deadly claws – more like talons than claws – slid from the creature's furry paws as it advanced towards them with a great roar which sent the Chervah scampering into the woods, running for his life. Darkmane held his ground and grasped his sword with both hands. He had fought a Skunkbear once before. He moved slowly round to the left, keeping the fire between himself and the enraged creature. The Skunkbear roared again, dropped on to all fours, and leapt round the fire with astonishing speed. Darkmane drew his sword back to strike, then swept it across the creature's chest. The Skunkbear howled with pain as the blade drew blood. It slashed out at Darkmane ferociously with its razor-sharp claws, missing his sword-arm by a hair's breadth. Darkmane brought the blade back with a blow aimed at the Skunkbear's head, and this time the sword bit deep just below its ear. Bone crunched as the sword wedged itself in the creature's skull, and Darkmane struggled to pull it out. As he did so, the Skunkbear, now enraged to a rabid fury, lashed out at him. He cried in pain as the claws slashed across his midriff, ripping his tunic. He protected his stomach with his free arm and stepped back to gain his balance.

The Skunkbear turned its back on him and raised its tail. Darkmane had seen this happen before. He knew what was to come and he dived back into the bushes just as a spray of liquid pattered on the leaves in front of him. Taking a deep breath, the warrior gagged; the stink of the Skunkbear's spray was horrendous – the sewers of Port Blacksand were perfume compared to this foul stench. Darkmane staggered sideways as the creature turned towards him and advanced.

'Run, sire!'

Darkmane heard the Chervah's shrill voice. The little creature had found his courage and returned, crossbow at the ready, to aid his master. But then the smell of the Skunkbear spray reached his nostrils.

'Oh, ye mighty gods! The stinking breath from a drunken demon's belch! What a smell!'

A poorly aimed bolt from his crossbow missed the Skunkbear – but it did serve to divert the creature's attention while Darkmane readied himself. The Chervah's second bolt was more accurate. As the Skunkbear advanced towards Darkmane, the Chervah fired a shot that sank into its paw so deep that its point protruded from the other side. The creature roared in pain and Darkmane seized his chance. Holding his sword over his head, point forward, he charged the woeful beast and stabbed his weapon down at its neck. The Skunkbear opened its mouth to roar once again. The sword missed its original target and instead disappeared between the creature's jaws. The roar ended abruptly in a gurgle and the Skunkbear sank to the ground, the tip of

Darkmane's bloodied blade sticking out of the back of its throat.

The two adventurers fell to their knees, exhausted. They both stared at the beast's huge carcass.

It was the Chervah who spoke first. 'Well, sire, you did ask me to bring you back some meat . . .'

He looked up at Darkmane nervously. He realized that the creature that had followed him back to camp could just as easily now have been feasting on *them*.

Darkmane's solemn expression did not change as his stony face turned towards the little creature. He saw the apprehension in the Chervah's eyes. Creases appeared on either side of his mouth. His head rolled back and he laughed loudly.

'Aye, manservant,' he bellowed, 'that you did. And it seems you have brought me a selection. What is on the menu tonight?' He looked down at the net, still grasped in the Chervah's hand. 'What have we here? A skinny hare? A measly groundsnake? Not enough meat on either of those for a hearty meal. Tonight we will feast well. Here is our meat. Come, Chervah. First see to my wounds. Then you can chop up this Skunkbear and cook me my dinner.'

8

The Raid on Coven

Charnley Troone pushed open the door of his hut and took a deep breath before entering. His wife had prepared a pot of turnip stew which simmered on the fire. Toggi and Mindi, his two young sons, were playing in a corner of the hut. Each held a short stick. While Toggi held his stick stretched out before him with one end gripped in each hand, Mindi was trying to hit it with his own stick before Toggi could whip it quickly away. Their loud shrieks alternated between laughter and anger as they played. Shabitha Troone, nestling a squalling baby in her arms, pleaded with them to be quiet.

The game was forgotten when Charnley entered. Shabitha sighed with relief as the two boys dropped their sticks and rushed to greet their father, who scooped them up in his arms and hugged them tightly. He smiled at Shabitha. She knew him well; that weary smile meant he had had a hard day in the fields.

It was the season of harvest for the tuberbeets; back-breaking work, digging into the soil to find the fat underground plants, then the even more arduous tug-of-war against the tough root-strands to pull them out of the ground. The men of Coven saved their strength for the tuberbeet harvest, and when it was over they celebrated with their two-day Festival of the Limmannin. Charnley was looking forward to the celebrations next week but, until then, he and all the other field workers in the village could expect another five days of aches, pains, blisters and sweat.

'How many today, Da?' asked Toggi.

'Thirty-four.'

'*Thirty-four!* Coo! Let me see your hands.'

Toggi was fascinated by his father's hands after a hard day's work. If any new blisters had appeared his eyes would open wide in admiration, as a soldier's son might admire his father's war-wounds. Being the elder of the two, Toggi knew he would soon be helping his father in the fields; and he longed for the day when he too would work so hard that blisters would appear on his palms.

'Oooh! Look at this one, Mindi! Coo, it must be sore – is it, Da?'

His father nodded.

The Troones had lived in Coven all their lives and they could foresee no future other than remaining there. Charnley was not an ambitious man nor was he particularly bright. But he had a kindly face and a gentle manner, and he could tell a good story. He worked hard in the fields and he had built a fine hut on the edge of the village for his family. Its neatly thatched roof and clay-caked walls had so far withstood the hostilities of the elements.

Shabitha Troone kept their single room tidy and tended the goat and chickens they kept in their yard outside. She had borne Charnley three children: the

The Raid on Coven

two boys and their baby sister, Bethalee. Looking after the hut and the children was more than a full-time job for her and she always looked forward to Charnley's return from the fields so she could have a break from watching over the youngsters. She was now serving out the turnip stew into wooden bowls as the family took their seats round the fire.

'Word is there's trouble brewing,' said Charnley through gulps of his stew.

'What trouble?' asked Shabitha.

'Ever heard of Lord Balthus Dire?'

'No.'

'Seems he and the Lord Zharradan were scholars together. Now he lives to the south in the Cragrocks, in a large tower. Something happened between them – no one knows quite what – and they are at odds with each other. Folks say, if things get worse Lord Zharradan will be recruiting an army.'

Shabitha stopped eating and looked gravely at Charnley. 'An army?'

'That's what they say.'

'From Coven?'

' 'Aps from Coven. Or Salamonis. Or he may even bring in Flatlands mercenaries.'

His wife was frightened. Though they hated Zharradan Marr, he had undoubtedly brought peace to the village. Before his arrival, Coven had been a continual target for raiding bandits. But ever since he became their lord, the raids had stopped; no one *dared* attack his village.

Her eyes dropped to her lap. 'W-w-will . . . D-do you think *you* might be called on for this army of his?'

'I can't say.' Charnley's face was glum. 'But you know I cannot refuse if my lord calls on my services.

89

Even though I'm resentful – we all are – of having to serve such a black-hearted rogue.'

Shabitha was close to tears. The two boys had been silenced by the conversation and now stared, open-mouthed, at their father.

Charnley tried to comfort his wife. 'Don't fret, my dear. Who knows, this may be nothing more than a fanciful rumour. In any case, Lord Zharradan would not send us off during the tuberbeet harvest. 'Aps things may blow over before the harvest is done.'

They finished their meal in silence. Even Charnley himself was deep in thought, chewing over the fears which he had not dared express to Shabitha. He had never been called on for military service before. He had no sword, no armour. What chance did a peasant army have against trained soldiers?

'*Listen!*' Toggi's whisper broke the silence.

'What is it?' asked Shabitha.

'Ssssh.'

'I can't hear anything.'

'In the distance. Listen.'

They all listened hard.

'There!'

'Yes,' said Shabitha. 'I *can* hear something out there. It sounds like . . .'

'It's getting closer.'

'What is it?'

The sounds were indeed getting closer. From afar, an ominous rumbling noise was approaching. As it grew slowly louder, Charnley could pick out individual sounds: the distant tramping of feet; the chink of metal; an occasional high-pitched whistling, followed, as if in answer, by a rallying roar. Closer it came.

The Raid on Coven

A storm was gathering. A storm of evil.

Charnley rushed to the door of the hut, pushed it open, and stepped outside. Further down the dusty road, his neighbours' heads were appearing at their doors.

'Look!' shouted one. 'Out there! Coming towards us!'

The others ran to where he was standing and peered southwards, following the direction indicated by his trembling finger. He was pointing towards the Trolltooth Pass.

'See!' The tone of his voice had changed; he could not disguise the fear he felt. 'Oh my gods! There are hundreds of them! And all coming this way!'

In the distance Charnley could make out flickering lights. Torches! They were arranged in a line stretching right across his field of vision – and they were advancing! The dim light of the torches fell on the torch-bearers and behind them lit up a more terrifying sight. For following the torch-bearers were more figures – figures of all shapes and sizes. And the occasional flash as the torchlight glinted on metal could mean only one thing. These figures were dressed in battle-armour.

The sounds were now clearer; the steady progress of the marching army was unmistakable. The cries and grunts of the advancing creatures were picked up by the wind and carried to the ears of the terrified group of villagers. A rousing whistle sounded. It was answered first by a roar from the troops and then by a loud thumping as several hundred feet stamped on the ground in unison.

The villagers began shrieking.

'We are attacked!'

'Sound the alarm!'

'We must run!'

'No! We must stand and defend our homes and our families!'

'Alert the village!'

'Who will tell Lord Zharradan?'

'Shabitha! Gather the children!'

The last call came from Charnley Troone, who by now was racing back to his hut, his weariness forgotten. He flung open the door. Shabitha and the boys were standing beside the fire; they stared anxiously at him.

'What is it, Da?'

'Raiders!' he panted. 'Coming this way. Hundreds of them. Quick! We must flee! They will be here in minutes!'

'Oooooow!' Shabitha was rooted to the spot with fear.

'Quick, woman!' snapped Charnley. 'There is no time for fear. We must gather our things and leave if we are to escape with our lives!'

But his words had no effect. She remained where she stood, sobbing hysterically and desperately clutching baby Bethalee.

He grabbed her and shook her. 'Do you not hear me? They will be here! We must flee east into Knotoak Wood. Gather your senses, woman!'

She wailed again and fell, sobbing, into his arms. He held her tight, but then pushed her away. Too much had to be done, too quickly. He took the baby while she wiped her face.

She managed eventually to compose herself and began to fling their belongings into a dirty haversack. The boys were stuffing clothes and food into a grain sack. Charnley reached under his straw mattress and grabbed a small pouch containing the few copper pieces they had saved, and stuffed it into the pocket of his breeches. Still clutching Bethalee in one arm, he picked up a pitchfork in the other and urged Shabitha and the boys to hurry.

A bell began to ring from the run-down chapel to the north of the village; the alarm had finally been sounded. The village was now alerted, and the bustle got louder as the peasants scurried about, unsure what to do. Women wailed, children cried and men shouted angrily, tempers flaring. The whole of Coven was in a state of terrified confusion. The streets of the village were solid with people rushing this way and that. Some carried or dragged baskets and sacks overflowing with belongings. Some frantically cried out the names of friends and loved ones, lost in the crowds. Some, unwilling to leave their homes, had decided to barricade themselves in and were preparing their meagre defences against the invaders.

But the invading army had now reached the outskirts of Coven.

'CHARGE!' came the cry, followed by three shrill blasts on the whistlehorn. And the legions of hell itself descended in fury on the defenceless villagers.

Indescribable creatures of chaos and damnation swept into Coven wielding their weapons of mayhem: Hill Goblins with their shortswords and cutlasses; foul-mouthed Orcs with savage teeth. Black Hellhounds roared and spat flames around.

And the unknown terrors struck. Tall, two-headed creatures wrapped in armoured cloaks swung long-handled scythes, sweeping the way clear before them and leaving a trail of bodies as they advanced. Giant fly-creatures with hairy legs, sharp talons and cutting mandibles hovered in the air. Small, eyeless fiends with shaggy faces were armed with short bows which they fired in volleys, aiming with deadly accuracy at the fleeing villagers. And giant spider-beasts towered above the huts, stalking through the village on long, spindly legs.

'Mindi! Look out!' Charnley yelled.

He grabbed the boy and yanked him to one side just as a fat spider-beast proboscis thumped into the ground where he had been standing. Steam hissed from its slimy folds and it was sucked back into the

air, coiling up towards that hideous head in the sky above, now searching around for another victim.

'Are you all right, son?'

'Yes, Da, I'm fine. W-what was *that*?'

'I don't know. I've never seen anything like it. Where are the others?'

In the commotion Shabitha had been swept away with Toggi and Bethalee in the middle of the panicking crowd. She too had just realized that they had become separated from Charnley. 'Toggi! Can you see your father? Where's Mindi?'

'I don't know. *Mother! Look out!*'

A flat-nosed Orc let out a whoop as, racing through the crowd, he swung his cleaver dangerously close to

Shabitha. She avoided the blow and the cleaver blade bit deep into the side of an abandoned wooden cart. With a maniacal laugh, the Orc leapt past Shabitha and Toggi and on into the crowd.

'Where is Da? I can't see him!'

Toggi was sick with fright. From the darkness came more snarling Orcs. He carried no weapon; they could only run from the foul creatures. But wherever they turned, their way was blocked by panicking villagers.

He grabbed his mother's hand and tugged at it. 'Look! There's Da and Mindi!' Toggi caught a glimpse of Charnley standing in the middle of the road, desperately searching for his wife and son. 'Da! here we are!'

But Charnley could not hear Toggi in the chaos. He ducked just in time as a buzzing fly-creature the size of a winged dog swooped down, talons poised to grab him. The bristling beast wheeled around in the air and turned to strike once more. But this time Charnley was ready. He steadied himself and held his pitchfork in both hands. As the creature came within range, he jabbed up with the pitchfork, aiming at its underbelly. A blazing torch flew through the air, thrown by one of the chaos raiders. The winged horror dived quickly to avoid it and Charnley felt the heavy thump as it landed on his pitchfork. The monstrosity was impaled on the weapon's prongs, which had pierced its abdomen. It squealed in agony and a thick greenish brown liquid trickled down the pitchfork handle. Charnley felt a burning sensation as it reached his hands and he dropped the weapon.

The creature fell to the ground with a plop. Immediately two similar creatures darted down from the sky and landed on the fallen fly-beast, tearing hungrily at its black body, their mandibles clicking. Charnley backed off in horror and grabbed Mindi, turning him away from the sight. Suddenly he heard a familiar voice behind him.

'Da! Here! Here we are! Wait! Mindi!'

Toggi was rushing towards them, pushing his way through the crowd.

'Toggi! Here! Wai . . . NO! WATCH OUT!'

He had noticed one of the shaggy-faced archers taking aim in Toggi's direction. It drew back the bowstring and fired an arrow into the crowd of villagers.

'NO! No-o-o-o! TOGGI!' screamed Charnley Troone.

The crowd parted quickly as the arrow sped towards them. Miraculously, the arrow missed all of them and Charnley breathed a sigh of relief as he saw it *thunk* into the wall of a hut. But the parting crowd had swept Toggi off his feet. He was nowhere to be seen.

Shabitha was feeling faint. She had heard the cries but had not seen what had happened. All around, villagers were pushing past this way and that. She had completely lost her bearings and had no idea which way to flee. And little Bethalee, wrapped in her arms, was wailing with fright. She chose a direction and pushed forward, tears running down her cheeks. If only she could find Charnley!

She noticed a familiar face in the crowd – the bushy eyebrows, thick beard and woollen cap of Grummold Noomran. Grummold was a kindly old soul who lived alone, quite close to the Troones. Before settling in Coven, he had been a woodsman in Knotoak Wood, and the children loved to hear his stories of the creatures he had encountered – though most of his stories were probably more fantasy than fact.

For Shabitha, Grummold's face now seemed like a ray of light in the darkness. She pushed towards him. 'Grummold! Grummold Noomran! Help! Oh, please help! Have you seen Charnley? I've lost my husband. Please! Help me!'

He was shoving his way frantically through the crowd. His normally calm features had taken on an unfamiliar, aggressive – almost *savage* – look as he fought to break through the sea of people barring his way. His eyes darted towards Shabitha as he heard her cries, and for an instant his angry expression relaxed. But there was nothing he could do for her. It was each man for himself now. If he paused to help this woman, then no doubt both of them would be slaughtered by the raiders. His eyes turned away and he continued to battle his way through the crowd.

Shabitha was devastated. She turned, first one way then another. By now, she was so confused she was in a hopeless state. She stood in the centre of the road clutching her baby, unable to decide what to do or where to turn next. She seemed to be facing in the wrong direction. Now the fleeing villagers were all shoving past her, apparently running away from *something*. But Shabitha was past caring. She could do no more than stand, weep and clutch Bethalee tighter.

Charnley and Mindi turned a corner and arrived at the square in the centre of Coven. Their situation was hopeless. Charnley turned to see the awful devastation that had once been their home. Flames licked high into the sky. Columns of dark smoke arose from the dry huts as the raiders' torches set them alight.

The Raid on Coven

The sounds of battle filled their ears. Screams of murder and death still rang out and echoed in the distance. And the raiders were still advancing.

A crowd was milling about in the village square. It seemed to be a logical place for the people to head for, in order to decide what to do next. No one had any clear idea, but the words 'Knotoak Wood' could be heard among the general hubbub. The consensus seemed to be that the villagers should flee into the forest.

But Charnley could not escape. First he must find Shabitha, Toggi and Bethalee.

He pulled Mindi to him in front of the medicine man's hut. 'Mindi, I must try to find them. They may be in trouble.'

'Yes, Da. I help.'

'No, Mindi. It's too dangerous. You must wait here until I come back.'

'No, Da! I come with you.' There were tears in his eyes.

'I won't be long. You know how your mother gets so frightened. I'll find them sooner if you stay here.'

Mindi was silent, his eyes turned to the ground. Tears rolled down his cheeks.

'You must be brave, Mindi. I'll only be gone a few minutes. And if I am not back soon, follow the crowds into Knotoak Wood and I'll meet you there, with your mother, Toggi and little Bethalee. Will you do that for me?'

Mindi tried to be brave. He nodded, wiping his eyes with the back of his hand.

'Good boy. Take care. And remember: if I am not back soon, follow that road to the east and we'll see you in the wood. And I have a very important job for you. I want you to mind these for me.'

From his own pocket he pulled the pouch containing his copper pieces. He pressed it into Mindi's hand and closed his son's fingers around it. He kissed the top of his son's head, turned and headed back towards his hut to look for Shabitha. Mindi watched him go.

It was the last time Mindi Troone ever saw his father.

9

Battle Plans

The raid on Coven by Lord Balthus Dire's chaos hordes had been merciless. The few villagers who survived were forced to flee into Knotoak Wood and from there deeper into the Forest of Spiders. Some followed the trail and sought refuge at Lord Zharradan's Testing Grounds, where Thugruff ordered that only able-bodied men were to be allowed in; he had no use for women or children. Others left the paths and scoured the woods for a suitable site to build a makeshift camp as a temporary home. But the harrowing experience of the raid showed in their eyes. They had no idea how 'temporary' their new homes would be.

Coven itself had been razed to the ground. All that remained of the once peaceful little village was a scattering of smouldering embers, like so many burnt-out giant camp fires. And everywhere were the gruesome remains of those unfortunates who had not escaped. Some were limbless; some were half eaten; some had been decapitated. Most were barely recognizable as the simple peasants they had once been.

After the raiders had taken their pickings from the

ruins of Coven, they turned and made their way back towards the Cragrocks, still whooping with excitement at the carnage they had caused. It had been a good night.

The body count had shown that their casualties were minimal; almost insignificant. A couple of the giant fly-creatures had been impaled on makeshift spears; three Hill Goblins had been trapped as a flaming hut collapsed; and two angry Orcs had killed each other in a brawl, arguing over which of them could claim the axe-grinder's daughter as a prize. These casualties had been packed into sacks and taken off by Lord Zharradan's men.

Zharradan Marr seethed inwardly as he listened to their descriptions of the scene. Luckily the raiders had not discovered any of the entrances to Marr's underground domain. His dungeons – and his mines – were safe. But while he had always despised the weaklings who had inhabited the village, the crops they grew were needed to feed his army and his slaves.

His dark-red eyes narrowed as he sat back in his chair. The sergeant-at-arms tried to study his expression but found himself unable to look at Marr's eerie green face for more than a moment. It was as if he was being forced into a state of humility by Marr's very presence.

Finally the necromancer raised a single bony finger and scratched the point of his ear. 'Find Thugruff,' he hissed. 'Tell him to prepare the *Galleykeep*. Tomorrow we ride south!'

The *Galleykeep* was Zharradan Marr's ultimate fighting machine: a majestic sky-galleon with billowing black sails which caught the wind and drew the vessel smoothly through the air. As a spectacle, its magnificence was unsurpassed. Those on the ground who saw the *Galleykeep* pass above believed they were watching the gods themselves sail past. As a transport vessel it could carry a thousand troops or as much cargo as passed through Trolltooth Pass overland in ten weeks. As a battleship its power was awesome: it could be attacked only by cannonfire or by flying creatures – indeed it was Marr's trusted flying Tooki troops who had captured the *Galleykeep* in the first place. And it had an impressive range of deadly weapons, such as trident cannons and potash balloons, which were unique to the *Galleykeep*.

The sergeant-at-arms was scratching his chin as he left his lord's chamber. *The* Galleykeep, he thought. *Does this mean Lord Zharradan will sail direct to Craggen Rock and take Dire on in his own territory?* He shook his head. He did not believe they had sufficient advantage to risk such a daring attack. Nevertheless he set off to pass Zharradan's message on to Thugruff.

But Zharradan Marr knew that he did not dare risk the *Galleykeep* on a journey deep into Dire's territory. Balthus Dire was a sorcerer of great power and, were his magical resources used against the *Galleykeep*, Marr could not be certain of victory. It would be extremely unwise for Zharradan Marr to lay himself open like that. Like all generals, he would let his troops take the risks and fight the battles. He himself would simply close in to take the glory when the battle had already been won.

Instead he was planning to use the sky-galleon strategically. It was time to step up the battle. His troops must be sent out to war.

*

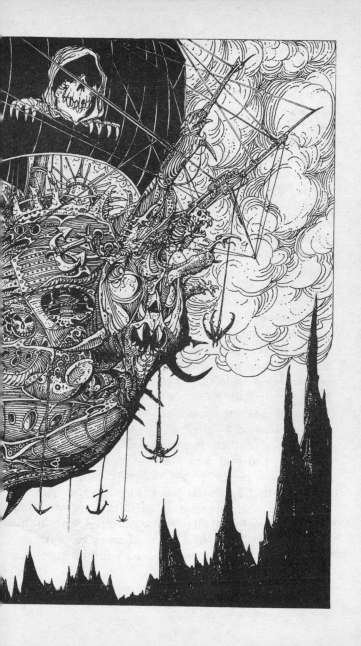

Balthus Dire's strength and his weakness both derived from the location of his headquarters. High up in the Cragrocks, it was a difficult military target; no army could storm it easily. And the journey, for any force large enough, would be extremely perilous. The slow going would allow hill scouts to plot an army's progress accurately, and there were too many opportunities for ambushes and rockfalls. Thugruff's raiding party had been lucky; Marr knew that Balthus Dire would by now have made arrangements to prevent another such raid.

The necromancer himself was not so well defended. The massacre at Coven had shown him just how close Balthus Dire was able to get. Though the raiders had not found the entrance to his dungeons, they had no doubt passed dangerously close to one or more of their secret locations.

But the very fact that the Black Tower *was* so inaccessible posed problems for Balthus Dire. It was difficult for his own troops to move about *en masse*. And his supply routes were easily sabotaged.

Marr was laying plans for besieging the Black Tower from a distance.

Supplies reached the citadel from the north and west. To the east and south was nothing but the inhospitable peaks of the Craggen Heights. Nothing grew in this area save rock mosses and scrawny bushes. It was true that a hardy type of mountain goat could be found all over the Craggen Heights, but they were difficult to hunt and were certainly not plentiful enough to provide food for all the Black Tower's inhabitants.

Over the next few weeks Zharradan Marr sent out troops on the *Galleykeep*. The first priority was to guard

Battle Plans

the narrows of the Trolltooth Pass. The Pass had to be patrolled at all times, for it would be difficult to prevent Dire sending raiding parties eastwards out of Craggen Heights to the southern side of the Pass.

Other troops were positioned along the banks of the Whitewater River, just south of the Vale of Willow. From there they could build rafts and boats to patrol the two tributaries which came down from the Cragrocks and fed the fast-flowing Whitewater. Supplies to the Black Tower *had* to cross these tributaries, and Marr's troops knew well what grim penalties they faced should they fail to prevent *all* supplies getting through.

The *Galleykeep* became Zharradan Marr's new war office. He could not risk another close encounter with his enemies. Though he preferred his underground sanctuary, necessity dictated that he take up his chambers aboard the sky-galleon.

Skirmishes and battles between the warring forces became everyday occurrences. At first Marr's troops were successful in cutting supply lines. Simple traders on their way up to the Black Tower were either turned back or slaughtered. Hill Goblins were sent to escort supplies through, and battles ensued all along the Whitewater tributaries. In the Vale of Willow, where the Whitewater passed through the Forest of Yore, folk told of days when the water could be seen to have a tinge to it: sometimes faintly pink, sometimes faintly green. And there was a marked effect on the vegetation growing along the riverbanks: flowers began to wither and the normal full green colour of the grasses and leafy plants seemed unhealthily pale for the time of year.

The Trolltooth Wars

Thus, much to Balthus Dire's chagrin, the Cragrock foothills became for a while the battleground of the Trolltooth Wars. He was on the defensive. He desperately needed supplies to get through. But only one supply caravan in four reached him safely, thanks to Zharradan Marr's 'attack and destroy' orders. Soon independent merchants would not risk a journey to the Black Tower – even at the high prices offered.

It was time for Balthus Dire to step up his campaign, time to take some risks – risks that could be disastrous for him or risks that could bring forces of untold power into the battle on his side.

It was time to use the cunnelwort.

10

Shazâar

'And look at *that*!' whispered the Chervah. 'What do you think *they're* doing?'

Darkmane followed his manservant's eyes. The Chervah was staring at two men standing in front of a building they were passing. One had long fingernails and was scratching strange shapes on to his own chest. The other was lying on a table, painting himself all over with a black dye.

He shrugged. Darkmane hadn't the faintest idea what they were doing.

They had arrived in Shazâar.

They were saddlesore and weary after their long ride from the Whitewater River across the dusty Southern Plain. The sun was ready to set as they rode into Shazâar. But their weariness was now forgotten. No visitor to the peculiar oasis town could fail to be amazed both by its strange beauty and by the bizarre behaviour of its inhabitants. At the entrance gate, a guard had given them directions to the Fatted Pig and had then waved them off with a strange farewell: 'May Logaan take your lucre . . .'

The two of them continued along Moon Street as the guard had directed them. And after entering the town of Shazâar, the sights they saw soon persuaded them that the town's bizarre reputation was no exaggeration.

The buildings were a strange mixture. Many were small, square dwelling-huts with plain fronts. These had been brightly painted in a multitude of splashes of colours – as if pots of paint had been thrown against the walls by naughty children. These smaller houses were interspersed with tall, sprawling buildings with unnatural spires and gables that jutted out from the central structures at all angles. It was as if their builders had chosen to tack on extensions, spires and stairways entirely at random, with no thought of practicality. These buildings looked as if they were organic, growing a little each season like great oak trees.

The place was a wonder to behold.

'Sire, look. The junction. There are the market stalls.' Through an archway, the Chervah had noticed the junction, and now he held out a hand and tugged his master's sleeve to attract his attention, pointing to it. Darkmane nodded and they rode on through the archway which, they discovered, was not a viaduct as they had assumed. Moon Street actually passed through a room of one of the larger houses.

They continued until they reached the junction.

'Look at these places,' chuckled the Chervah.

Behind the stalls were a number of shops. Each bore a sign advertising the services of its owner. The Chervah studied them and one in particular caught his attention.

'Hmmm. *Diseases and Deformities*. I'll wager that healer does a brisk business in this asinine place.'

Darkmane smiled. He pointed to the message written beneath the main banner.

The Chervah squinted and read it out loud: 'Hmm. I can't quite read it. Let me see. "Diseases and Deformities". *Leprosy for Sale*. What? *Mutilations Performed to Your Requirements*?' He turned to Darkmane with a look of horror on his face.

By now the warrior was laughing loudly. 'I don't understand it, Chervah,' he chuckled. 'This place is as strange to me as it is to you. Who knows what is going on? Come on, little friend. Let's keep moving.'

A number of tattered street hawkers had gathered round their horses. One of them held out a handful of rotten bomba fruits. Darkmane did not even look at him. He shoved the urchin away with his foot.

Another scruffy young lad was standing by the Chervah's horse, making stupid faces up at him.

The Chervah stared at him quizzically. 'What is he doing?' he asked Darkmane.

'I don't know. Perhaps he's simple.'

'Go away!' the Chervah shouted. 'We have no money. Don't bother us. Let us pass.'

They nudged their horses through the urchins. Shouts came from behind them but they did not look back.

Further along the road they came to the area of waste ground the guard had spoken of. A game of some sort was being played by a group of grubby young boys.

'Ogreball,' said the Chervah. 'I've seen it played before. See that lad in the middle? He's the flinger.

111

He flings the ball at that tree stump and tries to hit it. The striker – see, that one standing in front of the tree stump with the club? He tries to strike the ball away. If he hits it, he must run round that circuit of sacks. The flinger's getting ready. Watch.'

They reined in their horses and watched. The flinger twisted himself into a hunched-up position and then uncoiled, flinging the ball at the tree stump.

'Must be a good flinger,' said the Chervah. 'I couldn't even see the ball.'

The striker swung his club and began to run. In the field, the fetchers ran about, chasing after his hit. And the striker ran round the trail of sacks as quickly as he could.

They rode on past the Ogreball game and turned left. They passed a man carrying a dog over his shoulders and asked him the way to the Fatted Pig inn. The dog barked twice and raised a paw, pointing down the street.

The man stared at them blankly.

The road ahead narrowed as they trotted under an archway. After passing through, they entered what must have been the central part of Shazâar. Many more people and animals were milling around in the streets. No one took any notice of them.

A short distance further on, they reached their goal. A wide building stood on its own on the left-hand side of the road; its dark-green walls were criss-crossed with blue timbers. Suspended above the road from a pole hung a cage, and inside the cage was a large sow, lying contentedly asleep and swaying gently in the breeze.

Beneath the cage, the scene was not so peaceful, however. Sounds of merrymaking and the smell of

ale came from the inn and drifted along the street.
Men entered and left – walking as they entered and
staggering as they left.

They had reached the Fatted Pig.

They dismounted and tethered their horses outside
the inn. Darkmane's dry throat was urging him inside.
But the Chervah was wary of these drinking-houses;
he had been in them many times before and he
avoided them if he could. His size and his baby-like
Chervah features were usually the object of drunken
ridicule by the patrons of such places. He took his
time fingering the horse's ties.

Darkmane was growing impatient. 'Chervah! Come
on! I'm parched. Hurry yourself!'

'Er, you go on ahead, master. I will wait here and
tend the horses.'

'Don't be foolish. The horses will look after themselves. Let's go inside and wet our whistles. Get
yourself over here. Now!'

The Chervah finished tying up his horse and
walked slowly over to Darkmane. Together they
entered the Fatted Pig.

The tavern was packed with customers. Inside, the
air hung heavy with smoking-weed fumes, and the
hubbub was deafening until their ears grew accustomed to it. The Chervah coughed uncomfortably as
he followed Darkmane through the crowd. Beady
eyes from all corners of the dingy room followed them
as they made their way to the bar. They squeezed
between wooden tables and round three-legged
stools. One of the drinkers was accidentally jostled as
Darkmane pushed past him. In a flash he stood up,
bottle in hand, and grabbed Darkmane's shoulder.

The Chervah gasped, but Darkmane merely flashed the man an icy glare. The man sat down again slowly, mumbling to himself. Wisely, he had decided against taking on the tall Salamonian warrior.

'I-I don't like this place one bit,' stammered the Chervah.

'Relax, little friend. Have a mug of ale. Have two! No one in this room will bother you. *Innkeeper!*'

'Thank you, sire. But I would prefer canefruit nectar. It . . . it is much more nourishing than ale. Perhaps you might even like to try it yourself . . .'

Behind the bar stood a well-rounded man with a balding head. He wore an apron that had no doubt begun the day a clean white colour; but a day's bar

work in the Fatted Pig made this difficult to believe. He turned from serving another customer and stepped up to Darkmane, rolling his sleeves up.

'Yaahhh?'

'A flagon of ale, innkeeper. And my little friend here wonders whether you have . . . what was it, Chervah?'

'Er, canefruit nectar, sire,' answered the Chervah, nervously. 'But please don't go to any trouble. I would just as soon wait outside . . .'

'Canefruit nectar,' laughed Darkmane. 'Do you have any canefruit nectar, innkeeper?'

The burly innkeeper shook his head.

'Then *two* flagons of ale. And can you find us

a table? We have travelled from the Whitewater River and we wish to rest here.'

'Two flagons of ale.' The innkeeper had already filled the flagons and he put them on the bar. 'Six pieces of silver. Find your own table.'

Darkmane raised an eyebrow. This innkeeper had the manners of a Blacksander. He fished out six coins and placed them on the man's outstretched palm. But as the innkeeper closed his fingers on the money, Darkmane gripped his wrist tightly.

'Calorne Manitus,' he whispered. 'The census-taker. He stays here. Which room?'

'His business. Not yours.' The innkeeper snatched his hand away and turned from Darkmane to serve another customer.

'Here! Master! Over here!' The Chervah had found two free stools at a table.

Darkmane brought over the drinks and they both sat down.

'I fear you have wasted your money, sire. I cannot drink a flagon of this ale. I-I actually find the smell rather repulsive. Please. Drink mine as well. I am not as thirsty as you are.'

'Nonsense,' laughed Darkmane. 'If you are half as thirsty as I am, you will down this flagon in one gulp. Try it.'

'No, master, I couldn't.'

'Go on, Chervah. Extinguish your thirst.'

'I would rather not, sire.'

'I insist!'

'Well . . .'

The little creature gripped the flagon gingerly. He held it under his small nose and sniffed. His face contorted itself into an expression of disgust.

116

Shazâar

Darkmane laughed again. 'Go on, Chervah. It may not be canefruit nectar, but it will certainly satisfy your thirst. Drink!'

Eventually the Chervah's thirst overcame his reluctance. He tried the ale. At first just a sip, then a mouthful, then he took several gulps. He spluttered and grimaced. The rest of the flagon followed.

Darkmane congratulated him as he thumped the empty flagon down on the table: 'That's it, Chervah! We'll make a man of you yet!'

'Sire, that was an experience I would rather *not* repeat.'

Darkmane finished his own ale and rose to purchase another round for them. As he did so, his eyes fell on a solitary figure sitting in the corner of the tavern.

He recognized the familiar features of Calorne Manitus.

'Calorne Manitus!'
'Chadda Darkmane!'

The two friends grasped arms and hugged each other warmly. Calorne Manitus was a gentle man with a kindly face. He had the advantage of many years over Darkmane, but his mind was still as sharp as it had ever been. He was a smart dresser with a preference for blue silks, and he also favoured wearing a hooded cloak. A perpetual wanderer, he had managed to persuade the various rulers of Western Allansia that they ought to acquire more information about the races and peoples within their kingdoms. Surprisingly, each had agreed. In this way Calorne created for himself the job of census-taker, travelling throughout Western Allansia, collecting information on its inhabitants – at a leisurely pace, of course.

117

Calorne Manitus probably knew more about the people and the goings-on in Western Allansia than any other human alive.

Calorne's eyes fell on the Chervah, standing by Darkmane's side. By now the little creature was feeling the effects of his ale; his eyes were rolling from side to side and he had grabbed hold of Darkmane's leg to steady himself.

Darkmane slapped him on the back with a blow to rattle the Chervah's teeth and introduced him. 'And this is my manservant. A Chervah.'

'Sroo . . . er, Sroonagh Morrow . . . Monnow Pirrashathasha, at your shervice, sir. But you . . . Please call me "Chervah". I will take no offence – of course not – though you would, were I to call you "human". Our names are diff . . . difficult for outsiders to pronounce. Oh dear! You must ekshcuse me.'

'I am pleased to meet you, Sroonow . . . er, Pisha . . . Yes. You are right. I shall call you Chervah. Pleased to meet you, Chervah.'

'Our Chervah has just been introduced to Shazâar ale,' chuckled Darkmane.

Calorne Manitus smiled and turned to the warrior. 'Now tell me, Chadda Darkmane: what brings you out into the Southern Plains?'

'We have travelled to Shazâar from Salamonis in search of *you*, friend. For I am in need of your help.'

'Just tell me how I can be of help, Darkmane.' The census-taker remembered well how the tall warrior had helped him escape several years before, when Calorne Manitus had been carried off by brigands into the Craggen Heights. Alone, with a two-handed sword, Darkmane held off six of the rogues while Calorne untied their horses and sent them galloping off, holding two back for the warrior and himself to make good their own escape.

'Let's sit down. I shall tell you of my mission. But no one else must know of it. Swear to me that our discussion here will never be repeated.'

'I swear it. I swear it on my family name. And I swear it on my Amonour. Whatever you tell me shall travel no further on my lips.'

'Good. Now listen to what I have to say, for I need your advice . . .'

The three of them sat round the table and Darkmane told the census-taker about the war boiling up between the two sorcerers. He enumerated the king's fears and explained how he had been sent on a mission to find a way to ensure the safety of Salamonis when this war had been won.

'. . . and my plan is this: I must make contact with both sides in this war; both must regard me as an ally – a mercenary for hire. I shall serve both sides well. And I shall offer to both plans for the conquest of Salamonis when they have defeated their enemies. I shall ensure that neither side gains too great an advantage. The war will be prolonged until neither side has the strength left to challenge Salamonis.'

Darkmane looked deep into Calorne Manitus's eyes.

'But this is where I need your advice, my friend,' he whispered. 'You are the information-gatherer of these parts. You more than anyone know about the people of the area; their loyalties, their strengths and their weaknesses. Please. Search your mind. Tell me who may be of help to me, and who may bring me closer to Balthus Dire and Zharradan Marr.'

The census-taker was silent, his eyes staring out into the distance. Eventually he spoke.

'Chadda Darkmane,' he began, 'the mission you have set yourself upon is noble and just. But I fear it is also foolhardy and it will end in tragedy; your own tragedy. You are but one man. These two warlords have harnessed the powers of evil. Balthus Dire has chosen chaos as his ally. Zharradan Marr is a necromancer; his is the power of life and death. They are both surrounded by their troops, heavily guarded in their own fortified strongholds. What chance do you have, standing as one man against their might? I would not wager a single copper piece against a nugget of pure gold for your chances of success.'

'My friend, you must not fear for me,' replied the warrior. 'Fate has chosen me for this mission and I will succeed. The Allseeing Three selected me. King Salamon himself has placed his faith in me. And I know in my heart that I am *destined* to succeed. No, fear not for my safety, Calorne. And take up that wager if you wish to become a rich man!'

'Proud words, Darkmane. But your pride will not help you steal into the Black Tower unseen, nor protect you from the undead horrors in Marr's underground netherworld. You should return to Salamonis and advise your king to mount an army. Let the king's army fight first against one side and then against the other. His army would stand a better chance of winning this war than you do single-handed.'

'A plan of this kind has been considered already. The risks are too great. The king cannot know for sure the size of either side's army. Dire's troops are scattered across the Cragrocks, ready to serve him at an instant's notice – and who knows how many they number? And Zharradan Marr calls on the undead to fight his battles – perhaps their numbers are limitless. No, Salamonis is safe for the time being, until one side is victorious. Far better to let the two sorcerers fight it out between them for as long as possible, before entering the battle.'

'But you risk certain death!'

'Without your help, that may be so.'

'Even *with* my help, which I shall gladly give, you cannot hope to succeed.'

'You should not concern yourself with my fate, my friend, for there are many things you do not know. I am destined to serve the people of Salamonis and to gain their respect in a way that few others have ever done in the past. You have heard of Hallan Wardalus?'

'The prophet?'

'The same. He now lives as a recluse in the Cragrock Foothills. He is old but his wisdom is unsurpassed, though his sight is failing. He is attended by a small tribe of Thagralites, who see him as some kind of mystical priest.'

'But how did you find him?' Manitus was astonished. 'In my census I have him recorded as dead, for no one has seen or heard of him since his meeting with Rosina in Dree.'

Darkmane smiled. He had tricked one of the hag-witches of Dree into giving him the information. 'I wished to visit Hallan Wardalus for a sign from him . . . a prophecy. I was nineteen years of age. My Amonour had yet to be developed; but my fame was growing. You know that a Salamonian cannot rest, once the desire for Amonour has touched him. I was eager to find out what the gods had in store for me.

I sought out the ageing prophet, found him and bade him look into my future.'

'Yes?'

Both Calorne Manitus and the Chervah were by now engrossed in Darkmane's tale. Hallan Wardalus had been the king's most trusted sage; some say his prophecies and warnings had done more to bolster up the continuing state of peace and prosperity in Salamonis than even the king's judgement. In good time he had foreseen and warned the king of the Strongarm uprising that was brewing. The king had cleverly defused the situation by inviting a gathering of pan-Allansian trading caravans into Salamonis to attend a special market trading week. Naturally the caravans needed Strongarm guards when they left with their fat profits. And thus, by the end of the week, the problem was solved. With most of the Strongarms riding with their caravans to the furthest reaches of Allansia there were hardly enough mercenaries left to organize a bar-room brawl, let alone an assault on the royal palace! Whether his powers were god-given, or whether he was simply a shrewd observer of life in Salamonis, was of no matter; Hallan Wardalus's Amonour was among the highest in the kingdom.

Yet his curiosity had got the better of him when he made the mistake of visiting Dree, the village of the witch-women: he had never returned from his journey to Dree, and he was assumed to be dead. Until, that is, he had been sought out by the young Chadda Darkmane.

'At first Hallan Wardalus would not welcome me. I was an intruder in his simple, new world. He wished to be left to live out his life in seclusion. But something happened that made him change his mind.

'While we were speaking he stumbled; I grabbed his arm to support him. When his hands touched me, there was energy flowing between us. I could feel it! An emotion swelled up inside me; I had no idea what it was, nor have I felt it since. It was a feeling of . . . of *glory*. It made me want to drop to my knees and yell out loud to the world! I felt as if I could leap into the sky and come to rest on the clouds themselves!

'We looked at each other and I could see that he had felt it too. Tears were running down his cheeks. We both felt as if we had known each other for a lifetime – yet we had met only moments earlier. For a long time we stood there, gripping each other's arm and staring without blinking into each other's eyes.

'He invited me in. I stayed with him for several days and we became friends. *Special* friends. He was as a father to me, and I was the son he had never had. He taught me much of the wisdom of the world; and I brought him the joy of life; the joy of youth. He would hold me spellbound for hours with tales of the past. And I would make him laugh with boyish pranks.

'Before I left, he explained to me that the energy which had passed between us was a sign. It was, he said, as if I were an individual with a *destiny*. His power lay in his sensitivity to such things. And he likened our encounter on that first day to a magnetic lodestone touching a weapon of iron.

'He also made me swear that I would never reveal to anyone his whereabouts. When he had left Salamonis, his Amonour was at its highest point. Since then he had grown old and fragile. His powers were fading. He did not wish to return to Salamonis and allow the people there to watch him weaken as senility

overcame him. He wished to be remembered only as
a great prophet – not as a dying, once-great old man.
I swore to keep his secret.'

There was a long silence among the three of them.
The noise of the inn was the merest background
whisper. But they were abruptly startled from their
silence by a burly rogue, dressed in the dark leather
armour of a footpad, who stepped up to the table and
grabbed the Chervah's arm.

'Here!' he yelled across the bar. 'Here's a stool! This
one'll do.' He picked up the Chervah with one hand
and held the terrified creature dangling in the air in
front of him. His dirty mouth opened to a broken-
toothed grin. 'Get on your feet, runt. I want this seat.
I'm taking it for my mate. You've no objections, have
you?'

'N-n-no . . .'

Darkmane reacted as quick as a flash. His right foot
catapulted up from the floor, deep into the rogue's
fat stomach. The footpad dropped the Chervah and
doubled over, clutching his belly. As his head
dropped down, Darkmane whipped his right arm
over the man's shoulders and round his neck, holding
him in a tight lock. With a single jerk he slammed the
rogue's face down on the table, nose first. Another
jerk pulled his head back up. The Chervah shuddered
at the expression of agony on the man's face and saw
a thick trickle of blood oozing from his broken nose.
Darkmane tightened his grip and brought the rogue's
head down again. But this time it was not pulled
down on to the table. Instead Darkmane jerked it
down towards his left hand which was now grasping
a sharp throwing knife. He stopped expertly, the
point of the blade not more than two centimetres from

the man's right eye. The footpad shrieked, panic-stricken.

'You are in error,' Darkmane said coolly. 'That stool is occupied. Perhaps you cannot see my friend sitting on it. Would you like my blade to scratch the fog from your eyes?' He switched his grip: his right hand grabbed the man's hair and yanked his head back. His knife blade was now resting along the footpad's neck.

Beads of sweat appeared across the man's forehead and rolled down his face. 'I-I-I am sorry, my lord,' stammered the rogue. 'Y-y-you are quite right. I will have to find another stool. A thousand pardons.'

'Then begone. And do not bother us again.' He let go the man's hair and pushed him on to the floor.

A crowd had gathered to watch the incident. Dark-mane looked at the faces round him; eyes darted furtively away as he caught their stares. Eventually they resumed their drinking. Darkmane returned to his conversation.

The Chervah was visibly shaking in his seat.

Calorne Manitus had remained silent throughout the whole incident. At last he spoke. 'You are quick, Darkmane, very quick. But one is foolish to cause trouble at the Fatted Pig. You will have made enemies tonight.'

'I have no fear of making enemies. And now, look. Our flagons are empty. What say you, shall we have another drink?' Darkmane pushed himself up from his stool and went over to the bar.

The Chervah had recovered his composure by now and was anxious to learn more of the strange customs of Shazâar. 'Er, Calorne,' he began, 'tell me – if you don't mind, of course – this place: Shazâar. It's . . . rather *unusual*, wouldn't you say? I mean, the people who live here. Why do they do such strange things?'

Calorne laughed. 'Your first time in Shazâar, eh, Chervah?'

'Er, yes. I mean, the first time I've actually *been* here. Of course I've heard a lot about the city in the desert. But really, nothing I've heard can compare with seeing this place with my own eyes. On the way in, we passed a place – I thought it was a healer's – offering diseases for sale! Who on Titan would want to pay to become sick?' The Chervah's wrinkled face twisted itself into an expression of total bewilderment.

Again Calorne laughed. 'You'd be surprised,' replied the census-taker. 'I know the place you mean, of course. All kinds of people want to buy diseases. Curse-witches, for a start. They're not much use if they have to cast their curses over a great distance, but if they can actually *come into contact* with their victims . . . Buying a small vial of the disease to cast over their victim is much more convenient – and sometimes more effective – than spending hours preparing their cursing broths.' The Chervah grimaced. Calorne continued: 'Beggars, too. Their begging is much more profitable if they really are diseased than if they have to pretend. More recently, too, some diseases and disfigurements have become *fashionable* here in Shazâar. Myself, I feel that these fashions were started by the disease merchants themselves.'

'I see.' The Chervah nodded. 'But then, what of the strange behaviour of some Shazâarians? On the way in we saw a man scratching designs on to his chest with his long fingernails. And a woman walking along the street with her hands over her ears.'

Again Calorne smiled. 'Ah yes. This place is well known as the City of Madness. Some of these acts, it is true, are pure insanity. But most are no more than religious rituals. In Salamonis you think nothing of holy men who shave their heads, or who wander through the streets singing and dancing, or who chastise themselves with whips. In Shazâar there are over a hundred religious sects, and each has its own peculiar rituals. Some of these may be acts of penance, others are methods of prayer. Have you come across the Logaan-worshippers since you arrived?'

The Chervah shrugged.

'The members of this cult must, this week and the same week every year, reduce their wealth to nothing by giving it away to anyone who has less than they have.'

'But how do they survive?'

'Well, they are not exactly the wealthiest citizens of Shazâar! They work hard all year, earning as much as possible, then have to give it all away during Lucre Week. It is a field-day for beggars, of course, who flock out into the streets of Shazâar for the rich pickings to be had. Some of the shrewder Logaan-worshippers have found ways round the practice. Anyone with any real wealth makes sure they have a good friend who is not a Logaan-worshipper. This way they can give all their possessions and most of their money to this friend just before Lucre Week. They save a small amount of cash to give away, to ease their conscience. And after Lucre Week, they get their friends to hand back all their possessions again. There have been instances when these "friends" have been badly chosen and have demanded a portion of the worshipper's wealth before agreeing to hand it back. And there was one famous incident when one of these "friends" got himself converted – he actually *became* a Logaan-worshipper *during* Lucre Week! Gave away all his friend's money!'

Darkmane returned with three flagons of ale; large ones for himself and for Calorne Manitus, and a smaller one for the Chervah.

The census-taker took a sip. 'Aaah. Shazâarian ale. The finest in Allansia. Yes, most of this seemingly odd behaviour can be traced back to religious origins. But more recently, when tales of Shazâar spread across Allansia – sometimes grossly exaggerated – artists, crazies and strange fellows from all over the place began arriving, to see the city for themselves. Many of them made their homes here. And they began to introduce their own ideas of eccentric behaviour. What you see around you now in Shazâar is a mixture of all these influences.'

Darkmane snorted. He despised those who wasted their time with nonsense. 'Well, this inn looks ordinary enough,' he sneered. 'Like any other tavern in Allansia.'

'You wait,' said Calorne Manitus. 'There are always those who will seize the opportunity for a little blatant exhibitionism . . .'

As if his words had been heard right across the bar-room, a sudden commotion erupted in the far corner. Two thin, pale-skinned creatures – perhaps of an Elven race – pushed out into the middle of the floor, bowling over some of the others who were standing around, drinking. The locals sensed a brawl and a circle was rapidly cleared round them.

One of the two, dressed in a dark-green cloak, reached down to his belt and grabbed a stiletto. In a squeaky, high-pitched voice he screamed at the other: 'Galee Eredil, I am sick and tired of your insults. You may mock me, but you shall not discredit my family. My blade will see to it that I never have to listen to your indignities again.'

The crowd cheered.

The second Elf also drew out a knife, and they faced each other. The green-cloaked Elf held his knife aloft. As the blade came down, however, the other Elf grabbed his knife-arm and held it back. He brandished his own knife and said: 'Neela Imuria, the only way you will escape me is to the heavens!'

'NO!'

Neela Imuria grabbed Eredil's wrist, and the two Elves wrestled. The brawl continued, to the delight of the crowd, each Elf trying desperately to kill the other.

Darkmane noticed a table near the scene of the brawl, at which two men were sitting. They were completely ignoring the disturbance going on around them and were engrossed in deep conversation. The smaller of the two was facing towards Darkmane. He was a well-proportioned, clean-looking fellow, neatly dressed in a brown leather jerkin. His partner at the table was just the opposite: this man was fat – so large in fact that, perched on the small bar-stool, his backside spilled over it and he kept shifting uncomfortably from side to side. Rolls of fat disguised exactly where his neck ended and his head began.

The brawling Elves were still locked solidly together; each was trying to prevent the other's knife from striking home while at the same time trying to plunge his own knife into his adversary's chest. The onlookers jostled them, egging them on. A hand from the crowd gave them a sideways shove, and Galee Eredil tripped over a loose floorboard. The two of them went flying, crashing into the fat man with enough impact to knock him off his stool to the floor. Gasps went up from the onlookers, then a sudden hush spread across the tavern.

The fat man heaved himself up from the floor. The Elves had stopped their fighting and stood open-mouthed before him. Back on his feet, he towered above them and Darkmane saw on his face an expression of fury, accentuated by a deep scar that ran across his cheek. He was a sight to make even the bravest man cower in fear.

He reached out and grabbed the two Elves by their necks. His powerful fingers gripped tightly. The two unfortunate Elves were powerless against the man's strength. They choked and gagged, clutching desperately at his fingers. He raised his arms and lifted them easily into the air. Then, with a loud roar, he swung his outstretched arms together, bringing the two Elves towards each other, head to head. There was a sickening crunch and the Elves' struggling bodies went limp. The fat man tossed them aside.

He turned back to the table, took a last swig from his flagon, and reached into his pocket. He tossed a couple of coins on the table, nodded to his former drinking companion and pushed his way through the crowd and out of the inn. The onlookers watched him go in silence.

The Chervah was terrified.

Darkmane turned to Calorne Manitus, but before he could speak Calorne pointed a finger at the smaller man; he was still sitting at the table, obviously as shocked as the rest of the onlookers by what had happened.

'Observe that man,' said Calorne. 'That is Jamut Mantrapper. Now *he* may be your man.'

Shazâar

Darkmane studied him across the bar-room. A well-dressed man, with sharp eyes; probably quite intelligent. Although not tall, he had broad shoulders, and he gave the impression of being someone able to look after himself. A sword with an ornate hilt hung by his side. He was deep in thought.

Darkmane turned back to his friend. 'Tell me more about him, Calorne.'

'Jamut Mantrapper is an adventurer and mercenary. He has travelled far and wide across Allansia and knows the land well. If the fee is high enough, and the quest sufficiently interesting, then he is for hire. He has quite a colourful history and is well known to Allansian nobles. Daring rescues, robbery, assassination, soldiery – these are his skills. And by all accounts he is an accomplished craftsman in these skills. Remember how Shannack, overpriest of Zengis, was found in his bed one morning with his throat slit? Despite the presence of a hundred specially trained guards protecting him? It is rumoured that Mantrapper was his assassin. And the fearsome Sea Ogre which plagued merchant ships in Port Blacksand for Lord Azzur? Its body was found washed up in the harbour, but without a scratch on it. Folk say that, too, was the work of Jamut Mantrapper.'

'But what of the man himself?' asked Darkmane. 'Is he reliable? I distrust these mercenary adventurers; their loyalties change if their fee is raised.'

'Well, that's as may be,' nodded Calorne. 'Who knows how to secure their loyalties above the temptation of a larger bag of gold? But Jamut Mantrapper is reputed to be expensive, very expensive. And for this price you buy not only his sword but also his honour. He has a good reputation in mercenary circles as far as

131

that is concerned. And from what I know of him, he generally fights on the side of right. Rumour has it that he was swindled badly by Shareella the Snow Witch after capturing and enslaving the meddling explorer, Harlak Erlisson, for her. But I agree, there can be no guarantee of loyalty from any of these adventurers, though I think you would find Jamut Mantrapper has more scruples than most; he was educated by the priests of Silverton. Why not talk to him yourself?'

Darkmane nodded. He ran a risk with any strangers but, from what Calorne had told him, this Jamut Mantrapper's credentials sounded promising.

He stood up from the table. The Chervah stood up with him, but Darkmane waved him back down and the little creature complied. The warrior pushed across the room and stood by Jamut Mantrapper's table.

'Jamut Mantrapper?'

The man seated at the table was drinking. He put his flagon down and turned slowly to look up at Darkmane. 'Who wants to know?'

'I am Chadda Darkmane of Salamonis. I am here on a mission; a mission which could be of interest – and of reward – to Jamut Mantrapper, the mercenary adventurer. Are you he?'

Jamut Mantrapper's right hand moved slowly to grasp his sword-hilt. He took no chances with strangers. 'Aye, I am he. But you waste your time. My sword is already hired.'

Darkmane ignored the rejection, pulled up a stool and sat down at the table, opposite Jamut Mantrapper. No matter how lucrative Mantrapper's current mission might be, Darkmane could offer more.

The mercenary scowled at his impudence and began to rise, but Darkmane's pacifying gesture encouraged him to sit down again. He might as well hear what the warrior had to offer. Darkmane too was thinking carefully how he should approach the mercenary; he dare not tell him too much concerning his mission.

'I am on a mission for King Salamon,' he began. 'The king wishes me to gain audience with Lord Balthus Dire of the Cragrocks. I travel with my man-servant, but I need another travelling companion – one skilled in the arts of stealth and skirmish. My journey through the Cragrocks will have its dangers, so I need someone who will fight by my side and who, should I fail in my quest, will either take over my mission or return to the court at Salamonis to tell the king of my death. I am told that you know Allansia well. I need someone to guide me through the Craggen Heights to the Black Tower.'

Darkmane waited for a response.

Jamut Mantrapper looked casually at his flagon, which was nearly empty, and fingered it absent-mindedly. 'Hmm. A perilous journey perhaps. Although some ways through the Cragrocks are less perilous than others. But it matters not. As I say, my sword has been hired. I am riding north first thing tomorrow morning. Even if I were interested in your mission, it will be some weeks before I return to Shazâar. And if this were still acceptable . . . perhaps you have heard something of my reputation? I am not cheap. And you could have fifty Strongarms from Salamonis for the price of Jamut Mantrapper.'

'And how do you think Balthus Dire would react to an army of Strongarms marching through the Cragrocks? A small party not only has a much better chance of reaching the Black Tower undetected, but such a party would also pose no threat to Lord Dire. And Strongarms are brawn without brain; I require brawn *and* brain.'

'Well then, let me see. Such a mission hardly generates much excitement in me: a few saddle-weary days on horseback; perhaps a little Goblin-skewering to liven things up a bit – but then if we are particularly careful and take my route, we may even avoid *any* encounters. No, I do not see the prospect of much *adventure* on this mission. I suggest you find yourself another sword for hire.' He took a swig from his flagon and looked away from Darkmane.

The warrior's expressionless gaze was fixed on him. 'The fee is three hundred gold pieces.'

Jamut Mantrapper choked on his ale. This was a lot of money for a relatively simple mission!

Darkmane added: 'One hundred and fifty now; the rest when we return.'

Jamut Mantrapper composed himself quickly. 'Four hundred.'

'Four hundred it is. But we must leave tomorrow.'

'Five hundred.'

Darkmane gave him a cold stare and said nothing. The impudent mercenary had already named his price and Darkmane had agreed. The matter of price had been settled and was no longer open to further bargaining.

But Mantrapper, encouraged by the three flagons of ale he had already drunk, was enjoying the bartering, though he realized he had overstepped himself. 'I will give your proposal my consideration, Darkmane.'

Darkmane was growing angry at Jamut Mantrapper's cocky insolence. He did not like being toyed with. 'I need your answer now.'

'You will have it tomorrow.'

Without warning, Darkmane's hand grasped his sword, the long blade flashed from his belt and in one furious motion he had bounded across the table. Reacting at once, Jamut Mantrapper's weapon was also drawn to defend himself.

The commotion caught the attention of the other customers in the bar; another brawl was about to break out! It was as if time had stopped: Jamut Mantrapper's sword-point was poised a hair's breadth from Darkmane's neck; Darkmane's own sword was held motionless above the mercenary's head.

But Darkmane's eyes were not on Jamut Mantrapper. A split second earlier he had seen the gleam of a dagger in the hand of a black-cloaked assassin lurking behind the mercenary. As the dagger came down, aimed at Jamut Mantrapper's neck, he had reacted instinctively. His sharp blade was now the only thing standing between the descending dagger and his drinking companion's neck!

An ear-splitting scream of agony came from the sinister figure in black standing behind the mercenary. At the same time the assassin's severed hand, still clutching the dagger, landed with a thump on the table. Jamut Mantrapper's eyes opened wide as he realized what had happened. Had he reacted differently and decided to thrust his own sword into Darkmane's throat, the scene would have been entirely different: both he *and* Darkmane would now be lying dead on the tavern table, while the assassin would be making off through the crowd and out into the street, his mission completed. Mantrapper's sword drew away from Darkmane's neck.

'Follow him!' roared Darkmane, pointing after the assassin.

The two men jumped to their feet and leapt in hot pursuit of the fleeing assassin. A side door opened and closed. They rushed up to it and found a bloody smear, still wet, just above the handle, where the assassin had pushed it open. Darkmane opened the door and the two men ran out into the street.

It was dark outside. They looked left, then right, but could see no sign of the fleeing assassin.

'On the ground!' shouted Darkmane. 'Look for the drips!'

The two men searched around but could find no bloodstains on the ground. There was no clue as to which way the assassin had turned. And by now he was no doubt well away. He had escaped them.

'Grang!' Jamut Mantrapper swore. 'Gone! The scum! I'll wager I know whose gutter he crawled out of, though . . .' He turned to Darkmane. 'My friend. And to think I nearly made a tragic mistake – tragic for both of us. But instead you have preserved me from that black worm's knife. And his days as a hired assassin are over now! You have saved my life. Tell me how I may repay you.'

The two men looked at each other. Each knew what form the payment should take.

A solemn expression spread over Jamut Mantrapper's face. 'Of course,' he said quietly. 'But, alas, this is one repayment I am unable to make. The price is too high. There are certain *problems*. But let me work out how I may help you with your mission. I must talk to some people. Take a room for the night at the Fatted Pig, and I will visit you in the morning . . .'

11

A Warning from Lissamina

Darkmane awoke with a jolt.

He was sitting bolt upright in his bed, beads of sweat glistening on his forehead. His hair was tousled and he was breathing hard.

'M-master!' the squeaky voice of the little Chervah sounded in the darkness. 'Are you . . . Is there anything I can do? Do those sleep demons torment you?'

Darkmane sighed.

'No, Chervah,' he said at last. 'Just a bad dream. Gods! It was only a nightmare – but so vivid! I actually *felt* that blade . . . But no. Just a dream.' He stared round the room as if to convince himself that he really was only dreaming. He recognized his own clothes draped over a wooden stool; and there stood a half-finished mug of cold broth on the bedside table, next to the candle, both of which the innkeeper of the Fatted Pig had given them on their way up to the room.

The Chervah's quivering voice broke the silence. 'What sort of dream, sire?'

'A strange one. You and I and that Jamut Man-

A Warning from Lissamina

trapper were making our way through the Craggen Heights towards the Black Tower. Mantrapper had suggested we take a special route he knew – round the side of a mountain, it was. Several hours along it, we could see the spire of the Black Tower reaching into the sky. It was close. Very close.

'The path led under a precarious overhang. I can remember looking up at the overhang as we walked the horses beneath it. The jagged rocks hanging down looked like the teeth of a ferocious rock-beast and we were walking across its tongue!'

The Chervah shivered at the thought.

Darkmane continued: 'Up ahead, a rock-slide had recently fallen across the trail, destroying most of it. *We* could climb over, but we would never get the horses over. We discussed whether to leave the horses and continue on foot or turn back with the horses and waste another half-day. I wanted to continue; you two wanted to turn back. But you allowed me to have my way – and I led us all into the ambush.

'With horses we would have escaped the charging Hill Goblins easily. They were armed and waiting for us . . . expecting us. We all turned to run. But we were encumbered with our packs and they caught up with us easily as we scrambled back over the rock-slide. You collapsed as an arrow tore through the back of your knee. I felt two pairs of rough hands with broken claws grab my waist. My sword freed me that time. Then another two; then more. Eventually they held me. Ugh! I can remember the smell of their stinking breath. Then their chief approached me and muttered something like: "You try run. We stop." This appeared to amuse him. And one of his henchmen drew a knife.'

On the other bed, the Chervah was wondering whether asking Darkmane about his dream had been such a good idea after all. He wished a candle was lit. He kept on reassuring himself that this had been simply Darkmane's dream.

'While the others held me still, this Goblin began to draw his blade slowly across the back of my ankles just above the heel, cutting through the sinews. That was when I woke up.'

This time the Chervah sighed. He was glad the story had come to an end. 'Er, ah . . . W-what a t-terrible dream! But that's all it was, sire, a dream. You can rest again now.'

The warrior lowered his head back on to the mattress. The images of his dream were still there. And he had not told the Chervah what became of Mantrapper in his dream. He had not mentioned that the mercenary had stopped to watch as Darkmane was captured and had stood among the Hill Goblins, a faint smile on his lips, as the henchman's knife bit into his heels. It was, after all, only a dream. It meant nothing . . .

Darkmane drifted off into sleep once more.

He began to dream again. But this time he dreamed of a distant fire, burning in the sky. A single, tall, red flame hovered high above the treetops. It flickered defiantly in the wind, hesitated, then sprang forward through the air like a speeding arrow, straight towards him.

It stopped above him and burned with a rich scarlet colour. The shape of the flame altered gradually, until at last he could discern a human form within the flame, wrapped in a flimsy silk. Her arms were folded and her face was hidden by the waves and curls of

A Warning from Lissamina

golden locks that hung down. Slowly she lifted her hands to her forehead and her thumbs found a centre parting. She separated the two sides of her tresses and tossed her head, first to one side, then to the other, to clear the hair from her face.

Two large green eyes opened slowly and gazed frankly at Darkmane. A soft smile spread across her face. His heart fluttered as he recognized the sylph-like features of the sorceress in the Forest of Yore. Lissamina was visiting him in his dream.

As she took on her human form, Darkmane was transfixed. He could not help but watch every movement of this exquisite creature: each step she took; each carefree toss of her head; even the way she drew her robe round her; he was watching poetry in motion. When she moved, she moved slowly and deliberately. Each movement seemed to blend into the next, as if she were a royal shadow dancer of many years' experience.

Finally, his trance was broken by her voice, as soft as a warm breeze: 'Darkmane, I have made this journey to bring you further news. You should know that the war is escalating. Lord Balthus Dire sent chaos raiders to Coven and the village has been destroyed. Lord Zharradan Marr has taken to the skies in his *Galleykeep*. He has stationed troops along the White-water River in order to starve out the chaotics. King Salamon fears that, if Marr's plan succeeds, many of his troops will be perfectly positioned for an invasion of the Vale of Willow. There have even been some reports of Marr's troops raiding the Vale farms for food.'

Darkmane noticed emotions apparent in her voice which her face was trying not to show. She was evidently deeply worried that Marr's troops were so close to Salamonis. And there was something else in her voice, which sounded slightly flat and drawn. The last time they met she had been bubbling and excited. She had not been able – nor had she tried – to hide her enthusiasm at being given such an important task. But now her voice was a little drawn. A little *tired*.

'I have again been watching your progress. You are planning to take Jamut Mantrapper into the Craggen Heights, to visit Balthus Dire – this I know. When you announced this intention, I decided I must use my powers to test this plan.

'Darkmane, I know you distrust sorcery. And you probably distrust me. But I implore you: *do not embark on this journey!* You believe you have just had a dream, a nightmare. That was no dream. *That was a vision of the future.*

'I have described to you my powers, bestowed on me by Gelda Wane in Silverton. I am able to create visions of future *possibilities.* Perhaps you do not accept much of what you hear of gypsy sorcery. But you must believe me when I tell you that your trip to the Black Tower will be disastrous. You have seen with your own eyes the deathly fate that may lie in store for you in the Cragrocks.

'Now I hear you say: "*We may avoid the danger altogether. If we should reach the rock-slide, we will simply turn round and take another route.*" But you should not take your dream to be a glimpse of the absolute future. My visions are mere indications of the likely possibilities. All prediction must work only like this. For otherwise anyone with a knowledge of that future could certainly change its course.

'No. Future-sight can only work rather like the

fisherman who, having cast his line into the sea, finds to his good fortune a school of fish swimming under his boat. The fisherman will certainly catch *a* fish, but he cannot know beforehand which one he will catch.

'My visions of the future may be likened to a single fish in that school. And of course it *is* possible that this single fish may be the one caught by that fisherman. But the message of the vision must be read on a broader scale: to undertake this journey to Dire's citadel would be a dangerous mission. The ways in which this danger may show itself can be as varied as the number of fish in the school. But just as the fisherman *knows* that he will catch one of the fish, so the danger is just as certain. I urge you: *please do not continue this journey!*'

Her last words were spoken with a quiver in her voice which revealed the restraint she was using to control herself. Her eyes were glistening with moisture.

Quickly she regained her composure and continued: 'Perhaps you will heed my warning; perhaps not. But remember this: if you should come to grief, you will have failed in your mission and your efforts to aid the people of Salamonis will have been as naught. And I have an alternative suggestion. It is well known that Balthus Dire and Zharradan Marr were pupils together under the tutelage of Volgera Darkstorm. Few know that Darkstorm had a third pupil at that time: a young sorcerer known as Zagor. On Darkstorm's death – at the hands of the other two – Zagor made his own way north into Kay-Pong and there established a life for himself as a semi-recluse in the Moonstone Hills. It is said that he was resentful and despised the other two for murdering their master. Perhaps he will know of ways to help defeat them.

'I cannot say for certain where this Zagor lives, but I suspect that if you ride north to Chalice or Stonebridge, home of the Dwarfs, you may learn of his whereabouts.'

Lissamina's attention was diverted to the silky cape she was wearing, which was beginning to flicker. A small redness burst into flames on one of the sleeves; then another came alight on the hem by her ankle. The flames grew.

She raised her head again. 'And now I must go, brave Darkmane. But before I leave, I implore you to heed my warnings . . .'

The flames had grown larger. She smiled at him and lowered her head, throwing her golden hair forward to cover her face. She grasped her burning sleeves, then lifted them high, finally bringing them down carefully, one on each shoulder. By now she was a single red flame, burning fiercely. The flame spun round, rose into the air, and moved towards him. Then the fire began to dwindle, becoming quickly extinguished. In an instant it had vanished!

Darkmane once again sat bolt upright in his bed. Another equally vivid dream! The faint perfume of Lissamina's hair still lingered in his nostrils and he could feel the comfortable warmth of the red flame.

'What is it, master? Another dream? Not quite so frightening this time, I hope.' The Chervah was awake with him.

'No, little friend. No more nightmares. Not this time.'

Darkmane lay back again on the bed. The dawn was breaking and soon he would have to rise.

A Warning from Lissamina

But first he had some decisions to make.

The future-sight dream had a profound effect on Darkmane. During the first hour of daylight he was silent, preoccupied with his visions of the night before. Had he really been given a glimpse of the future from Lissamina, or had he just had a particularly vivid dream?

The Chervah was sensitive to his mood and tried to get him to talk about what was concerning him. Darkmane remained tight-lipped, however. He had to make up his mind whether to take this mysterious advice or ignore it. He would have preferred not to have a decision to make at all – especially when the advice came from a sorceress.

It was two hours later when Mantrapper's knock sounded at the door.

At least the man is true to his word, thought Darkmane. *He has come as he promised.*

'Enter!'

Mantrapper entered with a flourish. He was wearing a colourful Shazâarian tunic festooned with ruffs, pleats and pads which made him look twice the size round his chest; the tunic tapered neatly at the waist. His trousers were skin-tight. Darkmane's immediate impression was that the mercenary resembled a minstrel rather than a sword for hire, but there was something about Mantrapper's manner which made him look more like a noble of the court. They exchanged greetings. Darkmane told the Chervah to prepare them a drink and the little creature set about making a pot of Valeherb tea.

As he was returning with two mugs full of the

lemon-scented liquid, Jamut Mantrapper pulled a scroll from his pack. 'Thank you.' He took the tea and sipped it. 'Look. Here is a map. See? This is the Black Tower and the hill trails are marked. I suggest you take this route . . .'

'You will not be accompanying us?'

'I cannot.' Mantrapper hung his head. He was evidently torn between two loyalties. 'As I have told you already, my sword has been hired – and I am a man of honour. Instead, I can only offer you advice and this map.'

'I thank you for your help, mercenary.' Darkmane was disappointed. 'But I have had to change my plans. King Salamon no longer wishes me to speak with Balthus Dire, but instead with another. Have you ever heard of Zagor?'

Mantrapper spluttered and coughed a mouthful of Valeherb tea back into his mug. 'Grang! This tea is hot!' The mercenary wiped his mouth. 'Who did you say? *Zagor*? No. Never come across a Zagor before. Whereabouts does he live?'

'I don't know. Perhaps around Kay-Pong? I was hoping you might know something of him.'

'No. Never heard of him. Look, when are you leaving?'

'When we have found a suitable travelling companion. Someone who can help us find this Zagor.'

Mantrapper quickly rolled up his map and rose to leave. 'Look, I must go now. But I'll see if I can learn anything about Zagor. Meet me downstairs in the tavern this evening . . .'

As the mercenary left, Darkmane and the Chervah looked at each other.

'I think,' said Darkmane, stroking his chin, 'that

we should keep an eye on Jamut Mantrapper.
Follow him, Chervah. Let's see what he gets up to
today . . .'

The bar-room at the Fatted Pig was the same as ever
that evening – noisy, smoky and dirty. The same faces
were crowded into the bustling bar. It was no wonder
that tempers flared, but so far there had been no actual
brawls. Darkmane and the Chervah were seated at
a table in the corner – a table where the noise was not
so deafening and where they hoped they would not
be disturbed. Two half-empty flagons of Shazâarian
ale were on the table before them. The Chervah was
developing a taste for the brew and, as on the previous
night, it was having the same effect of loosening his
tongue. He had just returned from his day's vigil and
was giving his report to Darkmane: '. . . He went
straight to the Singing Minstrel, sire, and spent some
time in there. I could see him at a window, talking to
somebody. But I couldn't see who it was. Then he left
and walked halfway across Shazâar. Oh, sire, the
things I have seen today! This place . . . *And* I was
attacked by a *washer-woman*! She grabbed me for no
reason. Pulling at my clothes like a wild dog, she was!
I nearly lost track of that Mantrapper. But finally he
arrived at a house – a very grand house, I suppose,
by Shazâarian standards. He spent a long time in
there. I asked a passer-by who lived there and he
said it belonged to Lord Tanneth of Shazâar. Those
demons of impatience nearly took me while I was
waiting there, but, just as I was about to leave, Mantrapper appeared at the door and set off once more
back to the Singing Minstrel. But he never came out.
At least I never saw him leave. Perhaps he went out

by a back door? I don't know. After waiting until I was sure, I came straight back here.'

Darkmane was deep in thought, considering whether there was any significance to be read into these visits. His eyes scanned the bar again, looking for Calorne Manitus who also had promised to join them.

Jamut Mantrapper was the first to arrive. 'Darkmane! And hello, little Chervah. I see you prefer Shazâarian ale to your herbal teas. Ha-ha!'

Mantrapper sat down with them. His temperament seemed to have changed; somehow it seemed *brighter*. His smile was wider, his eyes more eager . . . Something had happened to him during the day. Darkmane wondered what.

The mercenary offered his hand. 'Fellows, I am at your service. If you would like me to join you, my sword is yours for hire!'

The other two looked at each other.

'And what of your previous mission?' asked Darkmane.

'I have managed to, ah . . . to *postpone* it. Let us go and find your Zagor!'

'But you said you knew nothing of him,' said Darkmane suspiciously.

'That is true. Today I have questioned several people, but not one could tell me anything of Zagor. But I know of one who *will* know . . .'

'Go on,' said Darkmane, sternly.

'Well now, just rein in for a minute!' Mantrapper grinned. 'This is something of a change of plan. The way I see it, a journey to the Black Tower was one thing. But a search for an unknown person – that's an entirely different matter. We could be looking for weeks. It's an expensive trip for someone such as myself . . .'

Darkmane realized what the mercenary was up to. Although the warrior's expression changed little, Mantrapper sensed an explosion building up inside him, but Jamut Mantrapper was a mercenary; he was used to heated bargaining and was skilled in the craft.

'Now calm yourself, my friend,' he began, a relaxed smile on his face. 'I have not forgotten that I am indebted to you. But if you were in my boots, you would think likewise. Here is what I suggest.

'I have an acquaintance who will doubtless be able to point us towards this Zagor. We will visit my friend and, if he is able to help, you will then have two choices. You can decide to set off on your own to find the wizard, and if you do we will part company and I will charge you only one hundred gold pieces. Or, if you then wish to hire me again for this new mission, my fee will increase to four hundred – plus my journeying costs. The choice will be yours.'

Darkmane considered his words. It was true that a journey to find Zagor might indeed take much longer than the trip to Dire's citadel. Mantrapper's timing could perhaps have been more subtle but, as Darkmane was finding out, the mercenary spoke directly and spoke his mind. He admired that. Did he want Jamut Mantrapper with him on this trip?

'Very well,' said Darkmane eventually. 'I accept your terms. But tell me, mercenary, why have you decided to join us? This morning such a change of plans was impossible.'

Mantrapper beamed a wide grin at Darkmane. 'You wished to hire my sword. And now you have it. Why should my decision concern you?' he asked. There was no change in the warrior's expression; this explanation was not adequate. Mantrapper added quickly: 'All right, then. I must confess I find myself intrigued by your mission. No one I have asked here in Shazâar has even heard of this magic-user. This is a challenge! I have earned the name "Mantrapper" through my abilities – and my successes – in quests such as this. And, of course, let us not forget the events of last night in this very place. I would not be here now had it not been for your quick thinking . . .' He broke off, waiting for a reaction from the warrior.

At first there was none. But finally Darkmane spoke. 'I see. So be it. Now tell me of this friend of yours.'

'Ah yes. We should leave now and head north,' said the mercenary. 'At the southern end of Darkwood Forest stands a fine tower of white stone. It is the home of my friend.'

'And what is his name?'

'His name is Yaztromo. His practice is the magical arts.'

Darkmane grimaced. Yet another magic-user to contend with!

The Chervah, however, was deep in thought. He was considering Mantrapper's words. Had Darkmane also caught the slip? He must mention it to him later. Jamut Mantrapper himself had never heard of Zagor. Nor had anyone he had spoken to during the day.

How then did he know that Zagor was a *magic-user*?

12

A Spiritual Journey

Balthus Dire was sitting on the floor in a deep trance. His wife, the black sorceress Lucretia, sat cross-legged before him, watching him closely. Round her head was strapped a peculiar leather half-mask. From the mask's mouthpiece a long flexible pipe snaked across the floor and out of a window – a breathing device of some kind.

The candles flickered as a soft breeze blew across the room and she checked them to make sure they were all still alight, but their deep glow had been only momentarily disturbed. They bathed the centre of the room in a fluorescent green glow which cocooned the sorcerer and seemed to focus on his face. Outside the circle of sand in which Balthus Dire sat, motionless, she could see nothing but blackness.

Lucretia's eyes fixed on her husband's, which were closed tight. Every so often her gaze would drop to the ornate bowl set before him on the ground. The liquid inside continued to bubble slowly; the white vapours which rose from the concoction and bathed Dire's face appeared green in the candlelight. Within the bowl she could also see flakes of herb swirling

A Spiritual Journey

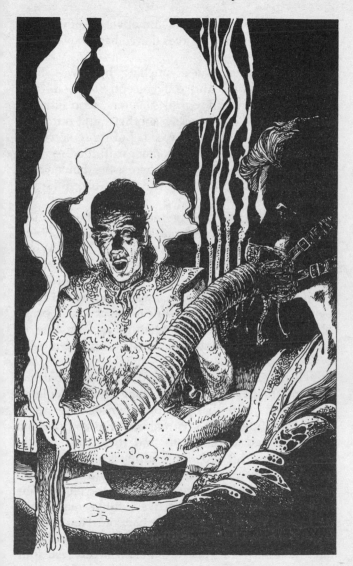

about in the boiling liquid. Cunnelwort! Balthus Dire twitched, and Lucretia's eyes darted back to watch for any signs of ill-effects.

The mysterious, sweet-smelling herb was little known in Allansia and only recently were its real powers becoming known to sorcerers, who hitherto had thought of it as merely another mind-numbing herb, rather like smoking-weed. But those sorcerers of Allansia who had close contact with the heavenly deities, and those who probed across the dimensional barriers, were beginning to learn more about its true nature.

Cunnelwort grew only on the eastern shore of Lake Nykosa, where the K'Amoole, a type of Marsh Goblin, protected it and regarded it as a holy herb. When dried and mixed with certain other herbs and potions, however, cunnelwort could become much more than a simple smoking-herb. To those who had trained their minds for journeys in the universal void, a properly prepared cunnelwort mixture was capable of opening the mental gateways into the spirit planes.

This discovery had been passed on to both Balthus Dire and Zharradan Marr by their teacher, Volgera Darkstorm – though Darkstorm himself had never dared experiment with cunnelwort. But its potential had fascinated both pupils and they had secretly vowed to seek out and obtain supplies of cunnelwort. The race had begun in earnest many years later, when news spread round Salamonis that a travelling merchant from Wolftown had arrived with a small quantity of the herb. Unwittingly, he had sold it too cheaply to a group of boisterous Strongarms, who had mistaken it for a new type of smoking-weed. All four

A Spiritual Journey

Strongarms had died within a week, but not before this strange dried plant had become known to the local herbalists.

Balthus Dire made the mistake of sending two Citadel Guards in pursuit of the merchant. Their interrogation of him was totally unsuccessful, the unfortunate man dying of fright before they could get any useful information out of him. Afraid for their own lives, they told Balthus Dire that the merchant had arrived from Frostholm; consequently, Dire sent several parties of scouts on wild-goose chases to the north-eastern reaches of Allansia, to Fangthane, Vynheim and the Forest of Night – areas where the climate is much too cold for the sensitive cunnelwort plants to survive.

Zharradan Marr tried a different approach. He had the body of one of the Strongarms dug up out of its grave and brought to him. The necromancer succeeded in briefly restoring some life to the corpse – for just long enough to learn how the herb had been purchased and where it came from. With this information, he immediately sent a caravan eastwards to Lake Nykosa.

Though both sorcerers relished the prospect of exploring the spirit planes, they each had a different intention for the cunnelwort. Zharradan Marr already existed in the netherworld of his enchanted mirror. This mirror was his only gateway to the physical universe and the world of Titan. The universe *inside* his mirror was limited, though in it he was safe from physical harm. Marr desired to communicate with beings on other planes. He thirsted for knowledge of new universes and, in particular, he yearned to make contact with the sources of power. Who knew what

knowledge could be learnt from these other
dimensions? But this much he did know: that anyone
with access to such a wealth of new knowledge would
surely be master of all he surveyed. Such a being,
aided by the spirit creatures, would be unstoppable
in the material plane.

Balthus Dire, on the other hand, had already had
his own glimpse of the spirit planes through his talks
with the Ganjees, themselves other-dimensional creatures. He found it difficult to absorb and understand
many of the concepts they used in their conversation.
But they had convinced him that his own immortality
would be assured if he gained access to the spirit
planes. This prospect filled him with insane and gloat-
ing longing.

He had studied closely the preparations that would
be needed for such inter-dimensional trips – the exact
blend of minor herbs and potions which had to be
mixed with the cunnelwort; the state of mind he must
achieve before embarking on his mental journey; and
also the correct conditions of ritual and safety, should
anything go wrong.

Thus Balthus Dire now found himself, in the dark of
night, seated on a rush mat high up in his citadel,
being watched over by his most trusted companion.
His physical body, though apparently peaceful, was
inwardly racked with torment as his spiritual being
was wrested away from its human form. The struggle
was always most arduous the first time, but Dire's
alchemy and preparations had been faultless. His
ghostly spirit tore itself from his body and entered the
spiritual dimensions.

His first sensation was a rush of light-sound-colour-silence. Then again: light-sound-colour-silence. He fought desperately to make some sense of what was happening to him. But the experiences he was feeling had no words to express them in his own human language. It was as if, with his meagre five senses, he was as useless as a blind deaf-mute in this world of fresh experiences. Sensations that passed through him triggered off random emotions: at one moment he felt happiness so intensely that he wanted to scream out for joy – but then just as suddenly his scream became one of agony. In another instant he was struck by a sort of divine comprehension; everything he saw and felt seemed to fit neatly into place in his understanding. Then, just as suddenly, he understood nothing. For a second he felt calm and relaxed. Then panic struck – this was something he had to fight to get out of.

All this was happening instantaneously within his mind as he passed through the dimensional barrier. Soon, however, the confusion was replaced by blankness and calm. He felt as if he were floating weightlessly in a void. There were no sensations to disturb him. He could see nothing, feel nothing, hear nothing, smell nothing. He settled into a peaceful sleep.

But some time after going to sleep – perhaps moments or perhaps an eternity – he began to dream. Familiar images swirled and sped past him in all directions. People, places, things – even large-scale events – were appearing before his eyes, then fading to nothing. But these images were not accurate. His citadel now had *two* towers and it was located in a desert waste. Walking ahead of him, through the air, was a slender woman with long, dark hair. Lucretia! He reached for her shoulder and she turned round to face him. Her familiar features were a great comfort. She smiled at him. The smile grew larger and turned into a grin, the grin into a leer. Her mouth grew in size until her head shrank away behind it, mutating to the reptilian features of a Lizard-creature. He turned his head away in horror!

His eyes zoomed in towards the Black Tower as if he were hurtling through the air towards it. A figure was at one of the windows, beckoning him to approach. Closer he came . . . closer! The figure was familiar. Zharradan Marr! He tried to stop. Impossible. Closer! SMASH!! The mirror shattered! Blackness . . .

A strange noise began. A high-pitched twittering sound slowed down until it became a deep, low bass sound, then twittered again like a bird. An invisible missile swooshed past him. Then another. But all was still black. He could see nothing. A third *swoosh* as yet another missile passed him . . . and he began to hear sounds coming from somewhere, yet from everywhere; perhaps from inside his head or perhaps from all round him.

At first they were just an incomprehensible jumble of noise, then they became more distinct. They seemed to switch rapidly, changing in pitch, hesitating, then changing quickly again, as if somehow searching for one particular tone. Noises started taking shape. He began to recognize certain patterns which recurred regularly. He strained to follow them, to listen more carefully.

The sounds grew more distinct: 'Aaaaasssmyyye . . .' The hissing tone shifted its pitch. 'Pppaaassmyye . . . Dddaassmmyyrrre . . . Dddaambussmmyyrrre . . .' It became deeper and more distinct.

A Spiritual Journey

'Bbbaambusss Mmyrrre . . . Bbbaandusss Mmmy-yrrre . . . Bbbaanthusss Ssstyyrrre . . .' He realized that two distinct words were being formed. And as if in response to this, the words were repeated more rapidly. 'Bbbaanthusss Ssstyrrre. Bbbaanthusss Ssstyrrre. Bbbaathusss Sstyrre. Bbbalthuss Tyrre. Bbbathusss Dyrrre. *Bbbalthusss Dyrre!*' Hearing his own name jolted him.

Back in his study, Lucretia watched his physical body twitch, then relax.

He could still *see* nothing but blackness. But he began to pick out various shades of black. Shapes were now whooshing past him; shapes in vague, grey colours.

'*Bbbalthusss Dire! Bbbalthusss Dire!*'

The calling continued. He was now able to associate it with the shapes of grey that flew round him. It grew louder as a shape approached and fainter as it passed him. He felt a mixture of excitement – for he had surely entered another dimensional reality – and fear. He could still see nothing but vague grey shapes swirling in an infinite blackness. He focused his mind to speak.

'I am he!' His own words sounded strange, as if he was hearing another's voice speaking for him.

In response to his call, the swirling accelerated excitedly, then slowed down. More words, groaning and hissing, came from the blackness: 'Wwwee havvve mmmade connntacttt.'

Balthus Dire's heart leapt. His cunnelwort experiment had been a success!

Back in his study, Lucretia noticed a faint smile on her husband's lips.

13

Yaztromo's Tower

'Knock on the door, Darkmane.' Jamut Mantrapper stroked his chin thoughtfully. 'I shall try to surprise the wizard.'

Darkmane stared at his face, trying to read his thoughts. Was Jamut Mantrapper using Darkmane to test for hidden dangers? However, he saw nothing in the mercenary's eyes and turned slowly to the door.

The huge oak door was strong enough to keep an invading army out. In the middle, at eye level, was a shining brass bell coiled on a spring. Beneath the bell was a large gong of similar colour. A small leather-headed striker was hanging by the side of the door; evidently it could be used on either the bell or the gong. Darkmane picked it up and thought for a moment. He struck the gong.

The resonating BONGGGGG made the Chervah shiver. The little creature was standing behind Darkmane. 'I would rather you had rung the bell, sire,' he said. 'The sound of a gong has a somewhat mystical ring to it. Seems to set the scene for magic, if you understand my meaning. Almost . . .'

'Who is there?'

Yaztromo's Tower

The voice of an old man cut the Chervah short. A small panel in the door had slid to one side and two eyes were surveying Darkmane and his manservant.

'I am called Chadda Darkmane.' The warrior spoke out boldly. 'And this is my manservant, a Chervah. We would talk with you on a matter of some urgency.'

'You want my help? You wish me to perform magic to help you?'

'Your help, yes. But we do not require your magic. Though I respect your art, I myself distrust sorcery, sir. The help we require concerns only your knowledge of the land.'

The wizard behind the door snorted. 'Distrust sorcery, eh? Well, Darkmaid, I can see you are one who speaks his mind. If you wish to ask questions, then ask. I am listening.'

Darkmane looked down at the Chervah. The little creature noticed his jaw tightening. Darkmane was getting angry.

'*Slangg!*' he cursed under his breath. '*The sorcerer will not even open the door to us! These magic-users have the manners of Mountain Ogres.*'

Jamut Mantrapper had been listening to the exchange from behind a tree. He stepped out, hands on hips, and a wide grin spread across his face. 'Gereth Yaztromo!' he called. 'Where are your manners? Do you greet all your friends thus? You are like a Jib-Jib in its cave, talking to us through your door! You old hermit! Open up and offer us your hospitality, you miserable wretch. Have I travelled all the way from Shazâar to talk to my old friend through his door?'

'*Mantrapper!*' The eyes in the door-panel opened wide and the three travellers heard the sound of bolts sliding. Eventually the heavy door swung open and the old wizard emerged from the tower. Jamut Mantrapper stepped forward and the two men embraced warmly.

Darkmane studied the old wizard carefully. *A harmless old hermit*, Mantrapper had told him, *but beware of crossing him, for his magical powers are awesome*. He certainly seemed harmless. His clothes were well worn, even bordering on the ragged. His red robe had holes in the elbows and faded streaks down the creases. His slippers were threadbare and his skullcap sat on his head as if it were a permanent fixture. He was bent with age, and so was much shorter than Mantrapper. Indeed, in the mercenary's arms he looked a frail creature, and Mantrapper held him carefully as one might a favourite elderly uncle.

Beneath Yaztromo's bushy eyebrows, Darkmane could see the pleasure in the old wizard's eyes as he greeted his friend. Jamut Mantrapper had spoken often of the times he and the wizard had faced adversaries together. The two men stepped back from their embrace and looked each other over.

'Ah, Yaztromo! The great Yaztromo! My heavens, but you look well! Have you been working again on your Potion of Eternal Youth? It looks to me as if you have perfected it. Ha-ha!'

'Ach, young Jamut. Your impudence grows with your belly. Never have I met one with such impudence. But come, my friend. Now it is *you* who are lacking in manners. Will you not introduce me to your companions? And then let us go upstairs to talk. I am sure Vermithrax will wish to see you again.'

Mantrapper clasped his arms round Yaztromo's shoulders in a friendly gesture, but one which was perhaps a little too strong for the ageing wizard. He introduced first Darkmane, and then even managed to introduce the Chervah by his full name. Then the four of them entered Yaztromo's white stone tower and climbed the circular staircase to the fourth floor.

The Chervah's eyes opened wide as they climbed up past each floor. From the outside Yaztromo's tower seemed such an elegant residence, but it was hopelessly untidy inside. It was full to bursting with things collected during the wizard's lifetime: books, trophies, charts, tapestries, knick-knacks and ornaments covered every available square centimetre of wall, shelf and table space. Everywhere he looked, the Chervah could see scientific instruments and magical devices, most of which baffled him as he tried to guess their purpose. Darkmane was less fascinated. He wondered how the old man could bear to live surrounded by so much clutter. In his eyes, an untidy house was the product of an untidy mind. He shook his head. He could not understand the ways of sorcerers.

They continued climbing until they finally reached the wizard's study. Leather-bound books lined the walls from floor to ceiling; others lay open on the shelves while some had been pushed back into their places upside down. And the whole room was covered in dust. Yaztromo seated himself behind a desk that was covered in papers, maps and open books. The three adventurers took chairs from around the room and sat down to face him across the desk.

The wizard was the first to speak. 'So tell me, Jamut. What brings you here to Darkwood Forest . . . ?'

Yaztromo was leaning forward on the desk, his hands cupped under his chin. He looked from his friend to

the tall, black-haired warrior and then to the perky little creature at Darkmane's side, who glanced nervously back at him and then round the room as he caught Yaztromo's stare.

The old wizard nodded. 'Yes,' he said at last. 'I know of this Zagor you seek. But your journey to find him will be perilous. He lives to the north of here, deep within a mountain near the edge of the Moonstone Hills. You may find it easily, for its peak is tinted a ruddy hue. And thus its name is derived: *Firetop Mountain*.' Darkmane nodded slowly and intently. Yaztromo continued: 'I may even be able to show you this place. Above us, at the top of the tower, next to my aviary, is my observatory. In this room stands my viewing-scope. With this device I am able to see over great distances. Come. Let us see what we can see.'

The four of them rose together.

Yaztromo hesitated and turned to Darkmane. 'Of course,' he said, 'my services in the affairs of the world are bought at a price. You may consider that I am in the same profession as our friend Jamut here. But today is a happy day for me – I am glad to see my friend once more. The only payment I ask is therefore a courtesy rather than a fee. Perhaps, before we go upstairs, you will buy from me one of the magical items which I offer for sale?'

Darkmane was about to speak, but his eyes caught sight of the Chervah, who was staring at the old wizard, his eyes alive with excitement at the thought of Yaztromo's magical items.

Darkmane glanced at Jamut Mantrapper, who nodded discreetly. 'Of course, Yaztromo,' he said finally. 'Jamut here has told me of your skills in creating these treasures. It would be an honour to carry works from such a master magician. Please show them to us – and perhaps you will also suggest which one would be of most help to us.'

Both the mercenary and the Chervah stared at Darkmane in disbelief. Never before had they heard such courteous tones from the warrior.

Yaztromo straightened slightly, appreciating Darkmane's compliments. 'Very well, then,' he beamed. 'I will take you down to my stores.'

They followed him down five flights of stairs, until they eventually reached his storeroom, in a cellar below ground level. The Chervah could hardly contain himself. From floor to ceiling, shelves lining the walls were littered untidily with walking-sticks, rings, weapons, bottles, sacks, garments, books . . . all of which, according to Yaztromo, had been magically enchanted. He darted about from shelf to shelf, picking up this object and that, studying it and then asking Yaztromo what its purpose was.

Both Mantrapper and the wizard himself were amused by the little creature's excitement, but Yaztromo also noticed the look of disapproval on Darkmane's face as he surveyed the room. His expression revealed the contempt he felt for sorcery in all its forms.

'Come on then, Gereth,' said Mantrapper eventually, 'tell us what you have been working on. If I know you, no doubt you have just what we need for our journey – and at a bargain price, too!'

'Hrrmmph,' snorted the wizard. 'Yes. Well, I *was* going to recommend that you take something like a Ring of Light. You may need it if you enter Zagor's mountain. Or perhaps this net; it is a Net of Entanglement, and you should be able to snare most creatures with it . . .'

'What's this?' The Chervah's squeaky voice interrupted Yaztromo and all eyes turned to him. 'Oh . . . sorry. Er, what's this, sire?'

He held up a clear bottle inside which was a tiny, perfectly formed tree with minute leaves and wiry roots which were set into black powder in the base of the bottle.

'Ho ho! Be careful with that, little one.' Yaztromo took the bottle from his hands. 'If that bottle should break, I would soon have a great oak tree growing in the middle of my tower!'

He put the bottle down carefully on a shelf, then stroked his chin thoughtfully.

'Jamut, you have seen many of my creations. And of course, I cannot send you off with anything but the best. Many of these objects are no more than trinkets, that I must admit. It amuses me to conjure a little magic into them, and every so often I am visited by a fool who will pay me well for something to impress his lady – or his lord. But you three are bound on a dangerous mission. Zagor is a powerful sorcerer – and I do not wish this to be the last time I may see my friend the Mantrapper again.

'I suggest you take one item and no more. However, the object I recommend – as do all magical items of great power – will drain a part of your strength each time you use it. The temptation to use magic is always strong when it is to hand, but for one unskilled in the magic arts – as you are – the risks are high. No. Take one object and concentrate your minds only on the power of this item.

'I am suggesting this knife: an Orukk dagger. Its

purpose is twofold. First, as a throwing dagger, its accuracy is faultless. If you aim for the heart of your foe, only a greater magic will prevent its reaching its goal. Its second function will be vital if you are to find your way into Zagor's inner sanctum. Hold the dagger level with the ground, then balance the hilt at this point and ask the dagger to point in whichever direction your goal lies. It will show you which route to take. Thus.'

Yaztromo took a quill-pen from a table behind him and held it, nib upwards, between his fingers. He found the small recess in the dagger's hilt and placed it carefully on the nib of the quill. The dagger wobbled about but kept its balance, swaying to and fro.

Yaztromo spoke softly to it: 'Show me the one who doubts you . . .'

The dagger wobbled again and swung around towards the adventurers. When it had steadied itself, it was still trembling slightly, but was clearly pointing straight at Darkmane.

'Gereth! That is wonderf . . .' Mantrapper's words trailed off when he saw the expression on the wizard's face. Yaztromo's eyes were tightly closed and the muscles in his face were obviously trying hard to fight off an inner pain of some sort. The mercenary leapt to his assistance.

'No. It's all right . . .' The wizard spoke with some difficulty. 'As . . . As I said, these magic conjurings will drain strength, and my . . . my strength is not great at the outset. One with the strength of youth like yourself will hardly feel the strain – unless you come to rely on the dagger too heavily.'

Yaztromo slowly recovered. Mantrapper's concern was evident, but he tried not to show it as he said:

'Well, Gereth, our thanks for showing us your fine wares. Come, Darkmane, pay the man his price, and then let us all go up to Yaztromo's observing-room. I for one am anxious to see what awaits us up there!'

Yaztromo took forty gold pieces for the Orukk dagger and then led them upstairs again. They climbed up very nearly to the top of the tower. The air was lighter and cooler up here.

Yaztromo paused to catch his breath; he was much older than the others and his years objected to such exertions. 'Phew! Excuse me!' puffed the wizard. 'Jamut, you are right. I must concentrate my efforts on a Youth Potion! Foof! Nearly there. We just have to climb up through this trapdoor.'

They were standing in a workroom of some kind. A sturdy bench in the middle of the room was covered in and surrounded by tools and wood chippings. Near one wall a ladder led up through the ceiling to the next level. The smell of wood and sawdust told them that this room was constantly in use. The Chervah was surprised to see such a room in a wizard's home; he had always assumed that magic-users performed most tasks requiring physical effort with their spells.

'Ah, little one,' said the wizard, 'I can see you are puzzled. Perhaps because you see a craftsman's tools being used by a wizard? This room is where I make many of my magic items. Why do I not create them by magic? Magic is far too precious to waste on humble tasks like sawing and carving. No, I *make* them in here and enchant them downstairs. To tell the truth, I *enjoy* working with these tools . . .'

'But he doesn't enjoy cleaning up after his work – as you can see!' Jamut Mantrapper grinned at the wizard.

'Up here,' said Yaztromo, pointing to the ladder. 'Let us climb up into my observatory.'

As they entered the room above, the Chervah had occasion once again to express his astonishment. On clambering through the trapdoor entrance, he came face to face with a peculiar-looking mechanism of iron cogs and wheels which rose from the floor to support a thick, heavy, metal tube, angled up towards a wide skylight. Handles, pulleys, rods and knobs protruded from the tube, serving unfathomable functions.

This room was a little neater than the others. Charts of the heavens were tacked carelessly to the walls at odd angles but, apart from these and a wooden cabinet, the only other things in the room were the strange metal cannon-like device and a tall chair, positioned at one end.

Yaztromo was again catching his breath. He rested one hand on the chair and smiled proudly at the others. 'May I present . . . my viewing-scope!' The three observers smiled politely, unsure exactly how to react. Yaztromo continued: 'I can see that you are puzzled. This piece of apparatus is the only one of its kind in Allansia. With this viewing-scope I can see northwards to the Icefinger Mountains and on a clear day I can see Balthus Dire's citadel to the south. The machine's magic is held within the crystals that are set at each end. These crystals were cut for me from the crystalline rock found in the caves at Daddu-Yadu on the Earthend coastline in Kakhabad – the same crystal as is polished into Allansia's crystal balls, in fact. But this viewing-scope is no mere crystal ball. Here, you may look. Sit on this chair and place one eye to the end of the tube, there.'

Darkmane stood firm. He would have nothing to

do with this device. The Chervah took a half-step forward, noticed Darkmane's reaction and stepped back.

Jamut Mantrapper did not hesitate. He sat down on the chair and began to squint through one eye as he tried to make himself comfortable. 'Where do I look, Gereth? Through here?'

'That's it. If you see nothing, twist this knob here.'

They all watched as Mantrapper fumbled awkwardly with the device.

'What do you mean . . . Oh! What was that? That's better . . . Wha . . .? Logaan! What trickery is this?'

His mouth hung wide open. He was watching the image of a leather-clad horseman trotting along a crowded street past a small group of youngsters. The horseman rode on and Mantrapper watched him turn and disappear from sight round a corner. There was a building at the corner and hanging from the building was a sign. Though he could not read the letters on the sign, there was no mistaking the crest in the middle – a large black lobster.

'The Black Lobster!' he exclaimed. 'So close that I could step through the door and smell the stench of its stale ale! But how can this be? The Black Lobster is in Port Blacksand. And Port Blacksand is two weeks' ride from here!'

Darkmane looked round inquiringly at Yaztromo.

The old wizard smiled. 'My viewing-scope is my current preoccupation. Through its crystal lenses I can survey Allansia, from the Icefinger Mountains to the Desert of Skulls, from the Western Ocean to the Flatlands. From my seat here I have watched Baron Sukumvit sending eager contestants to their deaths at the yearly Trial of Champions in Fang. I have watched

Balthus Dire strolling outside his citadel walls with his lady, Lucretia. I can see out as far as . . .'

He stopped in mid-sentence. It was evident that the three adventurers were concentrating, not on his words, but on the viewing-scope. Even Darkmane was now showing impatience, anxious to have a look through the eyepiece, and the Chervah was almost frothing at the mouth with excitement!

Eventually, Mantrapper stepped away from the device and Darkmane took his turn. But he had a more serious purpose for Yaztromo's device than mere sightseeing.

'How may I view Salamonis?' he asked.

'Salamonis? Ah, let me see . . .' Yaztromo rustled through a pile of maps that were scattered on the cabinet, found one, and studied it. 'Yes. I think . . . If we point the viewing-scope in *that* direction!' He pointed a finger in a south-easterly direction.

The heavy viewing-scope could be moved around only with some difficulty, but eventually they had it pointing in roughly the right direction. Yaztromo took the seat, squinted through the eyepiece and fiddled with various knobs, trying to find the city of Salamonis.

'Ah! There! *There* is Salamonis!'

Darkmane took over the chair and peered through the eyepiece. He recognized the city gate and the silhouette of the buildings and towers behind the wall; it was, after all, a skyline that was most familiar to him. Astonished at the sight, he caught his breath. 'Can I get closer?' he asked.

Yaztromo showed him which knobs to turn. As he twisted them, the city moved quickly towards him. It was as if he were a bird, flying over the walls and round the buildings into the centre of Salamonis, glancing down at places – even people – that he recognized. The royal castle loomed up ahead. Suddenly he was looking into a courtyard inside the palace. Two figures were standing, talking, by a well. His hand stopped manipulating the controls and he watched silently in awe. The elder of the two he was observing was a man dressed in fine yellow robes. His tall physique, square face and short beard were unmistakable: *King Salamon!* The king was talking to a younger woman – a woman of beauty, of poise and of grace. The hairs on Darkmane's neck prickled as he recognized the golden hair and sylph-like features of the sorceress, Lissamina!

The two were deep in conversation. The king appeared at first to be anxious, but then Lissamina spoke and seemed to calm him with her words. How Darkmane wished he could hear what they were saying! The king gestured with his hands to emphasize a point: he held them apart, the fingers curved inwards, as if he were gripping a great beast around his neck. Then he looked at the sorceress and spoke, tightening his grip on the invisible beast as he did so, until finally his two hands came together. She nodded and spoke once again. The king sighed. Finally he held his hand out to her. She kissed it, curtseying as she did so. He laid his other hand on her head in an almost fatherly manner and then turned to leave. He walked out of Darkmane's view.

Lissamina remained by the well for a moment, wrapped in thought. Suddenly she cocked her head to one side: it was as if she could *feel* something in the air. She looked up. Frowning, she looked around as if searching for something – only she wasn't sure quite *what*. As her glance swept the horizon, from time to time she appeared to be staring straight into the viewing-scope at Darkmane and he had to resist an impulse to call out to her. At last her gaze came to rest in his direction and he found himself looking into her deep green eyes. The frown-lines vanished from her face and a warm smile crept across her lips. *She knew he was watching her!* She moved away from the well and out of the viewing-scope's sights.

Darkmane stood up quickly, away from the eye-piece, in a state of shock.

'Are you all right, master?' the Chervah asked.

'Wha . . . ? Oh, yes. Yes. I am . . . all right.' He composed himself and turned to Yaztromo. 'The visions I see through this enchanted contraption – they are real?'

'Of course.' The old wizard scowled. Darkmane's scepticism irritated him. Were it not for his friendship with Jamut Mantrapper, he would have no hesitation in ushering the warrior out. Instead, however, he added: 'And now that you have had the chance to use my *enchanted contraption* for yourself . . .' Yaztromo threw an icy glare at Darkmane ' . . . let us see if it can help you on your quest.' He returned to his charts, found a large map and began to study it.

The Chervah pouted. He was hoping to have his turn on the device. If it could see great distances, perhaps he could even glimpse the twisting spires of Rimon, his home town, far away to the south. But the others ignored him.

'We must move the viewing-scope to point towards the north,' Yaztromo said eventually. 'Then turn it a little to the east. There we may find what we are looking for.'

Yaztromo's Tower

They wheeled the heavy instrument around as the wizard directed. Yaztromo took his place on the chair and peered into the eyepiece. His hands took up their positions on the knobs and he nimbly began making adjustments.

'Hmmm. Should be around here . . . oh dear. Mist. Mist in the Moonstones. Hold . . . Ah, what's this? Yes. There. A red peak. Here we are! *There!*'

He leaned back proudly, then rose from the chair to allow the others to look. Mantrapper was the first to reach the eyepiece, and he squinted into it.

The excited Chervah could contain himself no longer. 'W-What can you see? May I look?' he squeaked.

'Mountains. A range of mountain-peaks shrouded in mist. Or perhaps clouds. Zorna's eyes, Yaztromo, I feel giddy! Have I become a hovering Nighthawk, stalking my prey?'

'Let *me* see.' Darkmane settled himself in the chair as Mantrapper stepped away.

He studied the panorama of mountains visible in the eyepiece. One peak to the left caught his attention.

'How do I make it come closer to me?' he demanded impatiently.

Yaztromo again placed the warrior's great hands on two of the knobs. Darkmane twisted them awkwardly and the peak jumped back, then appeared to leap towards him. He could now see clearly that it was different from the others. The tip of the mountain was tinged by a dull red fuzz, as if the gods had dropped a gigantic woolly cone on to it. And the very top of the mountain was not pointed, but almost flattened. Darkmane could see wisps of smoke floating up into the air. He sat back in the chair.

175

'Let me see again . . .' Mantrapper insisted, but then he noticed the Chervah. The excited little creature was straining desperately to control his excitement and frustration. The mercenary laughed loudly. 'Ha-ha! All right, Chervah, take the seat. Look into the viewing-scope. And quickly, before your own eyes pop out of your head and beat you to it!'

The Chervah scrambled frantically on to the chair. He was too small to reach the eyepiece and the others had to lift both him and the chair until he could see into the viewing-scope.

'Faa . . . Oh, look! Aaah! Mountains! Teeth! Like giant teeth! Heee! They're . . . Ah! I am a god! Oh dear! It's like . . . It's just like seeing through the eyes of a god!'

The others smiled as the Chervah went on burbling enthusiastically. Eventually Mantrapper turned to the wizard. 'So tell us more of this Firetop Mountain, Gereth. How do we reach it?'

'It is a safe ride if you skirt Darkwood Forest – perhaps three days, maybe four. If you choose to take the east side of Darkwood, you will find a trail that runs along the foothills of the Moonstones and takes you to the Crossing at the Crossing, where the Red River and the Catfish River meet. At this point you should ask the Dwarfs for directions, as the way onwards is into the hills.'

'Will you show us on your viewing-scope, Gereth?'

'Aye! A fine idea. Let us plan your route . . .'

For the next few hours, until darkness descended, they trained the viewing-scope along the route they planned to take. They were to head east from Yaztromo's tower, avoiding Darkwood Forest. Although the way through the forest was more direct, it was far more dangerous: Gremlins, Orcs, wild beasts and deadly Shape Changers lived in Darkwood Forest. Instead, Yaztromo advised them to follow the path between the edge of the forest and the lower reaches of the Moonstone Hills. This was a well-used path and was much safer.

The viewing-scope picked out the busy Crossing at the Crossing, where a ferry service would take them across to the north bank. Yaztromo swung the scope westwards to pick out Stonebridge, home of the Dwarfs. He managed to pick out Gillibran and suggested that, if the party ran into trouble, they should call on him for help. Then he returned to the matter of their route: it began to rise into the Moonstone foothills and was difficult to follow with the viewing-scope. But Yaztromo showed them several small villages where they could ask for directions to Firetop Mountain.

The Chervah drew up a map as they plotted their route, noting all that the wizard told them about the dangers along the way, likely fruits, plants and animals they would be able to find to eat, and the places where they might encounter friendly races.

When at last they had exhausted their questions, Yaztromo led them back down one floor from the observatory. He paused on the landing and stepped over to a door which had the word 'Aviary' inscribed on it. He gripped the door handle. 'Before we go down, Jamut,' he said, 'perhaps you would like to meet a friend of yours once again?'

A breeze blew past them as Yaztromo opened the door; a large window in the room inside was wide open to allow his birds to fly in and out of the tower.

'Ah, Vermithrax,' said the wizard to a large black

crow that was perched on the branch of a tree which grew inside the room. 'Look who has come to visit us!'

'C-c-r-rawk!' answered the bird. 'Mantrapper! Good afternoon! C-c-r-rawk!'

'Hello, Vermithrax!' laughed the mercenary. 'How goes it in Darkwood, you scruffy-feathered sparrow!'

'*R-r-r-oark!* I see your manners are still as poor as your taste in wenches! C-c-r-rawk!'

Mantrapper laughed. The last time he had visited the wizard's tower, he had been on his way to Stonebridge, home of the Dwarfs, accompanied by a bad-tempered Dwarf maiden who had run away from her family. She had fled to Silverton to avoid an arranged marriage with a Dwarf whom she despised. Her well-to-do father had hired the mercenary to find her and bring her back. Yaztromo had to drag her, kicking and screaming, all the way from Silverton, and they had stayed overnight at Yaztromo's tower on the journey there. She shrieked and fought all evening. When the old wizard grew tired of the Dwarf maiden's tantrums, he had locked the ill-mannered creature in an outhouse for the night – but not before she had met Vermithrax. The two had taken an instant dislike to each other.

'So how goes it in the forest? Is all calm in Darkwood?'

'C-c-r-rawk! Today I have been eavesdropping in Chalice for news of what is happening around the Pass. C-c-rawk! The Elves and the Dwarfs of Darkwood are nervous. C-c-rawk! Especially the Elves. C-c-r-awk! They fear the trouble may spread to Stittle Woad in the Forest of Spiders.'

Mantrapper nodded. 'And what have you heard?'

'C-c-r-rawk! Many things, Mantrapper, many things. C-r-rawk! But do *you* give *your* services as charity? C-c-r-rawk!'

Jamut Mantrapper laughed. He pulled a gold piece from his pocket and flipped it through the air at the crow, which leapt up and caught it in its claws.

'Same old Vermithrax! All right, then. Give us your news!'

'C-c-r-r-awk! Thank you. C-c-roak!' The bird settled on a branch and calmed down. When it next spoke, its voice had a more serious tone to it. 'C-crawk. The bloody war continues, but it seems the tide is turning . . .'

14

The Coming of the Sorq

The tide had indeed been turning; a new force had entered the battle. Balthus Dire could not have imagined what would follow when he decided to experiment with the cunnelwort herb. He could not have foreseen the dangers of opening up a gateway to the spirit plane.

Into the material world they came. The strange spirit beings which he had encountered emerged from the dimensional gateway into an unsuspecting world. At first Balthus Dire was convinced he was their master. He had sought them out and opened up the gateway: they must obey his commands.

He soon discovered that their powers were infinitely greater than his own.

When they entered the material plane, the Sorq Spirits disappeared immediately from the Dark Tower. Though Balthus Dire despaired, thinking they had gone for ever, they returned the next day. He learnt they had simply been determined to find out about this new world and during their absence had journeyed the length and breadth of Allansia. At each place they visited they sought out a prominent person, be he noble, rich merchant, or magic-user, and assimilated his knowledge into their own minds. The minds of their poor victims had not merely been *tapped*; they had been *stolen* while they slept. When they awoke the next morning, they were found to be little better than imbeciles.

The Sorq Spirits absorbed the newly acquired information rapidly. They were fascinated by the new world they found themselves in. They thirsted for more and more knowledge. But when they had learnt their fill, they returned to Balthus Dire's citadel. They now knew who he was. They had discovered that this primitive human evidently wielded some power in this new dimension and he was a respected magic-user. Perhaps he would be able to teach them more about the material world and the secrets of its sorcery. They also knew all about his struggle with Zharradan Marr. It would amuse them to assist him in this struggle . . . but only for as long as it suited them.

Their own spirit plane was devoid of *things*. They were masters of time and space; they were also masters of the intellectual skills – but here were *physical objects*! Mountains, trees, cities, buildings, people, animals . . . To the Sorq Spirits, travelling round Allansia was as wondrous as it might be to a blind man who has just had the darkness lifted from his eyes.

They returned to the Black Tower and co-operated in Balthus Dire's plans. He told them about the supply blockade and sought their help in clearing the Cragrock foothills of Zharradan Marr's troops. They immediately set off north to the Trolltooth Pass.

It was late evening. A small troop of Marr's legionaries were huddled round a camp fire on the banks of the

Whitewater River at a point where a natural ford made crossing possible. The Rhino-Men had bullied their ways to the warmest spots nearest the fire, and the Black Elves behind them were grumbling at being forced out; with Rhino-Men sitting round the fire, very little warmth penetrated through to them.

It was pitch-black. The only sounds to be heard were the incessant roar of the Whitewater River as it flowed past on its way to Oyster Bay and the monotonous moans that came from the nearby stockade. This was where the Soulless Ones were locked up. The miserable undead wretches would have to remain in their stockade until a caravan was sighted.

The legionaries had found that their job was now easy. Very few caravans came through with supplies for the Black Tower and those that did could easily be captured, simply by releasing the Soulless Ones; there was no need for the legionaries to risk themselves in battle at all. Instead, they slept, exchanged stories, gambled and argued.

It was a young Black Elf who heard the splashings first. He held up his hand and signalled for silence from the others. They listened. Horses were crossing the river!

The fire was quickly extinguished with dirt and the legionaries crept down to the river-bank. As their eyes grew accustomed to the darkness, they could see the faint image of a horse-drawn wagon carefully picking its way across the ford.

'Get the Soulless Ones!' The order prompted another argument among the legionaries, but eventually one of the Rhino-Men stumbled off to the stockade.

The Coming of the Sorq

The wagon looked easy prey. On a seat at the front was a cowled figure and there were four horses. A handful of creatures the size of Goblins were pushing at the cartwheels, lightening the horses' burden. The wagon was covered, so they could not see what was inside, but presumably this was just more supplies for the Black Tower. Easy prey. The legionaries would simply let the wagon cross the river and then, with all the Goblin-guards exhausted, they would release the Soulless Ones. They remained crouched behind bushes on the river-bank and waited.

Eventually the wagon reached the southern bank. The horses were allowed to rest for a moment, their heavy panting steaming out into the cool night air. The guards too sat down on the bank to catch their breath.

'Release them!'

The Rhino-Man's order pierced the silence like a shrill whistle. The wagon guards leapt to their feet and grabbed at their swords as two hundred Soulless Ones shuffled towards them down the bank. Their situation was hopeless. Though the Soulless Ones were unarmed, their sheer numbers were sufficient to overwhelm the defenders. And the hideous sight of so many living corpses, rotting and stinking, moaning and shambling towards them, was enough to freeze the heart of any guard, however dutiful. The creatures encircling them were long dead and, by the looks of agony in their pure white eyes, had no conception of fear or any idea of what they were doing. Expendable killing machines was what they were. Indeed, that was how Zharradan Marr himself saw his Soulless Ones.

They moved in closer. The guards began to tremble.

The drawhorses snorted and whinnied. The legionaries smiled and stepped out from behind the bushes
to watch the massacre at closer range. Soulless Ones
at the end of the line spread themselves out to encircle
the wagon. The circle tightened. It was not until the
Soulless Ones were within ten metres of the caravan
that the wagon driver stood up and threw off his
cowl.

In the next few instants, the scenario was utterly
transformed: hunter became hunted, victim became
victor, as the Sorq Spirits struck.

The cowl dropped to the ground and all eyes focused on the hideous creature gripping the horses'
reins. Though all saw it and gasped simultaneously,
each legionary saw a *different* figure, for the Sorq had
reached into every creature's mind and for each had
created the worst horror imaginable.

Some of the legionaries were confronting a demonic
creature from their own tribal mythologies; others
were seeing a vision from their own worst nightmare;
yet others were facing a ferocious beast of legend.
Terror struck the hearts of all the legionaries.

The Soulless Ones stood, silent and motionless, in
their tracks. Their enslaved souls were as one, seeing
before them the most terrifying vision imaginable in
their minds: the image of Zharradan Marr.

The Sorq cracked its whip and drove the wagon
forward into the pack of Soulless Ones. But the wagon
was no longer being drawn by mere horses. The four
drawhorses had turned into snarling and slavering
beasts of hell! They charged into the wretched Soulless
Ones, their powerful jaws snapping and crunching at
bone and ripping limbs from bodies like scythes in a
cornfield. Wherever the beasts charged, the Soulless

The Coming of the Sorq

Ones fell like ninepins. Those that had managed to avoid the charge stood confused. It was Zharradan Marr who stood tall on the wagon – and they could not attack their master!

The carnage continued.

The Sorq guards could keep up the pretence no longer; it was time for them to join in the mayhem. They metamorphosed themselves from the simple Goblin-creatures they had mimicked into winged demons and flew up into the air and after the legionaries, who by now were fleeing for their lives along the banks of the Whitewater. Swooping down on their victims like birds of prey, they lashed out with razor-sharp swords and talons. A Rhino-Man dropped to the ground screaming, clutching the wound in the middle of his face where his snout had once been. A Black Elf died instantly as a fierce blow from one of the demons collapsed his puny chest. The legionaries were cut down ruthlessly as they fled.

Then, abruptly, the Sorq ceased their attack. Their plan was complete: the Soulless Ones had been destroyed; many of the legionaries had been killed. They had no wish to kill *all* the fleeing troops. How otherwise would news of the massacre spread?

They returned to the wagon and watched the remaining legionaries escape into the night.

News of the massacre did indeed spread, and spread rapidly. Within a few days, panic had engulfed Marr's troops along the Whitewater River and in the Cragrock Foothills. The Sorq struck twice more: once in the north and once in the west. Their strategy was an overwhelming success. Faced with severe losses, low

The Coming of the Sorq

morale and the occasional mutiny, Zharradan Marr was forced to withdraw his troops.

The flow of supplies to the Black Tower was restored.

But Marr was no fool. From the information he acquired concerning the massacres, he soon realized that it was no worldly magic at work here. When tortured, his prisoners from the Black Tower also began to leak stories of these 'strange spirit creatures'.

He turned to the Ganjees for advice. The Ganjees recognized immediately the work of their kindred spirits. But the news of the arrival of the Sorq angered them greatly.

Zharradan Marr had been most disappointed with his new guests. Since he had enticed them into his household, they had proved most unwelcome visitors. They may have delighted in playing wicked practical jokes on Marr's minions, but to date they had offered no information concerning their battle-magic. They showed no interest at all in the developing war and sought only to learn all about Marr's marrangha experiments. Zharradan Marr consoled himself with the knowledge that at least they were not aiding Balthus Dire. And he kept his explanations of marrangha to a superficial level only.

But all this changed when the Ganjees discovered that the Sorq had arrived in the material plane. They ordered Zharradan Marr to set up a confrontation with the Sorq. He was to send a regiment of legionaries and Soulless Ones to the Whitewater ford – to the same place as the first massacre – and the Ganjees would accompany them.

Marr was outraged at receiving such an 'order'. But

if he was to destroy the Sorq, then the Ganjees were probably the only creatures who would be able to match them. He made the arrangements as they had demanded.

When it took place, the encounter cost him the lives of three hundred Soulless Ones and fifty-two legionaries before, in the height of the battle, the Ganjees revealed themselves!

The wagon they used was abandoned and the remaining legionaries watched incredulously as the two races of spirit-creatures locked in battle. The sky was alight with colour as disembodied shapes flashed through the air. Explosions sent out shock-waves which knocked all the onlookers to the ground. Giant ghostly shapes appeared in the sky, howling with the strength of a gale-force wind. Then they shot out of sight. Shadowy demons hung in the air, locked in combat, then faded. Lightning-bolts ripped the sky apart. Clouds pursued each other across the heavens. It was an awesome spectacle.

Suddenly a low, resonant sound filled all ears; it grew ever louder. High in the sky, a darkly shimmering void appeared. The spirit shapes paused in their battle for a moment and seemed to look up at the void. Then, in one mad, frantic rush, they were *sucked into it*!

Moments later, all was calm. The Ganjees – and the Sorq – had returned to the spirit plane to continue the battle there.

Balthus Dire cursed at the news. Now his advantage was lost. The Sorq had freed his supply line, and together they had laid plans for an attack on Marr's

The Coming of the Sorq

Galleykeep. Zharradan Marr had been forced on to the defensive while his troops were being continually driven back. The tide of war had turned.

And Dire, pressing his initiative, had already ordered Orcleaver, the Goblin battle-sergeant who had taken over from Foulblade as commander of his troops, to gather together an army of Goblins, Orcs and chaotics, and to march down into the Pass and secure it. But total victory would be certain and quick with the Sorq to aid him.

There was only one thing for it now. He would have to take another cunnelwort journey.

But the dangers were considerable. He decided first to wait and see how Orcleaver's army fared in the Pass. Then, if necessary, he would use the cunnelwort again.

What he did not know was that Zharradan Marr, faced with a weakening position, had taken desperate measures.

At that very moment, Thugruff was leading Marr's own army southwards. The two armies would meet in the Pass at any moment.

15

Into the Mountain

A cold wind was making the morning mist swirl. The Chervah looked up and shivered. From where they stood, the mountain resembled a huge stone titan towering above them. Rocky crags on its higher reaches made vague shapes and features, and the little creature's attention was fixed on what looked like two angry eyes glaring down at him.

He forced himself to peer higher up the mountainside. The tip of Firetop Mountain was obscured by clouds, but he could clearly see the strange reddish colour at the peak glistening as sunlight penetrated the clouds and lit up the early-morning dew decorating the crimson moss that gave the mountain its name.

The three of them approached the cave entrance and peered into the dark depths of Firetop Mountain. The Chervah held up a lantern they had bought from the Dwarfs of Stonebridge. The passage narrowed a little as the route through the cave disappeared into the blackness. Slimy walls glistened as the lantern's light fell upon them. Drips from the ceiling fell into small pools on the rocky floor, making splashes that

190

re-echoed off the walls. The sudden light had caused a flurry of scamperings across the floor as unseen small creatures ran for cover, but the adventurers could see no immediate danger.

Darkmane stepped forward and gestured for the others to follow him. The warrior led, with the Chervah following close at his heels flashing the lantern from side to side. Jamut Mantrapper took up his position at the rear of the party. He ran his hand along the wall to feel the damp. He smeared the oily liquid between his fingers and wiped it off on his tunic.

'A junction,' said Darkmane in a hushed voice. 'Careful! Wait here.'

He pressed up against the wall and peered cautiously round the corner. To the right, the passage continued; to the left it turned another corner. But this way he could also see a dull light.

He turned to Mantrapper. 'Try the Orukk dagger.'

Mantrapper stepped up and balanced the dagger in a dimple on his sword hilt. He whispered to it: *'Which way to Zagor's chambers?'*

The dagger began to quiver. It rocked gently from side to side as if trying to sniff out the correct direction. Finally it swung to the left.

'Left. The dagger – ' A shock of pain ran through him and cut his sentence short.

'Are you all right?' asked Darkmane. Mantrapper nodded and shoved the dagger back in his belt. They turned left and followed the wall round cautiously.

The Chervah heard a sudden noise and grabbed Darkmane's leg.

'What is it?'

'I-I c-can hear a sound!'

They all listened. The sound was faint, but they

all heard it distinctly, coming from the passageway ahead, round the corner. It was the low, rhythmical sound of something breathing!

A dull red glow illuminated the corner ahead, where the passageway turned to the right. Darkmane again kept to the wall and slowly edged his head out to look round the corner. The noise was louder here.

He took a quick look, then pulled his head back rapidly. 'Ssshh,' he warned. 'There's something asleep just round the corner. Slowly. We must not wake it.'

The other two followed as he tiptoed round the corner. The Chervah gasped when he saw the ugly creature slumped asleep in a stone crevice in the rock. Its skin was dark and warty and its hands and feet ended in horny claws. As its chest heaved up and down, its lower lip opened to reveal dirty – but sharp – teeth. The Orc sentry wore patchy leather armour, and a wooden spear rested between his knees and against the stone wall.

Darkmane advanced slowly, stepping carefully past the sentry towards the passageway ahead. Mantrapper, who had gone ahead of the Chervah, followed him. But the little creature was rooted to the spot, unable to move through fear.

'Chervah!' Darkmane hissed. 'Quickly. Come on.'

His master's words snapped him out of his trance. His foot inched forward. The whole of his body was shaking. He took another step. Then another . . .

CRACK!

The Chervah groaned as he looked down at the broken twig beneath his foot. The sound of the breaking wood resonated round the stony corridor. Frozen in his tracks, he glanced nervously at the Orc.

Into the Mountain

Its eyes fluttered and snapped open!

'*Rrraawwk!*' It saw the little creature standing quaking in front of it and grabbed its spear. The Chervah was unable to move.

Mantrapper sprang into action. The Orc's spear was mere centimetres from the Chervah's chest when Mantrapper's blade cut through it, shattering the wood. The ugly creature's eyes opened wide and it reached for its own sword, which was hanging in a scabbard round its belt. But Mantrapper moved more quickly and his blade cut deep into the Orc's forearm. The sentry pulled his arm away instinctively and held it up to view the damage. Dark blood oozed from the wound, soaked the Orc's sleeve and dripped on to the ground. The hand and forearm fell to one side, hinged by the last remaining sinews that Mantrapper's sword had left intact.

The Orc opened its jaws to scream but, before a sound could emerge from its throat, the point of the mercenary's sword pierced its neck. The sound emerged as a bubbling gurgle and the Orc fell to the floor, dead.

'Come quickly, Chervah,' Jamut Mantrapper panted. 'And for Slangg's sake, take care!'

The Chervah shook himself and followed. His head hung low as he realized the trouble he had caused. Perhaps the sentry's cry had warned others? He followed Darkmane and Mantrapper up the passageway.

They passed a door in the left-hand wall and stopped, a few paces on, by a second door. Darkmane bade them be quiet and turned his ear to the passage ahead. He could hear something coming.

He stepped over to the door and pressed his ear to

the wood. He heard nothing inside. 'In here,' he whispered to the others.

The noise from further down the passageway was growing louder: solid footsteps coming their way.

Darkmane turned the handle and stepped boldly through the doorway, sword at the ready. The room was empty. The others followed him in and closed the door behind them.

The room was lit by a single candle that stood on a small table. *Sleeping quarters*, thought Mantrapper as he saw the dirty straw mattress in the corner. *I hope they are not the sleeping quarters for whatever is out there.*

The Chervah noticed a small box lying under the table and he picked it up. It looked like a jewellery box of some kind, finished in snakeskin and with a small metal clasp holding it shut. He shook the box. Something rattled inside. *I am going to open it!* he thought, and he took the clasp between his fingers. *Wait! It might be dangerous!* said a little voice inside him. But the words were ignored as his fingers unhooked the clasp and flicked open the lid.

'*Aaaaahhh!*' he cried as the little snake inside reared up and bit his hand. The other two adventurers sprang across to his aid. The Chervah's fingers lost their grip on the box and it fell to the floor, spilling its contents: the small snake, a piece of red silk, and a bronze-coloured key which had been hidden away underneath the silk.

Mantrapper crushed the snake beneath his heel and bent down to pick up the box and its contents. 'Must have been an Orc's pet,' he said. 'But look at this key. What do you think? A key for this room? No – there is no lock on this door. But still, it might come in handy, don't you agree?'

Into the Mountain

Darkmane nodded, and Mantrapper slipped the key in his pocket. The Chervah put the silk square back in the box, laid the dead snake on top, closed it and put it back under the table.

Darkmane was standing by the door, listening for sounds in the passageway outside. All was quiet. They left, heading deeper into Firetop Mountain.

It was some time later when they arrived at the room of the Iron Cyclops. The corridor ended at a wooden door. They had taken a wrong turning at the previous junction – a mistake that could cost them dearly.

'Through here?' asked Darkmane.

'I don't know. It seems the only way. Let me listen.' Mantrapper placed his ear to the door and listened carefully for a few moments, then shrugged. 'Can't hear anything. I'll try the door.' He turned the handle slowly and pushed at the door.

It opened and, as it did so, light flooded out of the room into the passageway. The adventurers shielded their eyes and peered into the bright room.

They stood spellbound as they took in the ornate beauty of the room. The walls and floor were decorated with a mosaic of marble tiles that gleamed as they reflected the light coming from a bright point in the ceiling. In the centre of the room was a tall statue, standing on a pedestal.

'What is *that*?' gasped the Chervah.

'I don't know. Perhaps a statue of one of Zagor's creatures. All I do know is that I'm glad it *is* a statue, and not the beast itself!'

The great metallic statue was of a creature they had never seen before. It was man like in proportions, but stood on two hoofed feet. Its face was like that of a demon, with a forked tongue protruding between sharp teeth and a single eye in the middle of its forehead. But no representation of an eye had been sculpted in the socket. Instead, a huge sparkling jewel there caught the light and sent a myriad tiny sparkles round the room.

They entered cautiously and closed the door behind them, but Darkmane ordered the Chervah to go back outside to keep an ear and an eye open for Orcs. Meanwhile he moved slowly round the walls, searching for hidden doors or for any other clues as to the way onwards.

Mantrapper was transfixed by the iron statue. 'That jewel . . .' he sighed. 'Grang! It must be worth a king's ransom! I think I will just . . .'

'*Leave it!*'

The severity of Darkmane's tone stopped the mercenary in his tracks.

He turned to face the warrior. At first he was taken aback by the harshness of the order. Then his eyes narrowed. 'Let us get one thing straight!' Mantrapper's voice had a steely tone. 'You may be here on a mission to save your precious kingdom. But *I* am here for one thing only. You are paying me handsomely, that I don't deny. And while you are my paymaster, my services are at your disposal. But do you expect me simply to *ignore* a jewel the size of a rabbit's skull? And one moreover that is unguarded; simply *pleading* to be taken? Why, I could sell this jewel in Shazâar and live comfortably for a year on the proceeds.'

Darkmane scowled at the mercenary. 'We are not here as common thieves. First, we will find this Zagor – and that is our only purpose. Once we have found him and left this hellhole, then you will be free to return to plunder as you wish. But until then, nothing will distract us from our mission.'

'Oh, but of course!' mocked Mantrapper. 'The *great* Darkmane is a warrior of the court. What use has he for gold and riches? Well, Jamut Mantrapper is *not* in such a privileged position. I *will* take this jewel, and it will change my life for the better. What folly it would be to leave the jewel in place, hoping to return later to collect it! It is *here* and *now*! Look: it is practically in my hand! Anyway, we are wasting more time now arguing about it than it will take for me to prise it from the eye of the statue . . .'

'NO!' thundered Darkmane. '*While I pay your wage, you will obey my orders.* I do not trust this place. I sense danger in the air all around us. We are leaving this room *now!*'

It was a clash of wills. The two stared at each other, eyes blazing with their fiery anger. Outside the door, the Chervah could hear the raised voices and was dithering about whether to go inside and see what was going on. But at that moment the door opened and Jamut Mantrapper stepped out. His teeth were clenched together and the veins on his temples pulsed visibly, straining to contain the fury in his mind. Darkmane followed him out.

'We must retrace our steps back to the junction,' said Darkmane. 'And there we will turn right. I will lead. Chervah – get behind me. Let us go!'

They walked on in silence. It would take some time for the tempers of the two swordsmen to calm down. They continued round the corner until they arrived at the junction.

Darkmane stopped to consider which way to go.

'Mantrapper. Are you sure the dagger pointed this way?'

There was no reply.

Darkmane felt a swell of anger at the mercenary's unwillingness even to talk. He swung round to face Mantrapper . . .

Mantrapper had disappeared!

Darkmane looked down at the Chervah, who shrugged. He had neither seen nor heard anything. Suddenly, a succession of sounds broke the silence.

'Nnyyyaaaaaaahh!'

Claaannngg!

'Aaaaarrgghh!'

The yell came from behind them. It was the voice of Jamut Mantrapper! Darkmane raced back down the passageway, his sword already in his hand. When he turned the corner, the sight before his eyes stopped him in his tracks.

Mantrapper's rage and greed had evidently got the better of him. The mercenary had decided to ignore Darkmane's order and had quietly slipped back to the marbled room to steal the statue's jewel. And stolen it he had, as the warrior could clearly see through the open doorway to the room. He was holding it clasped tightly in his left hand. But the jewel had not been undefended. When it popped out of its mounting, Mantrapper had stooped to pick it up. From above him he had heard a creaking noise, like a slowly opening rusty iron gate. This sound was repeated once, then again. At first he thought it was the door opening, but when he looked up he found to his horror that the creakings were not coming from the door.

He gasped and for an instant was frozen in shock, unable to move. Above him, the limbs of the demonic statue were flexing themselves in jerky movements. Its great head twisted awkwardly on its neck as if searching the room for something. One cloven hoof stepped forward a pace. The other did the same. The creature was stretching, bending and twisting as if flexing its iron muscles for the first time. It was as if a guardian demon-spirit had awoken inside the creature and was testing and learning what movements were possible in this new body.

Mantrapper came out of his trance and grabbed his sword and at the same moment the shining statue leapt to the ground from its pedestal! As the mercenary's blade slid out of its scabbard with a metallic ring, the creature cocked its head to one side. At the moment it was standing facing away from Mantrapper; but the sound of the sword being drawn from its sheath caught its attention. It swung its body round towards him and its mouth twisted into a snarl. The snake-like tongue darted and flashed in its throat and it raised both hands, ready to grasp its terrified human prey.

'*Nnyyyaaaaaaahh!*' Mantrapper leapt forward, raised his blade over his head and brought it down with a savage chop across the statue's forearm.

Claaannngg! The ringing sound of steel on steel echoed round the room.

The shock-wave of the impact ran along the sword-blade, through the hilt and up Mantrapper's arm. The firm line of his eyebrows collapsed as his face twisted into an expression of pain. '*Aaaaarrgghh!*'

The statue moved in. It had learnt quickly how to control its new-found muscles and swatted fiercely at Mantrapper with its iron fist. The blow caught the mercenary on the left shoulder and sent him flying

across the room. He crashed into the wall with a force that would have stunned a lesser man. He shook his head and looked up at the advancing statue through glazed eyes. Miraculously, he had managed to hold on to the jewel, but his sword had been knocked from his hand and lay on the floor by the pedestal, well out of reach.

Mantrapper scrambled to his feet just as a clenched steel fist thudded into the wall where he had been lying. He summoned up all his energy and launched himself at the statue. It was off balance and now he might be able to bowl it over and give himself a chance to get back to his sword. His shoulder slammed into the creature's chest . . .

The move was not a wise one. Mantrapper cried out aloud in pain as his shoulder hit its target, but the statue scarcely felt the blow. Its open fist swung into the mercenary's stomach in a powerful punch which sent him reeling across the room. This time he was not so lucky at holding on to his possessions. The jewel fell from his grip and scudded across the marble floor into a corner. Mantrapper's backpack split open, spilling gold pieces and provisions round the room. Yaztromo's dagger twisted out of his belt and slid over to the pedestal.

The creature turned towards him. Its face was contorted into the snarl of a wild-cat and a steaming, hissing sound came from the back of its throat. It stepped jerkily towards him.

Mantrapper lay in a heap against the wall. He shook his dazed head slowly and blinked several times, as if trying to shake some sense back into his stunned brain. He raised his eyes to take in the situation. But the sweep of his gaze never reached the far side of the marbled room – it was cut off abruptly by the sight that confronted him not half a metre away. He focused quickly on the hideous, metallic, snarling face with its gaping eye-socket, silvery forked tongue that darted in and out, and the sound of steam hissing in its throat. Before he had even the chance to scream, a grip of iron circled his throat, and began tightening.

He coughed and spluttered, his own hands struggling valiantly to release the vice-like grip of the creature's hands. But what chance has flesh against iron? The mercenary began to gasp as the steely hands tightened further. His head started swimming and consciousness began to fade. Jamut Mantrapper's world was dissolving to blackness . . .

His last remembered view before passing out was of the creature's savage expression and its mutilated forehead where the missing jewel had been prised from the eye-socket. The blackened socket was immediately in front of his eyes; it was almost as if the creature was intentionally leaving him with a last reminder of his foolish crime as he paid the price and succumbed to his punishment. The eye-socket filled his vision. Its blackness became Mantrapper's blackness. A shaft of silver gleamed in the blackness. Consciousness left him . . .

16

The Battle of the Pass

That same morning, thick, dark clouds hung heavy in the skies over the Trolltooth Pass. It was as if the celestial gods themselves were scowling at the carnage to follow as the two armies came within sight of each other.

'Look! In sky. Big ship.'

Orcleaver's ugly face screwed into a squint as he followed the scout's pointing finger. '*Galleykeep*,' the battle-sergeant, now army commander, said quietly. 'Za'mar comes.'

Orcleaver and his five-thousand-strong army had reached their destination first and made their camp on a high plain to the south, overlooking the Trolltooth Pass. His army was composed of thirty-seven tribes of Hill Goblins, each led by its own tribal chief, disorganized bands of Orcs and a miscellaneous collection of the creatures of chaos which had ravaged the village of Coven.

Though continually squabbling and brawling among themselves, the Goblins were the closest thing Balthus Dire had to Zharradan Marr's legionaries. Each tribe was loyal to its chief and each chief was loyal

to his commander; thus it was possible to organize the
Goblins into regiments and plan battlefield man-
oeuvres—something that was totally impossible with
the Orcs. As soon as an Orc caught sight of its enemy,
any semblance of order was lost. Instead, as often as
not, they would immediately fly into a frenzy and
attack without any regard for orders – or even for
their own lives. And the same was true for the other
creatures of chaos: they were simply battle fodder.
They could, however, be relied upon to take a good
number of enemy troops with them before eventually
being struck down themselves. For this reason, the
Goblins tolerated 'hem.

Also scattered among Orcleaver's forces were far

The Battle of the Pass

more dangerous creatures, hated and feared by Goblins and Orcs alike: Black Elves, Barbarians of the Hills, Calacorms, Giant Insects, Hellhounds, deadly Eyeless Archers and a multitude of other chaotics. They had joined Orcleaver's army as it marched past their homes and caves. Some had joined out of a vague sense of loyalty to Balthus Dire, but most knew little and cared less about the Lord of the Black Tower. They understood only that such a gathering of troops meant just one thing: an impending battle. This they could not resist.

Orcleaver turned to his assembly of tribal chiefs. The dirty fabric of the makeshift tent was flapping in the

wind so hard that the Goblin commander had to raise
his voice to make himself heard.

'Za'mar comes,' he announced. 'With army. We
surprise. We attack first. Listen . . .'

The Goblin commander knew precious little about
strategy or tactics, but his plan was simple and sound.
They would wait quietly for Marr's troops to enter the
Pass and then descend on them. He had witnessed
this tactic being used before, and it had been a total
success. On that occasion Foulblade's ambush had
left just a single survivor. This time there would be
no survivors.

'Stoneback take tribe. Go east Pass. Stop escape.'

Stoneback lifted his hands off his fat belly in a
gesture of agreement. All his tribe were as gross as
their chief and shared his disgusting eating habits. A
dry smile exposed a mouthful of broken teeth as
Stoneback grinned proudly at the other chiefs. After
all, he and his troops had been chosen for a special
mission. But Orcleaver had not chosen Stoneback
and his overweight tribe because of their skills as
accomplished warriors; they were much too slow to
be of any use. He had chosen them simply because
the escape-route to the east was of least concern to
him; there was nothing out there but the Flatlands.

'Halfclaw take other end. West. No escape. Kill all.'

'NO!'

The chiefs turned as one towards the figure squat-
ting at the back of the assembly. Halfclaw had a
stubborn expression on his ugly face. He and his
troops were from a particularly vicious tribe to the
south of the Black Tower. They were widely known
as 'The Bloodlusters' because of their macabre customs and rituals. Each day the Goblins practised their

weapons skills religiously. Any judged to be under-achievers (actually, those who had antagonized the judges in some way) became the victims of a monthly man-hunt, to be pursued and slaughtered by the rest of the tribe. In his time, Halfclaw had killed a good number of his own people. He was not a creature to be trusted. He rose to his feet.

'No. Not come to guard. Come to *kill*.'

Orcleaver also rose. He must not allow this insubordination. His thin lips tightened. 'You obey order. Or we kill you. Go west. Attack Za'mar army *behind*. Plenty killing. But no escape.'

Halfclaw opened his mouth to speak but then he sensed the hostility coming from the other chiefs, who were glad to have him distanced from the main battle – and away from their own tribes. He hesitated, then lifted his three-clawed hand in the recognized gesture of agreement. Murmurs of relief went up from the assembly as Halfclaw sat down again.

'Good,' continued Orcleaver. 'All others with me. Hide in hills. Wait my signal. Then attack.'

'Drones.' A gruff voice came from Orcleaver's left. 'What about Drones?'

The Goblins referred to the Orcs, Black Elves and other creatures not controlled by Goblin chiefs as 'Drones'. In a surprise attack they were a constant liability. As like as not, they would be unable to control their patience and would rush in to the attack prematurely.

'Scouts tell them. They not attack.' Orcleaver spoke with authority and confidence. 'Not until ready.'

This reply seemed to satisfy the questioner, though Orcleaver himself could only hope that they would obey the instruction.

'Now go. Take position. Watch. And wait for signal.'

The thirty-seven Goblins rose noisily to their feet and bustled out of the tent. Today they would do some *killing*.

The figure at Thugruff's side had been silent all night . . . silent, that is, apart from the rhythmical *clip-clop* of his horse's hoofs. Several times Thugruff had turned towards him to offer water, or conversation, but neither had been accepted. Instead the ghostly creature simply stared ahead, wide-eyed and unblinking. The two of them, at the head of Zharradan Marr's army, continued in silence. Thugruff wondered what his companion's thoughts might be.

But no one knew for certain whether *any* thoughts at all passed through the mind of Darramouss, the keeper of Marr's dungeons. The mysterious Half-Elf had been summoned to join Thugruff and to bring with him some of the creatures under his command. Though he obeyed the order, he disliked being in the open air and hated the sunlight. His dry skin, stretched tight over his bones, felt uncomfortable in daylight. He preferred the cold and damp of his underground domain.

His lord, Zharradan Marr, had decreed that this war must be decided and decided quickly. He had no patience for a drawn-out war of attrition. Thugruff had been training an army of legionaries at the Testing Grounds in Knotoak Wood. Balthus Dire's army, he knew, had had no such training. The longer he left it, the more time Dire would have to organize his troops. There was only one risk: Thugruff's troops were not great in number – a thousand legionaries

The Battle of the Pass

and perhaps half that number of Soulless Ones. If he struck immediately, before his enemy could gather his army together, there would be a good chance of finishing the war quickly and successfully. He did not know that both of them had given their battle commanders the same instructions at virtually the same time.

Thugruff and Darramouss rode slowly south towards the Cragrocks. Behind them, a thick wall of Rhino-Men, bristling with long spears, led the foot-soldiers. They were followed by three regiments of legionaries, grouped into races: the humans, the Lizard-Men and the Black Elves. Following the Black Elves was a regiment of mixed races: Goblins, Dwarfs, Kobolds, Craggeracks and Gorians.

Then followed the Soulless Ones, stumbling zombies who shuffled along in an unwieldy mass. Two dozen guards on horseback patrolled them continually, whipping them on. There was constant background noise, a mixture of sighs and moans as the undead monstrosities staggered onwards.

At the rear, pulled along behind a horse-drawn cart, were Darramouss's creatures. Each wore a spiked collar, from which a rope joined it safely to the cart. The clumsy band included Blood Orcs, Clawbeasts, Devourers and Manic Beasts. Though they now seemed to be docile as they followed behind the cart, each would become a fearless and deadly killer when Darramouss gave the order.

And high above, watching from the deck of the *Galleykeep*, was Zharradan Marr himself. A small band of trusted legionaries crewed the great vessel. At Marr's side stood a huge figure of a man with a savage scar down the side of his face: Vallaska Roue. Flying beside the *Galleykeep* were a dozen Tooki. These were huge winged Griffons – half eagle, half lion – being ridden by stern Blood Orc archers sitting proudly on their backs, their bows carried across their chests. The Tooki bobbed up and down beside the ship as the Griffons slowly flapped their wings.

It was Vallaska Roue who pointed out the movement below as Thugruff's army entered the Pass; he noticed the swarm of black ants that were Orcleaver's troops scrambling about in the hills. Marr gave the word and the *Galleykeep*, with its escort of Tooki, began to descend. A red flag was hoisted quickly up the mast – the signal of warning to the ground troops below.

'Thugruff! Look!' Tankasun, the one-armed Gorian sergeant-at-arms, galloped to the head of the line. His horse's clattering hoofs echoed along the Pass. 'See? On the *Galleykeep*. A red flag. A warning!'

Thugruff turned to look up at the black-sailed sky-galleon. As he caught sight of the flag, his pulse quickened. He also noticed that the strange creature behind him had turned his gaze skyward and then immediately wheeled his horse round and headed off towards the rear of the troop. Thugruff turned to study the steep rock-faces on either side of them. He had heard about the incident which had sparked off the war. Were Dire's accursed Hill Goblins planning another ambush?

He raised his hand to halt the march. The first thing he had to do was scout out the Pass. But it was too late. They were already in the Pass and the rocks to their right were thick with Goblins.

'ATTACK! This side! Down! *Kill!*'

The Battle of the Pass

Orcleaver screamed his orders and the trumpets sounded. The black horde poured down the slopes as if a huge cauldron of pitch had been overturned. The Goblins whooped and cried as they flung themselves down at the legionaries below, standing open-mouthed and unprepared.

Thugruff spurred his horse and rushed down the line, barking orders as he rode. The Rhino-Men closed ranks to form a tight phalanx, spears held firmly outwards. No creature, not even a Goblin, would surely dare face such a wall of death. The others drew their weapons and turned to face their attackers. Darramouss was already giving the order to unleash his dungeon horrors.

Thugruff pulled his horse up quickly by the wretched Soulless Ones, who seemed not even to have noticed the attack in progress.

'Go! Fight! Kill!' he bellowed at them, pointing with his sword at the cliffs.

Five hundred wretched heads moaned as the undead turned southwards. They staggered towards the Goblins who by now were reaching the floor of the Pass and were rushing into battle – straight into the outstretched arms of the Soulless Ones.

Screams came from the Goblins as the undead creatures ripped and slashed at them with their claws. Goblin swords bit deep into zombie flesh, spraying foul slime about. But even when their limbs were cut and broken, the Soulless Ones fought on. They knew nothing of fear and pain but only of their order to attack. Their sheer numbers would overwhelm the first rush of Goblins and scatter the others, making it easier for the legionaries to begin a counterattack.

Halfclaw's Bloodlusters were already down in the

Pass behind Thugruff's army and were advancing on Darramouss's creatures. The Half-Elf watched impassively as the Goblins swamped his cart. But the ground was clearing from the centre of the mêlée as the Manic Beasts and Devourers forced the Goblins out into a circle. Then the Goblins tightened the ring . . .

Thugruff ordered the Rhino-Men forward, and the phalanx moved. Shoulder to shoulder they marched, in a perfect square. Their outstretched spears prevented any attacking Goblins from getting within striking distance, and Thugruff used the Rhino-Men to break up any organized defence. The Lizard-Men had charged into the Goblin horde and the two forces were locked together in a fierce sword-battle. The Rhino-Men advanced and caught the Goblins in their flank. They cut through the creatures, driving a neat line through the middle of their ranks and making it an easy matter for the Lizard-Men to chop down those Goblins left on their side of the line.

From his vantage point high up in the rocks, Orcleaver watched the battle. He had sent only about two-thirds of his troops into battle, keeping the rest back as reinforcements to be deployed wherever the battle seemed to be going badly. He scratched his chin and grunted as he saw the Rhino-Men once again drive a deep wedge through his troops.

'Must kill Rhino-Men!' The voice of Blackscar, his own battle-sergeant and one of his most senior officers, snapped him out of his musing.

'Grrnt.' Orcleaver was surprised at his own noncommittal reply. Of course the officer was right. The Rhino-Men were wreaking havoc and had to be attacked – the phalanx had to be broken. Orcleaver also knew exactly what must be done: the Eyeless Archers must rain their arrows down into the centre of the phalanx. All he had to do was give the word . . .

But Orcleaver's expression suddenly became vacant. Within his own mind he struggled to keep control. But his thoughts were drifting, drifting from the scene below to another scene, deep in his memory. A burning camp fire. A sack of herbs. His old commander, Foulblade, giving the order to sleep.

He could see himself walking off into the darkness, pausing by a bush. Then . . .

'Aaargh!'

He fell backwards to the ground, his face frozen in an expression of horror!

'Orcleaver! What this? We kill Rhino-Men. Must use arrowers. Lose more troops now. Order it. You say.' Blackscar dropped to his knees beside his commander, grabbed him by the shoulders and shook him.

'W-w-what? What happen me?' Orcleaver's eyes fluttered and he shook his head.

'Must give order. Use arrowers. Look! Rhino-Men kill more!'

Down below, the Rhino-Men were continuing their work of devastation. Though the Goblins were pushing back the Soulless Ones, the Rhino-Men were ruthless, halting their progress: the Goblins were falling before them like flies. At the entrance to the Pass, Darramouss's creatures were holding off the circle of Halfclaw's Bloodlusters. The Goblins were now being joined by some of the Drones, who saw unarmoured creatures carrying no weapons as easier prey. But they soon learnt differently when a single Clawbeast's swipe broke three Orc necks and a Devourer savaged two others.

The officer was still pleading with his commander. 'Must give order! Not wait!'

'Grmmph.' Orcleaver shook his head again and turned to look at the young Goblin officer. His expression was vague and distant as if he had just awoken from a deep sleep.

Finally he gave the order:

'Arrowers. Rrrmph. Kill Rhino-Men . . .'

A furious battle was developing between three Goblin tribes locked in combat with the human legionaries. Casualties on both sides screamed loudly as they fell, clutching here a broken arm, there a bloody face. The two sides were so entangled that it was difficult to tell which had the upper hand. But when two more Goblin tribes joined in the battle, the humans could not hope to maintain their position. They were driven back towards the wall of the Pass and cut down as they retreated.

Thugruff saw the danger and signalled to the Rhino-Men. The phalanx wheeled and headed towards the Goblins, maintaining their perfect square. The Rhino-Men cut a swathe through the Goblins, until at last the Eyeless Archers found their range. Then a hail of ripping arrows rained down into the phalanx, their jagged blades cutting through the Rhino-Men's armour and tough hide.

Panic broke out in the Rhino-Men's ranks. Krravaak, their sergeant-in-command, bellowed his orders. If the formation broke, they would be slaughtered without mercy by the Goblins surrounding them; but, being such an easy target *en masse*, they were being slaughtered anyway by the deadly arrows. They tried valiantly to obey their sergeant's orders but, as wave after wave of arrows showered down upon them, the formation finally broke. The surviving Rhino-Men, in hopeless disarray, found themselves fighting with vicious Goblins armed with swords. Their own spears were of no use to them in such a close battle. They were cut down and hacked to pieces by the snub-nosed Goblins.

High in the sky, Zharradan Marr watched the progress of the battle from the *Galleykeep*. His troops had been doing well, holding off and pushing back a much larger force of Goblins and chaotics. But now, with the phalanx of Rhino-Men dispersed, the tide of battle might well change. Marr had his captain swing the ship around until it was sailing over a part of the rocks where a line of small black creatures were perched, each taking aim and firing deadly arrows one after another into the battle below.

As the shadow of the *Galleykeep* passed over the Eyeless Archers, the rock-face all round them erupted in a series of white-hot explosions. High above, Marr's legionaries were giving the creatures a taste of their own medicine as they hurled potash balloons over the railings and down on to the archers. These deadly missiles exploded on impact, scattering a shower of small burning fragments of potash which stuck to anything they touched, including skin.

The Eyeless Archers turned their aim to the sky, but no defence was possible against the deadly weapons which poured down among them. The legionaries below cheered loudly as they saw scores of burning black bodies dropping from the walls of the cliffs, to bounce down the rocks and land among the Goblin hordes.

Though the potash balloons had destroyed their position and left them few in number, the Eyeless Archers had already done their damage: the Rhino-Men phalanx had been dispersed. Their survivors were now surrounded by Goblins and were being slaughtered mercilessly. Thugruff's forces were being overwhelmed by the sheer numbers of Goblins. They desperately needed to regroup.

Thugruff considered his options and finally sounded the retreat, calling the Rhino-Men and the other legionaries out of the mêlée and away down the Pass. Looking eastwards along the Pass, he had decided on his next course of action: a single tribe of overweight Goblins stood blocking his passage to the east. Once they had forced their way through Stoneback's ungainly guards and then regrouped, they could mount an effective counterattack. His troops tore themselves free from their skirmishes with the Goblins and followed him down the Pass.

The *Galleykeep* took up its position above the Pass and potash balloons rained down on the pursuing Goblins. The pursuit halted. The Tooki swept down and fired their arrows into the mass. Trident cannons shot their deadly bolts into the hordes, and the Goblins fled to cover in the rocks.

Zharradan Marr knew his weapons would not last for ever. His ship could not hold the Goblins back for much longer; their sheer numbers would eventually force their way through. But he had another weapon which he could use against them, one which could be far more effective – if Quimmel Bone's efforts had been successful. The ship's physician was somewhat eccentric nowadays and could not always be relied upon. But Marr was certain that this Night Shadow creature could be their key to victory.

He sent Vallaska Roue down to see how the physician was progressing . . .

Stoneback's troops held their ground as the legionaries fled along the Pass towards them. They were hopelessly outnumbered and those on the front line were becoming agitated. A young warrior, not quite as fat as his chief, turned to Stoneback. 'Za'mar troops come. Too many. How we kill all?' he quavered.

Stoneback swung around to face him. 'We stay. Orcleaver keep tribes in hills. Ambush. Soon. You watch. Hold ground.'

But as Stoneback turned back towards the advancing legionaries, he had to admit to himself his own worst fears. What chance did his small tribe have against Thugruff's horde? They were outnumbered at least twenty to one. Again he thought about the reserves, holding their positions up among the rocks. Orcleaver was leaving it too late! Why didn't he spring the trap now?

High up in the Pass, Blackscar was pleading desperately with his commander. Down below, among the rocks, fifteen hundred frenzied Goblins were poised, waiting for the order to charge down upon the unsuspecting legionaries. 'Give order! Send tribes down! What matter? Stoneback tribe be killed!' The officer was frantic.

But Orcleaver's gaze was fixed somewhere out in space. He could not hear Blackscar's pleas. He could not see the massacre that was about to take place in the Pass below, as the full might of Thugruff's army reached a small band of less than seventy overweight Goblins. Nor could he see the fifteen hundred impatient Goblins waiting in their positions among the rocks above the legionaries, desperately waiting to be given the order to attack.

Orcleaver's mind was filled once more with the image of the night in the Cragrocks. He was writhing on the floor as he wrestled with the black shadow engulfing him. The more he struggled, the more he was becoming entangled. The harder he tried to breathe, the more difficult it became. His struggles were getting weaker. He was choking on the thick black shadow stuck in his throat. He could not move.

The Orcs and the creatures of chaos could wait no longer; they broke ranks and scrambled down the rocks, whooping and screaming. But the senseless creatures had no chance against the trained legionaries. Thugruff's forces turned, regrouped and calmly wiped out the Drones as they attacked. Then they turned about and charged Stoneback's terrified tribe, still awaiting reinforcements which never came.

Vallaska Roue returned to the deck of the *Galleykeep* and announced proudly to Zharradan Marr: 'Bone reports that the Night Shadow's power is working. Dire's Goblin commander is ours.'

Stoneback's tribe were cut down where they stood. The massacre was complete.

17

Zagor's Domain

'*Mantrapper!* Mantrapper, come on. Wake up!' The Chervah turned to speak to Darkmane. 'I don't know, sire, his pulse is weak. Those death demons are pulling at his soul. Perhaps we should leave him to recover at his own pace.'

'We have no time for that, Chervah. Keep trying. He'll come out of it. I should have left him to take his punishment. Fool!'

'Do not say such things, sire!' The Chervah looked shocked. 'I'm sure you are right. It *was* foolish – and greedy – to return for the jewel. But how was he to know the statue would come to life?'

'*Chervah!*' Darkmane's angry voice stung the little creature like a stiletto. The Chervah fell silent immediately. '*He disobeyed an order!* How can we hope to overcome the dangers before us if we act, not as a team, but with only our own selfish interests at heart? I cannot . . .'

Darkmane's words faded as he heard a sound coming from the mercenary's lips.

'Oooooohhhhh . . .'

Jamut Mantrapper's head rolled slowly from side

to side. His eyelids fluttered and at last remained open. He was looking directly up at Darkmane, who was standing over him. The warrior looked to him like a black spectre, until his eyes managed to get his face into focus.

'Whaa . . .?' He threw a brief glance around at his surroundings. They were all in the dark corridor outside the marbled room. 'Where . . .? Ooohh, my neck!'

'Sire, I fear you will have those red marks on your neck for some time to come.' The excited Chervah spoke quickly. He was glad that their companion seemed to be all right. 'But better that than the fate that was awaiting you, eh?'

'But what happened?' Mantrapper pushed himself up to a sitting position and rubbed his neck. He discovered that his shoulder, too, was painful. 'What happened in there? That creature . . . The statue!'

The Chervah looked up at Darkmane proudly. 'Sire, my master – *our* master . . .' Darkmane noticed the Chervah's ploy ' . . . saw off the creature, or statue, or whatever it was.'

Mantrapper turned to Darkmane. 'But . . . how? The thing was solid iron. My sword had no effect on it . . .'

Darkmane held out the Orukk dagger.

'I watched your struggle through the doorway. At first I was undecided whether or not I should enter the battle, since you had shown such insubordination. But then you became unable to defend yourself. The creature grabbed you round the throat . . . I could not hope to wound a creature made of solid iron. My concern was to find its weaknesses. I noticed two: the back of its throat and the eye-socket. I entered the room and picked up your dagger from the floor. I had to choose my target quickly, since your strength was fading and I would not get a chance for a second attack. I decided that the back of its throat was too risky as I would have to shove the dagger – and my fist – between its jaws. Instead I leapt on its back and plunged the blade into the eye-socket. It expired instantly.'

'Darkmane, my friend, once again I am indebted to you for my life. Thank you.'

Darkmane's expression remained unyielding. He had not forgotten how Mantrapper's foolishness had been the cause of the incident in the first place. The mercenary also realized this, and hung his head. Although his pride would not allow an immediate apology, they both knew it was implied.

The Chervah tried to cheer up Mantrapper's spirits. Quickly, he chirped: 'And when we examined the fallen statue, you'll never guess – '

'*Enough!*' Darkmane cut him short. 'Now . . . Now we must concentrate again on our purpose. Are you well enough to continue?'

Mantrapper nodded. But the Chervah's outburst had aroused his curiosity. 'The jewel,' he asked, hesitantly. 'Did you . . . ?'

'It remains with its fallen keeper,' said Darkmane. 'That cursed gem will cause us no more trouble.'

Mantrapper sighed. The whole incident had been for nothing. He thought vaguely about returning at once to collect it, but Darkmane's stern expression persuaded him that this was not a good idea.

He picked up his belongings, which the others had collected for him, rose to his feet and swung his pack on to his back. 'Let us continue, then,' he said.

The three adventurers set off down the passageway. Darkmane led, followed by Jamut Mantrapper, with the Chervah at the back. The mercenary walked awkwardly, adjusting to his bruises from the battle. There was something awkward and unknown in his pocket. He slipped his hand into the pocket and it closed around something that felt like a small rock. But this object was not quite like an ordinary rock; its shape was too regular – conical, pointed at one end and rounded at the other, and with smooth sides in between.

He turned to the Chervah. As he opened his mouth to speak, the manservant smiled, raised a bony finger and placed it across his lips, as a warning to keep silent. Then he pointed at Darkmane and winked. Mantrapper's heart leapt! He beamed a broad grin at the little creature, nodded, and turned to follow Darkmane.

Though the Chervah had slipped him the jewel, he had not mentioned that they also found a key: a small key, hidden in the statue's breastplate.

They continued through the caverns and passageways within Firetop Mountain. For the time being the danger was over, but they were soon to come across another of Zagor's creatures, in the labyrinth that was the Maze of Zagor . . .

'Listen!' Mantrapper whispered. 'Behind us! Footsteps. Can you hear them?'

'I hear nothing.' Darkmane held a hand up to his ear. 'And there can be nothing behind us. Remember the portcullis?'

'Perhaps it has raised itself.'

They picked up their pace and continued along the corridor until they reached a junction where another passageway, running north to south, crossed their own.

'Which way?' asked the Chervah.

'I don't know.' Darkmane considered the three possibilities. 'Perhaps we should use the Orukk dagger again.'

'Footsteps!' Mantrapper hissed. 'Coming closer. Quickly – shine the lantern behind us.'

The other two could now hear the footsteps. The Chervah flashed his lantern down the passage behind them and waited. The footsteps grew louder. They could hear heavy breathing. Darkmane and Mantrapper moved their hands to their sword-hilts. The hairs rose on the manservant's neck.

Suddenly, a figure appeared from the shadows into the flickering light. Not a human figure, but considerably larger. It was dressed in just a loincloth, and they could see that its bulky body was knotted with tough muscles. Its hands and feet were huge, ending in long horny nails that clattered on the rock as it moved. Its shaggy-haired face was gnarled like the trunk of an oak tree. As it entered the light, it snorted angrily. Its lips curled back to reveal sharp fangs.

'A Troll!' Mantrapper whispered. 'It cannot see us in the light. But we had better move quickly. Even three of us against that brute would only make it an evenly matched fight.'

The Troll roared and took a step forward.

Darkmane made an instant decision. 'Up here! Follow me.'

He had chosen the passage north. Slowly, Darkmane and Mantrapper backed up it, while the manservant kept the lantern light on the Troll for as long as possible. At the last minute, the Chervah blew out the lantern and followed the other two, hoping that this would confuse the creature.

The three of them moved slowly and quietly up the passage, feeling their way along the wall in the darkness. Darkmane eventually found his hand groping at a wooden door in front of them. There was no other way onward. He grasped the handle and turned it.

A dull light came from a slow-burning torch inside. It lit up a large but sparsely furnished room, littered with fragments of pottery. The three stepped quickly inside and closed the door, so that the light would not attract the blundering Troll behind them.

Mantrapper's eyes were immediately drawn to a corner of the room where a large vase, full of liquid, was standing. But this was not the object of the mercenary's attention. Beside the vase, a smaller bowl was lying on the floor – and this bowl was filled with what appeared to be gold coins!

'An excellent choice of direction, Dark . . .'

His sentence petered out for, behind him, he had heard a snorting sound. The three adventurers wheeled around together and their jaws dropped as they saw the creature standing in the shadows.

From the neck down, it was man-like, with powerful muscles flexing and heaving as its broad chest took heavy breaths. Naked save for a cloth wrapped round its waist, it was as tall as Darkmane himself – though even he stood in awe of the extraordinary strength implicit in its arms and thighs. But the wide girth of its neck was not human. Muscles and sinews strained beneath the skin, holding its great head erect – the head of a rampaging bull! Its huge red eyes glared at the adventurers like hot coals in a fire, while its moist snout opened and closed with each breath. It lowered its head, pointing two sharp horns at Mantrapper.

Then, with an angry bellowing roar, it charged!

The mercenary reacted slowly: the shock of the confrontation had made him sluggish. Darkmane, however, reacted at once. Seeing Mantrapper's frozen expression, he shoved him hard to one side, an instant before the Minotaur's horns could skewer him. Mantrapper fell awkwardly and the charging creature's knee caught him on the outside of his right thigh. He howled in pain and rolled across the floor, nursing his leg.

The Minotaur's momentum carried it across to the opposite corner of the room. It stopped, turned and prepared to charge at Darkmane. The warrior slid his sword from its sheath and stood ready. Seeing the weapon, the Minotaur paused. Instead of charging, it picked up the vase full of water and held it up over its head. The heavy vase seemed as light as a goblet in its hands. Water sloshed and spilled from the vase over the creature's head and on to the floor.

Without waiting to take aim, it flung the vase at Darkmane. The warrior had no time to react. The vase caught him in the chest, shattered and bowled him over backwards. His head thudded on the hard stone floor as he fell.

He lay motionless. A trickle of blood soaked through the hair on the back of his head and dripped down, forming a small pool by his ear.

The Minotaur let out a triumphant snort and turned to the fallen mercenary, who was struggling to climb to his feet despite the agony in his leg. Mantrapper gripped his sword and drew it out. As he did so, he

overbalanced; his leg refused to support him, and he dropped to the ground again, whimpering in pain.

The man-bull saw its chance and charged again, its head low and its horns set firmly in line for Mantrapper's chest. The mercenary looked up, to see the creature advancing, and squealed in panic. Keeping his injured leg straight, he kicked out desperately with the other, trying to push himself across the floor. But it was hopeless: he could not escape. The Minotaur was nearly on him, its head and horns about to crush his chest.

But then the charging beast stopped. Its head lifted up into the air. Its great lungs heaved and its eyes rolled up into its head. Its mouth dropped open and the bellow that came from its throat was louder than a fanfare of discordant trumpets: *'Hhhuunngh! Hhhuunngh!*

Hhhhhhnnnnneeeeeeee!' Its head shook violently and uncontrollably from side to side and it dropped to its knees. Another bellow rang through the room, though this time weaker than before: *'Hhnnneee . . .'*

Its legs twitched in reflex spasms. As they did so, the creature lost its balance, tottered, and slumped forward. Its head landed with a painful thump on Mantrapper's feet. Only then did it become clear to the mercenary what had happened – lodged in the back of the great beast's neck was a dagger.

Mantrapper's eyes scanned the room until finally they found the Chervah. The little creature was standing wide-eyed and open-mouthed behind the Minotaur. Beads of sweat were rolling down his high forehead. And he was shaking visibly.

'Chervah!' cried Man-

trapper ecstatically. 'You did it! Grang! You saved my life! You saved *all* our lives!'

The Chervah was silent.

Mantrapper pushed himself to his feet, and leant against a wall.

Darkmane was still motionless.

'I think my leg is broken,' Mantrapper groaned. 'Help me, Chervah.'

The manservant began to come to his senses. He shook his head and looked vacantly towards the mercenary.

'Come on, Chervah. Help me up.'

The call of duty snapped him out of it. The Chervah stepped over to help Mantrapper. 'I'm sorry, sire. I lost my senses. I have never done anything like *that* before.' He pointed at the fallen Minotaur.

'Well, you've done it now. Help me stand up.'

'There we are, sire. Is it painful? Can you bend it?'

'I don't know. There. Yes, I *can* bend it. By the gods, it's painful. It won't take my weight.'

'Be thankful, sire, that you can bend it. At least it's not broken. But I expect those pain demons are taunting you. Rest yourself for a minute and rub it. Lean against the wall. I'll help you.'

The Chervah helped him hobble to the corner of the room, where Mantrapper rested, leaning against the wall. Their attention turned to Darkmane.

'What of your master, Chervah? See to him, if it's not too late. I'll be all right here.'

The Chervah stepped across and placed his bony fingers on Darkmane's neck. 'There is a pulse! The gods be praised! But it is weak.'

The little creature scuttled over to the Minotaur and

ripped a length of cloth from round its waist; he soaked it in a puddle of water on the ground and then began mopping Darkmane's brow. While he was doing this, he noticed something lodged in a piece of pottery. 'Sire! Look at this! It must have been in the vase. It's a *key*!'

'Never mind the key, Chervah. What about that bowl in the corner? I'll take those gold pieces as a souvenir.'

Darkmane's eyelids began to flutter.

'He's coming back to us! Oh, sire. Can you see? We are here. The beast is dead!'

Slowly consciousness returned to the warrior. He rested, his head in the Chervah's lap, for several minutes while the manservant told him what had happened. He had broken the skin of his scalp on falling to the floor, but the graze was not serious. Apart from an aching head and a few minor cuts on his hands and face from the pottery shards, he was unhurt.

Mantrapper's leg was recovering, too. A huge bruise, running from hip to knee, made the leg very tender, but gradually he was able to put his weight on it.

His first move was to hobble over to the bowl of coins. 'Bah,' he grumbled. 'Pottery! These are not coins.'

The other two ignored him.

'Wait.' He picked up a coin and weighed it in his hand. 'This feels like gold. And another here. This is more like it.'

He found a handful of genuine gold coins and put them in his pocket. Then he looked at the other two. 'Er, eight gold pieces here. I think it is appropriate to split them among us. Two each. We can cast lots for the other two later.'

'And I think they all belong to the Chervah,' snapped Darkmane. 'It was he who killed that man-bull. Without the Chervah, you would have *no* coins. And no *life*.'

'Ah, erm, yes. Perhaps you're right. Here you are, Chervah. Darkmane's right. They *do* belong to you.'

'Oh, sire,' stuttered the manservant. 'I-I have no use for gold. My reward has been to see you two alive again.'

'Take them, Chervah,' said Darkmane. 'Or leave them behind. You have earned them.'

'W-well. I-if you *order* it . . .'

'I do.'

Mantrapper scowled and placed the gold pieces in the Chervah's scrawny hand. The thin palm was not big enough to hold them all, and a couple dropped to the floor. He picked them up and put them in his pocket, a look of embarrassment on his face.

Darkmane stood up. 'Now, if we are ready, we must press on with our journey. Chervah, do not forget the Orukk dagger.'

They gathered up their belongings and left the room. The Troll had disappeared. The Orukk dagger led them south, then west, then north again, and their journey continued uneventfully, following the seemingly endless passageways that made up the Maze of Zagor.

Eventually they came to a narrow opening, cut into the rock, through which a cold breeze was blowing. Darkmane, leading the party, squeezed through to explore. 'A cavern,' he whispered back to the others. 'A vast cavern with a high ceiling. And there is a wide hole in the top which opens to the sky. The place is lit by moonlight, though it is still dark.'

'Is it empty?'

'I saw nothing alive. But the cavern stretches back into the darkness. Who knows what may be lurking in the shadows? Keep quiet as we enter. Follow me.'

The other two crawled through the narrow gap until they all stood inside the cavern. Their footsteps echoed in the silence. The huge cavern was the size of a castle courtyard.

'Where do we go from here?'

'I'll use the dagger.'

'No, not yet. We'll look around first. There may be only one way out. We must not waste our strength. Cast the lantern around in the shadows. Let's see if there is a way through.'

Sure enough, the lantern lit up a passage leading away from the cavern. They crept quietly across to it.

'*Prrrmmph.*'

Darkmane stopped in his tracks. 'What was that?'

'Darkmane! Can you see anything? Be careful!'

The sound came from deep in the darkness behind them. It sounded like the snorting of some kind of creature – an extremely *large* creature. Darkmane broke into a run and the others followed him to the safety of the passageway.

They marched along until they reached a doorway. A notice drawn in arcane symbols was written on the door.

'Here we go again,' whispered Mantrapper rue-fully. 'Swords at the ready . . .' He grasped the handle and turned it.

The door opened and light flooded out into the passageway from the room beyond.

Inside was a cluttered room. Bookcases lined two of the walls: charts and parchments filled every square centimetre of wall-space not taken up with bookshelves. A warm fire was burning in a wide fireplace. Tables were piled high with miscellaneous bits and pieces: all three adventurers were reminded at once of Yaztromo's tower.

In the middle of the room stood a wooden table. A man was seated behind the table, and he looked up in surprise as he saw them enter. He was a kindly-looking old man, with long grey hair and a beard. His clothes were ragged. In his hand he held a pack of cards, which he was turning over one by one and arranging in patterns on the table.

'Greetings,' the old man smiled. 'And what can I do for you?'

'Who are you?' Mantrapper's tone was icy. His trust in strangers within Firetop Mountain had long since gone.

The old man returned his cold stare. His eyes seemed to glow with an inner fire.

Mantrapper blinked. He tried to break the old man's gaze but found that he could not. He was mesmerized.

'So!' spat the old man. 'You seek out Zagor. And I can read that your intentions are not friendly.'

As the man spoke, his voice started changing. The aged quiver had gone; instead, each word had a solid, steely ring. He stood up from the table, his eyes still fixed on Mantrapper's. As he rose he straightened and stood tall behind the table – much taller and straighter than a withered old man should have been. His appearance was also changing: his wrinkles were smoothing, his grey hair was darkening, and his rags were fading. As the old man disappeared, a quite different figure was forming before them. This man was younger, stronger, more imposing. He was dressed in robes of rich velvet and gold.

Though they had never seen the man before, they had no doubt about the identity of the sorcerer standing before them. Darkmane felt the Chervah's tiny hand on his arm. The manservant's mouth dropped open and a single word came from his lips in a whisper that could be heard only by Darkmane, standing beside him.

'*Zagor!*'

'Mantrapper! Behind you! Look out!' Darkmane's cry cut through the silence, startling them all.

Jamut Mantrapper snapped out of his trance and quickly spun round to face the danger behind him . . .

There was nothing there. Then he realized that this had been merely a ploy, to wrest his attention away from the hypnotic eyes of the sorcerer standing before them. He cursed himself for having been trapped so easily. And he cursed the warlock, Zagor, for coming so close to controlling his mind. His blood was boiling. As he turned back to face the sorcerer, there was a look of fury in his eyes.

Zagor's gaze again burned into his brain, cooling Mantrapper's temper. But this time the mercenary was resisting. In his mind a battle was being fought: his spirit wrestled to repel the invader, the probing will of the tall sorcerer. '*Yyyyyyyaaaaahhh!*' He broke free of the contest and sprang across the room at Zagor, raising his sword high over his head.

'Mantrapper!! Get back! Don't harm . . .'
Darkmane's anxious words were unnecessary.

Mantrapper's charge had been abruptly halted by some unseen force which grabbed him and threw him back against the wall. He landed heavily and the sword flew from his hand on to the floor.

'Zagor!' Darkmane spoke with authority. 'Forgive my friend. His impetuous behaviour on several occasions has already got him into more trouble than he bargained for. But we are not here to harm you. We have come to seek your advice.'

The sorcerer raised an eyebrow and turned to look at Darkmane. 'Fool. You cannot deceive me. I have been into your so-called friend's mind. You are nothing but common thieves – and murderers.'

'Jamut Mantrapper, who lies against that wall, is a hired mercenary, it is true. He was hired to lead me to you, and that he has done. But I am here on a mission from the noble King Salamon of Salamonis. I am Chadda Darkmane, emissary of the king; and this is . . .'

'I care nothing for your mission. You are trespassing on my territory. No doubt you have also left a trail of blood behind you – the blood of my guards. What reason can I have for helping you?'

'You trained with both Balthus Dire and Zharradan Marr, and without . . .'

'What!' Zagor's eyes narrowed. His next words were uttered in a whisper. 'What have you to do with those two?'

'Zagor, are you aware of what is going on round the Trolltooth Pass? Have you heard nothing of the ravages of the Trolltooth Wars?' The warrior waited for Zagor to speak.

No one was watching Mantrapper, however; his anger at being dealt with so roughly had mounted in a crescendo. Silently he picked up his sword and crept round behind the sorcerer. Then he sprang his attack! 'Filthy warlock!' he shrieked. 'You will regret the day you ever chose to cross Jamut Mantrapper!'

His sword chopped down towards the wizard's waist. In the nick of time, Zagor cast a spell which took effect just as the mercenary's sword struck his belt. Mantrapper's sword and the sorcerer's own belt both vanished!

The mercenary stood rigid in his battle pose, his eyes wide in amazement.

Zagor was furious. His voice thundered: '*Imbecile! Do you not comprehend the power which you presume to threaten? How can one as puny as you hope to challenge the might of Zagor? Your lunacy has cost me my belt. And now it shall cost you your life! And the lives of your companions.*'

The wizard stretched out his arms and threw his head back. Strange words came from his lips. As he spoke them, a deep rumbling sound resounded through the rock.

Darkmane's mind was racing. Was the warlock past the point when he could be reasoned with? Curse that Mantrapper and his temper! He must decide correctly and at once . . .

With a gigantic leap, he sprang across the room and landed on top of Zagor, bowling him over and breaking the spell. The Chervah followed him.

The four of them brawled. The warlock was astonishingly strong; he shrugged off Darkmane and the Chervah with little difficulty, and it was not until Mantrapper lent his muscle to the fray that they managed to hold him – but only for an instant. A moment later, they were grasping at thin air!

'*There!* There he is!'

The warlock had vanished and reappeared on the other side of the room. His mouth was open wide and on the tip of his tongue a burning fireball appeared. He cupped his hands round his mouth and spat the fireball at Mantrapper. The mercenary flung himself to one side and narrowly avoided being hit. The second missile was aimed at Darkmane and it singed his arm as he tried to sidestep it. He looked round for the Chervah.

The little creature had crept round the room and now he leapt up at Zagor. His foolhardy courage was wasted: a shrug from the wizard sent him flying across the room, and he landed heavily and painfully on the ground. Zagor turned again to Mantrapper. Another fireball appeared on his tongue.

The mercenary was on the ground. He would not be able to dodge this one if the wizard's aim was true. Desperately he searched for a shield . . . there was nothing. Putting his hand in his pocket, his hand grasped the jewel from the eye of the Cyclops. In a single movement he had pulled it out and swung his arm back, ready to hurl it . . .

The fireball disappeared from Zagor's mouth. His eyes were wide open, fixed on the jewel.

Mantrapper, realizing that something significant had interrupted the battle, lowered his hand. 'What's this?' he said. 'Is this jewel of interest, magic-man? Perhaps you would like a closer look?'

He held it out towards Zagor and smiled as the warlock struggled to remain calm; he was fighting to hide the pain within his chest. Darkmane at first had felt a flash of anger, seeing Mantrapper still with the forbidden jewel; but now he watched carefully.

Whatever was going on, the jewel evidently held some power over the sorcerer.

Beads of sweat appeared on the warlock's brow. He clutched himself and doubled over. From what the party could see, a transformation was taking place. He was ageing rapidly! His dark hair was becoming streaked with grey; his hands grew gnarled and wrinkled. When eventually Zagor raised his head, he was once again the old man they had first encountered. He remained silent.

'So!' Mantrapper mocked. 'Zagor has a secret. A secret fear. A weakness. *Now* who has the power, old man?'

'Give me the jewel, Mantrapper.' Darkmane held out his hand.

'No! The jewel belongs to me. And I will keep it. Logaan knows, I paid dearly for it.' The mercenary's words rang with an unyielding tone.

Wisely, Darkmane decided not to press his request; instead, the two of them discussed what to do next. They ordered Zagor to sit at the table and told the Chervah to keep close watch over him.

'Mind him carefully, Chervah,' warned Darkmane. 'He must not be allowed to leave. Once back in his underworld, his creatures will ensure that he makes good his escape. And remember the cavern. Remember the hole in the ceiling. Keep him here.'

A door on the far side of the room offered some privacy. Darkmane and Mantrapper stepped through into a small room which was empty except for a solitary large chest. Mantrapper's curiosity was aroused. 'What's this?'

'It is of no concern to us now. We must decide what to do with him.'

'In a moment, Darkmane. Look, it is locked. And with three locks. A treasure chest? Let's find where he keeps the key.'

'You think that he will simply tell us? The magic-user knows we need his help. We cannot harm him.'

'He sees us as thieves. His life rests in our hands.'

'Mantrapper, I need his help. His *willing* help. I have not fought my way this far simply to kill him. And even angering him, we risk his refusal to help us.'

'Not us. *You*.'

'Aye. That is right. Your side of the bargain is fulfilled. You have led me to Zagor. You are free to go.'

'Not without finding out what is in *there*.'

'So be it. But we will not – '

A cry from the Chervah startled them. They rushed back into the room. Zagor was making an escape! And he was once again transforming himself into a younger man. The effects of the jewel were wearing off. The Chervah was doing his best to hold the wizard, but his size made him no more than a mild obstacle as Zagor's strength returned. They both knew that, once through the door, he would be impossible to recapture. Darkmane rushed forward to help.

Mantrapper reacted quickly. A sly smile spread across his lips. He pulled out the Orukk dagger and flung it at the fleeing wizard. It sped towards its mark.

'Mantrapper! You fool! What are you doing?' Darkmane screamed. *'Chervah*, get away!'

At that moment, the Chervah tackled the wizard and the two of them rolled on the ground. The dagger hit its mark. Mantrapper sprang forward, jewel in hand.

Darkmane reached the scuffle and pulled the two

combatants apart. With unnatural strength he jerked Zagor to his feet and flung him towards Mantrapper. Then he knelt down beside the Chervah.

The Orukk dagger had once again proved deadly. The Chervah lay on the floor with the hilt standing erect on his chest.

The blade was lodged in his heart.

18

The Battle Is Won

Much to Blackscar's great relief, Orcleaver had finally recovered sufficient of his senses to give the order. The fifteen hundred hysterical Goblins had clambered down into the Pass. There they merged with the survivors of the earlier battle, and a huge black wave washed eastwards along the Pass towards Zharradan Marr's legionaries.

Thugruff's troops had taken up a position in Trolltooth Pass well to the east of the Goblin forces. And this time they were ready for the attack. A line of Rhino-Men, their numbers made up with humans, stretched two deep across the narrow valley. Each held his weapon stretched out towards the enemy. The dim-witted Goblins had only one thought in their heads. *Attack the enemy!* They charged headlong into a solid wall of spears and swords. The Rhino-Men stood firm.

The surviving Eyeless Archers recognized their previous targets and fired a fresh volley. But now they found the legionaries well out of range: Thugruff had made certain of that when he chose his new position. And they faced a new enemy as the Tooki bore down on them and picked them off with deadly accuracy.

The black wave struck the bristling wall. The line sagged as the legionaries absorbed the impact of the charge. Hundreds of Goblins at the front of the charge dropped, screaming, to the ground clutching their wounds. But wherever one dropped, two more took its place. The sheer force of their numbers seemed overwhelming.

But Thugruff chose his moment and gave the order; the Rhino-Men in the middle of the line began to step slowly and steadily backwards. As the wall changed from a straight line to a V-shape, reinforcements joined it from behind to make up the numbers in the centre. From the deck of the *Galleykeep*, hanging high above the battle, Zharradan Marr smiled. He could see the line stretching out into a funnel, drawing the Goblins along it until they were forced into its tight neck. There they were crowded so closely together that their weapons were useless; and they were now almost surrounded by enemy troops.

Those that did try to cut their way out found their swords striking down their own companions. Tempers flared and Goblin turned on Goblin. Dire's army was becoming disordered and confused. Behind the line of the funnel, the Black Elves flung spears and rocks over the line into the enemy. The Goblins fought desperately against the heavily armoured Rhino-Men to break the line.

Thugruff watched proudly as he saw his strategy working. Zharradan Marr would be pleased with him. It would be only a matter of time before the Goblins turned and fled. Victory would soon be his.

High up in his command position, Orcleaver himself

The Battle is Won

was now little better than a corpse. The Night Shadow had taken his mind. His body lay stretched out on the ground, alive but motionless. Blackscar had abandoned him and climbed down to join the battle.

When Darramouss first heard about the incident in the Cragrocks, he had had no idea that the mind which his Night Shadow now held in its power was that of the new Goblin commander. He had simply hoped that he would be able to probe the Goblin mind the shadow held captive, after they had returned to the dungeons beneath Coven. Perhaps he would be able to learn the details of the ambush in the Pass. He might possibly also discover the whereabouts of the cunnelwort. However, when he reported to Zharradan Marr both the name of the Night Shadow's victim and his position in Balthus Dire's army, the necromancer's thin lips had twisted into a wicked smile. The Night Shadow was ordered on to the *Galleykeep*, where Quimmel Bone could investigate the creature's powers further.

The Goblins were pressing the line of Rhino-Men hard. In the centre the line was beginning to break. Faced with a constant onslaught from the mass of frantic Goblins, Thugruff's troops were rapidly becoming exhausted. Here and there the Goblins broke through the line; they were set upon immediately by snarling Lizard-Men, who cut them down and filled the breaches. But the sharp lines of the V were wavering. The legionaries could not maintain their position much longer.

And they found themselves faced with a new threat from the Drones. The unruly Orcs had clambered over the rocks to try to attack the lines from behind.

Thugruff sent more Lizard-Men into the rocks to hold them back, but the filthy fly-creatures swarmed and struck. The spider-creatures on spindly legs spat out thick proboscises to engulf the enemy, sucking them screaming towards waiting mandibles, to be chopped into pieces and dropped back on top of their companions.

Finally the line broke at the apex of the V. The Goblins whooped and howled as they surged forward to confront the humans and a regiment of Gorians and Kobolds. The first wave of Goblins was far too exhausted to offer much of a battle; they were cut down easily. As the charge continued, however, the situation turned around and the Goblin hordes began pushing the legionaries further and further eastwards up the Pass towards Darramouss. Here the Half-Elf was standing on his cart like a spectral vision, waiting patiently for the moment to attack.

The legionaries parted; the humans to one side and the Gorians and Kobolds to the other. A single piercing sound came from between Darramouss's clenched teeth and the Clawbeasts and Devourers sprang forward. The huge shaggy Clawbeasts flailed with their long sharp claws, rending the Goblins' armour and flesh. The Devourers snapped and chewed with bone-crushing teeth. Bleeding, broken-limbed Goblins dropped before them.

The battle had now reached an impasse. In the rocks at the side, the Lizard-Men were locked in battle with the Orcs. The thick line of Goblins spread along the middle of the valley were attacked on both sides by the legionaries. For some time, the outcome was uncertain.

The turning-point came when Darramouss's

creatures began to force the Goblins back. The humans and the Gorians cut them down from the sides, and the line reformed across the Pass. Steadily it advanced westwards. With each step, the Goblins were pushed back. Thugruff positioned himself behind the advancing barrier of his troops, spurred his horse forward and urged them on. Their progress quickened. Each advancing step was taken over the bodies of fallen Goblins who could now do nothing to halt the advance. Moments later, the advance was becoming a rout.

Blackscar, who had assumed command of the Goblin forces, realized that the situation was hopeless. He gave the command for retreat, and the trumpet sounded. The Goblins fled in all directions. *I not blame for this*, he thought to himself. *Orcleaver commander – he blame. New commander. Lord Balthus make me commander. Must have troops to command. Must tell Lord Balthus.*

As they fled along the Pass and up into the rocks, the legionaries followed them. The Orcs and chaos monstrosities, seeing they were now on their own, also fled. Dire's panic-stricken army was in hopeless disarray – all except one small tribe of Goblins, who stood their ground against Thugruff's troops: Halfclaw's Bloodlusters.

A regiment of Lizard-Men were the first to come up against Halfclaw's tribe. They were horrified to find the frenzied Goblins chopping and hacking with a savagery they had not encountered before. But the Bloodlusters were too few. Halfclaw himself finally fell to the ground with a sword through his stomach. But before his death put an end to the Bloodlusters' valiant stand, he had taken six Lizard-Men and four humans with him.

The battle was won.

*

The Battle is Won

Zharradan Marr left the deck of the *Galleykeep* for his chambers. This battle was over. Thugruff had handled his troops admirably. But there was no time to waste – no time for his troops to rest. They must press on southwards and take full advantage of the victory. He would summon Thugruff on to the *Galleykeep*, and together they would make their plans for the final goal. They must march through the Cragrocks and storm Balthus Dire's Black Tower. If they managed to avoid delays, they could reach the citadel even before Dire knew the outcome of the battle. The *Galleykeep* dropped down into the Pass to allow the weary Half-Troll aboard.

But Marr's hope of keeping news of the result of the battle from his enemy was not to be. The ambitious Blackscar had set his sights on Orcleaver's position of command. The Goblin was already preparing his message to be sent by Nighthawk to Lord Balthus Dire. The outcome had been catastrophic for the Goblins; and, of course, Blackscar did inform his lord how Orcleaver's lapses into unconsciousness had twice cost them the chance of victory and had left his own troops frustrated and confused. In his own words, Orcleaver's incompetence had cost them the battle.

Balthus Dire cursed at the news. He could guess what Zharradan Marr's next move would be: he would press the initiative and advance on the Black Tower itself. With his own army defeated and only a handful of Citadel Guards to defend him, he needed allies, powerful allies. He must find the Sorq and bring them back to aid him.

He would have to take another cunnelwort journey.

In the palace at Salamonis, Lissamina woke up with

a start. She wiped the sweat from her forehead with a soft sheet. Another future-sight dream! And, worse, she had just seen the consequences of Balthus Dire making his second cunnelwort journey.

She was shaking – but this was only partly due to the mental effort of the dream. She was also frightened. Her dream had made one thing clear: she must not let Balthus Dire make the journey! How could she stop him? There was only one way.

She opened the door of her bedside table and pulled out a jar. Inside the jar was a dried herb. She twisted the ground-glass stopper, and a faint smell escaped into the air – a sweet smell that made her feel lightheaded.

Cunnelwort.

19

A Dark Secret

' . . . Your two fellow scholars are locked in a terrible war which is ravaging Allansia. My king's lands lie in the middle of the battleground. In his wisdom he fears that the carnage will not stop when the war is decided. Whoever is the victor will control territories to the north and south of his kingdom and it will simply be a matter of time before Salamonis also finds itself locked in a war against the forces of evil. I have sought you out in the hope that you would be able to put an end to this war. Either both or neither of the black sorcerers must be destroyed; if one is victorious, then he will surely be invincible.

'I mean you no harm. This quest has already cost the life of my manservant.' Darkmane looked sadly down at the body on the floor and then glared angrily at Mantrapper. 'But let not his death have been in vain. I most respectfully ask for your help.'

Zagor was deep in thought. He cared nothing for the fortunes of Salamonis, but the prospect of either Zharradan Marr or Balthus Dire extending his base of power *was* of concern. After Salamonis, the victor's armies would no doubt march northwards: through the Moonstone Hills, Darkwood Forest, Stonebridge and eventually to the lands surrounding Firetop Mountain. At Volgera Darkstorm's school, the three of them had been intense rivals. He knew that these old rivalries would re-emerge, and eventually the prospect of taking on Zagor himself would be irresistible to either of them.

'Hmmm.' Zagor, once again an old man in the presence of the jewel, clasped his hands together and leaned forward on the table. He rubbed his chin thoughtfully. 'Were I able to check your story, then perhaps I could help. But your own foolishness – at least, that of the mercenary – has made that impossible.

'The chest you doubtless observed in the small room there contains an orb which would allow me to test your statements. The keys to this chest were on my belt which, as you can see, I no longer possess. A duplicate set of keys was stolen from me some time ago by one of my servants whose greed persuaded him into disloyalty. He did not survive to gain the freedom he sought, but the keys . . . From then onwards, I carried the remaining keys with me at all times.'

Mantrapper's face lit up. 'Keys?' he cried. The enthusiasm left his expression as Darkmane's cold glare cut into him. 'But . . . but *we* have keys. Remember the Minotaur? And the snake in the box? Do you think they could be . . .'

'Silence, you murderous imbecile, lest the greed in your heart lead you to the same fate as Zagor's servant.'

Darkmane had managed to control the raging fury he felt for the mercenary following the death of the

A Dark Secret

Chervah. But each sentence that came from Mantrapper's lips caused it to swell up again. Nevertheless, this time his suggestion was sensible, though undoubtedly inspired by feelings no more noble than his own lust for riches.

He stood up from the table and stepped over to the corner where Mantrapper sat on a stool. He held his hand out. The mercenary dropped into his palm the key he had taken from the snake box. Darkmane himself had the key from the iron Cyclops, and he rummaged through the Chervah's pack for the key from the Minotaur's room.

He handed all three to the old wizard. 'Do you think these may be your keys?'

'I don't know. They *look* like the keys. We should try them. But first I want your word on two counts.'

'Name them.'

'You must give me your word that what rests within the chest is mine alone and will remain so.'

'You have my word. What else?'

Zagor pointed at the mercenary. 'And *he* must remain out here.'

'Don't listen to him!' Mantrapper stood up quickly. 'What right has *he* to dictate terms to *us*? He is our captive!'

Zagor smiled. His chest was booby-trapped with poisonous darts that would kill anyone trying to rob its contents. 'If *you* enter the room, then *you* must insert the keys,' he said.

'There is no need. Mantrapper will remain here.'

The mercenary scowled and sat down again.

Darkmane and Zagor turned to enter the back room. Inside, the warlock carefully inserted a key into each of the locks. One by one he turned them. One by one they clicked.

'You have recovered my keys. Fortune smiles on you. But I must ask you to turn away while I peruse the contents.'

'That I cannot do, Zagor. For you have yet to give me reason to trust you. I must be certain that what lies within is not a trap meant for me.'

Zagor nodded. He was beginning to get the impression that the tall warrior was a man of his word and that his intentions were good.

'Very well . . .'

He raised the lid slowly. As light fell on the contents, Darkmane realized the wisdom of Zagor's earlier request. It was not wise that such a sight be seen by the greedy mercenary, for the chest was full of gold coins, jewellery and richly decorated artefacts.

'You have seen what no other man has set eyes on,' he murmured. 'These treasures have been with my family since the days of my great-great-grandfather, Gallan Zagor. In those days he was rewarded richly for his skills in sorcery. You understand now why I have made my home in this place.'

He reached down into the chest and pulled out a crystal orb. In his hands it seemed to glisten with an unnatural sheen in the semi-darkness.

'The Moon Crystal.' Zagor held it proudly. 'With this we shall test the truth of your story.'

Darkmane noticed that the wizard's hands were becoming smoother, younger-looking. His hair was darkening. The jewelled eye of the Cyclops was with Mantrapper in Zagor's study. But he said nothing.

The warlock held the Moon Crystal cupped in his

hands before his face. The glow lit up his features. The transformation was almost complete. Darkmane's attention switched to the orb. A mist was swirling deep within it. Now it seemed like a giant pearl. Zagor was mumbling, his eyes closed. Darkmane recognized a word – no, a name – spoken by the warlock: *Zharradan Marr*.

The mists began to clear. An image appeared in the orb, faint at first, but then the focus became sharper. It was the image of a gigantic ship, a great galleon surrounded, not by water, but riding high up in the skies, its black sails billowing in the wind. The central sail bore the sign of a huge cowled skull: Zharradan Marr's insignia. This ship was the *Galleykeep*!

The ship loomed larger in the Moon Crystal. A heavily armoured Rhino-Man captain stood at the helm, clutching the ship's wheel firmly. Darkmane watched as the image moved from face to face of the men and creatures on the deck. A burly Half-Troll stood on the quarterdeck, staring ahead.

Zagor recognized the creature's ugly features and pitted skin. 'Thugruff,' he whispered. 'Marr's battle-sergeant. A brilliant strategist but with a heart as black as night. And there are some of his legionaries: Rhino-Men, Black Elves and Lizard-Men. Are there any Soulless Ones on board? No. I expect they would be chained up below.' A fat figure now filled the orb. 'And there's another of his trusted henchmen – Vallaska Roue, his recruiting officer.'

A veritable mountain of a man, Vallaska Roue stood on the bow, talking to a Rhino-Man. His clothes were untidy and ill-fitting, his face unshaven and mean-looking. He wore an eyepatch over one eye and a deep scar ran across the left side of his face. Dark-

A Dark Secret

mane's eyes widened as he peered into the globe at the face.

'But where is Marr himself?' Zagor asked under his breath. 'He must be below. Hmmm. So, Darkmane of Salamonis, perhaps your story has some truth to it! Let us see now if we can find Balthus Dire.'

Again Zagor mumbled into the Moon Crystal and the mists swirled. But this time it took much longer for any recognizable images to form and, when they did, they were dark and shadowy. Half-formed shapes darted across the picture and faint grey clouds billowed and dispersed. A human silhouette appeared – and then was gone. And another. Dull colours outlined vaguer entities. But little could be recognized.

'What is this?' Zagor spoke quietly. 'This is not the Black Tower. Nor Allansia. Something strange is . . . Wait! What is that?'

An image had held for an instant, just long enough to make out a human face. The distinctive high square forehead, topped with a knot of dark hair, gave away its identity. Balthus Dire! As quickly as it came, the image rippled and disappeared like a reflection in water disturbed by a stone. But the expression on Dire's face, captured in that instant, was not the usual image of cold control. Instead, it portrayed a man racked with agony; being subjected to some unknown torture.

Another fleeting image formed. This time it was a ghost-like image in white. Hazy at first, it focused just long enough for Darkmane to recognize it – or, rather, *her*.

He cried out as if in pain. 'Lissamina! The gods have mercy! What is *she* doing there? Zagor! Where is this place?'

Zagor shook his head. 'I cannot be sure. But I am certain of one thing: those two are not on this earth. Perhaps on the spirit plane . . . or perhaps in a dimensional limbo. Perhaps even in the heavens. It is difficult to say. But how . . .? Darkmane, does the cunnelwort herb mean anything to you?'

'Cunnelwort? Yes, of course! It has been said that the Trolltooth Wars started when a caravan carrying cunnelwort was ambushed in the Pass. Balthus Dire's Hill Goblins stole a sack of the herb from Marr's Strongarms. Why do you ask?'

But Zagor was deep in thought.

Eventually they returned to the warlock's study. Jamut Mantrapper was leaning back in a chair with his feet up and his eyes closed. The jewelled eye of the Cyclops was resting on the edge of the table. As they entered the room, Zagor clutched at his chest in pain. Each exposure to the jewel was having a stronger effect on him; his strength was fading. Driven by desperation, he made a reckless move: he lunged forward, stumbling across the room towards the table in an attempt to grab the jewel.

Mantrapper was not asleep. As the warlock staggered forward, one eye opened and a sinister leer spread across his lips. He leapt to his feet. The chair fell over behind him and clattered on the floor. He drew the Orukk dagger from his belt and raised it high.

Zagor fell forward and clutched desperately at the jewel. His fingertips touched its smooth surface, and faltered. It spun, rolled across the table and fell to the ground.

At the same instant, Mantrapper's blade flew down! The blow was aimed directly between the warlock's shoulder-blades. By rights it should have killed him instantly. And this it would have done, had Darkmane not reacted so quickly . . .

But something had clicked in Darkmane's mind.

The pieces fitted. At first he had blamed Mantrapper's temper for the mercenary's obsessive desire to kill the wizard from the moment they had entered the room. In that instant, however, he realized what Mantrapper's real objective was. He leapt across the room with his sword drawn and held it firmly, blade upwards, over Zagor's unprotected back.

The knife came swishing down. Inches from its mark, it fell from Mantrapper's hand. Screaming in pain, the mercenary clutched his wrist to try to stem the flow of blood pouring down his arm. Darkmane's blade had cut him deep.

He turned to the warrior, sobbing. 'Darkmane . . . Why . . . ?'

But the warrior was unrepentant. He raised his sword and pointed the tip at Mantrapper's throat. 'Get back, mercenary. Back against the wall. I have guessed your secret.'

Mantrapper stared incredulously at Darkmane's stern face, glaring at him over the hilt of his sword. Meanwhile Zagor seized his opportunity; he reached along the floor to grab the fallen jewel, then scurried across to the far side of the chamber. Darkmane was aware that the warlock was making his escape into the back room; but he was too preoccupied with the mercenary to consider stopping him.

'S-secret? What are you talking about?' Mantrapper stammered.

'Do not bother keeping up the pretence. Since we

entered this study, your every thought has been to destroy the wizard. Why? You knew I needed his help. Was this just your uncontrollable temper? I think not. Were you asleep? No. Why did you not simply pick up the jewel when Zagor rushed for it? Because you were creating an opportunity to stab him with your knife.'

'Darkmane!' The mercenary was sweating. 'Have you taken leave of your senses?'

'*Enough!*' Darkmane thundered. 'I will listen to no more of your lies. Why did I not realize something was amiss when your Orukk dagger struck the Chervah? A curse on you for deceiving me for so long. You know as well as I do: that dagger is enchanted. It never misses its mark. You *aimed* your throw at the *Chervah*! Tell me why!'

But the mercenary was silent and stared at the ground.

Darkmane continued: 'You have been using this quest for your own ends, for your own wish to find Zagor and kill him. My mission was simply a convenient way of battling through the horrors of Firetop Mountain with unpaid help until you found him. Thank the gods I realized all this before it was too late. How much are they paying you?'

'Darkmane, I . . .'

'*How much?*' Darkmane ground his teeth and pushed the tip of his sword up against the mercenary's neck. A small trickle of blood ran down on to his tunic.

'Agh! All right! You have guessed. But how did you know for sure?'

'In the warlock's Moon Crystal I saw the *Galleykeep*. Zharradan Marr's legionaries were on the deck; also on the deck was a face I thought I recognized. It was familiar, but I couldn't place it. It wasn't until a moment ago that I remembered who it was. Zagor called him Vallaska Roue, but that name meant nothing to me. I had seen him once before, though. In the Fatted Pig of Shazâar when Calorne Manitus first pointed you out to me, you were talking to a man . . . a fat brute with a scar running down the left side of his face . . .'

'It is true.' Mantrapper gulped and wiped the sweat from his brow. 'Vallaska Roue did speak to me before you approached my table. I couldn't believe my luck when you sat down afterwards. Roue had told me about a warrior who had been sent on a mission from Salamonis, a warrior whose purpose was to destroy Zharradan Marr. Their spies are many, Darkmane. It is difficult to keep anything from them; news carries to Marr's henchmen on the very wind itself. My task was to learn of your plan, and report to them. If you became dangerous I was to destroy you. Your original plan – to reach the Black Tower – suited them well. But when you changed direction and sought out Zagor, my orders changed too. Marr fears the warlock. He knows Marr's mind. And he is equally powerful as a sorcerer.

'This was a relief: you had saved my life and I had no wish to kill you. In fact I held you in deep respect. When we found Zagor, I had to devise a plan to kill him without arousing suspicion. Either that or I had to kill you all.'

'And the Chervah,' Darkmane asked. 'Why did you kill the manservant?'

'He was no manservant.' Mantrapper smiled weakly 'No. No manservant at all, though doubtless he didn't even realize it himself. ''The Eyes of the Gods'', he was known as to Zharradan Marr. I know no more, but my orders were to kill him before Zagor, as soon as his usefulness had come to an end. I took his usefulness to be ended as soon as we had fought our way through here.'

'And your reward for this treachery?'

Mantrapper's head hung low. He reached inside his shirt and drew out a small locket. 'This,' he said, unclipping it, 'is the price. An offer which I could not refuse.'

Darkmane lowered his sword and bent to examine the locket. Inside was a small portrait of a beautiful young woman.

'I am a fortune-hunter,' Mantrapper said sadly. 'You're well aware of that. But there is one thing that means more to me than gold, more to me than life itself. This lady is Hellena, daughter of Lord Tanneth in Shazâar. Ah, Darkmane, if you could only *see* her. Her skin is smooth as a silken sheet. Her hair is soft as gossamer. And her eyes – why, she can melt a man's heart with a single flutter of her eyelids. She is an angel from heaven. And I would willingly die for her.' The tone of Mantrapper's voice hardened. 'Instead, I was fated to *kill* for her. When Vallaska Roue spoke to me in Shazâar, first of all he offered me gold. When I refused, he showed me a golden locket, one similar to this one. Inside was a picture of me. And the picture was tarnished with three drops of blood . . . the blood of my lady.'

Tears appeared in the corners of his eyes. He stared vacantly at the locket for a moment.

'They had captured her and taken her to Marr's dungeons in Coven. No. My reward for killing Zagor

A Dark Secret

was not to be a sack of gold. It was Hellena's freedom. I had no choice. Would you have done otherwise?'

Darkmane was silent. The mercenary's story had touched his heart. His anger had turned to sympathy. He stepped back, away from Mantrapper and towards the table.

This was the opportunity the mercenary had been waiting for. In a single movement, he sprang up from the table and out of range of Darkmane's sword. In his hand he held the Orukk dagger, poised ready to throw!

Darkmane spoke quietly. 'Don't be a fool, Mantrapper,' he said. 'Remember the mission. We must stop the war, otherwise Allansia itself will fall under the control of . . .'

'I care nothing for Allansia,' Mantrapper cut him short, 'against the life of Hellena. I must free her first. Only *then* will I worry about the fate of Allansia.'

'Then join with me, help me. Once we have completed our mission, I give you my word I shall help find Hellena.'

'The risks are too high. What are Marr's creatures doing to her at this very moment? What more will they do while I waste time accompanying you?'

'Perhaps Zagor's Moon Crystal can tell you.'

It was only then that Mantrapper noticed that the wizard was no longer in the room. His eyes darted about until they fell on the half-open door. 'Warlock! Get back in here!'

The mercenary's eyes darted from the door to the table, then back to the door. His mind was racing. *Who is the greater threat? The warrior with his sword? No: the Orukk dagger will still keep Darkmane at a distance. The warlock, then? What has happened to him? Does he have the jewel? Have his powers returned?* He could hear no sound coming from the doorway. His attention returned to Darkmane.

The warrior stood at the opposite side of the room, sword in hand. He could not move for fear of the deadly Orukk dagger. Something was preventing Jamut Mantrapper from flinging the dagger and putting an end to things there and then; perhaps it was past loyalty, or respect for the dark warrior, now at his mercy. He hesitated. The two men stared at each other like two great rutting stags.

A slight breeze blew through the room and cooled their tempers. Mantrapper's grip on the dagger relaxed slightly. 'Darkmane . . . I . . .'

A slow creaking noise came from the door behind him. He whirled round, dagger poised. Darkmane saw his opportunity and leapt forward! The creak had been nothing but the breeze.

Mantrapper turned back and saw the warrior bounding towards him. In a flash, he aimed and threw the dagger.

Darkmane fell to the ground, his arms over his head. But there was no escaping the magical weapon. The Orukk dagger flew towards him, adjusting its flight downwards as the warrior fell. Its point was aimed straight at Darkmane's neck. His death was certain. Until the impossible happened.

Inches from its mark, the dagger stopped in mid-air. It just hung there for an instant. Mantrapper's jaw dropped in horror as the Orukk dagger turned around and flew back towards *him*! He jumped to one side to avoid it, but the dagger followed his every move, until . . .

'*Ungghh!*'

A Dark Secret

The blade pierced his throat and sank into his neck up to the hilt. Mantrapper's cry ended in a gurgle as blood from the wound choked him. He dropped to his knees, gagging and coughing.

Darkmane uncurled his arms and watched incredulously as the mercenary clutched with red-stained fingers at the dagger in his throat. He managed to pull it out and dropped it on to the ground, but he was already too far gone. In a fit of bloody coughing and jerking limbs, he rolled over and fell to the ground, dead.

'What . . .?' The word came out as a whisper. Darkmane could not believe what had happened. By rights, *he* should be lying dead on the floor.

Then a face appeared at the doorway . . . a face that explained all. It was Zagor. The warlock had resumed his youthful appearance. His magic powers had returned.

'Zagor! It was you . . .'

'Of course. Why do you look so shocked? Would you rather it was *you* lying there in a pool of your own blood? It can be arranged. No, I thought not. Then come with me. We have work to do.'

20

Into the *Galleykeep*

Darkmane awoke with a start. He looked around. The room was dark, but for the fire flickering and a single candle burning on the table. In the dim light Darkmane could see the fallen bookshelf, the chairs and the table, and the bodies of the Chervah and Jamut Mantrapper lying on the floor. He was in the warlock's study. He wiped the tiredness from his face; exhaustion had finally caught up with him and he had fallen asleep.

Zagor was seated at the table, engrossed in an ancient tome. He heard Darkmane stir and turned towards him. 'So. The warrior wakes. Gather your wits, Chadda Darkmane. Let me tell you what I have discovered and what we must do. And hurry; time is of the utmost urgency. The *Galleykeep* is even now nearing Craggen Rock. Your greatest challenge is yet to come.'

Darkmane pulled himself to his feet and eased his aching limbs. How long had he been asleep? And what had Zagor discovered?

He stepped over to the table and sat down, facing the warlock. 'I am ready. Explain what must be done.'

Into the *Galleykeep*

Zagor closed his book and sat back in his chair. 'Balthus Dire is lost to this world,' he began. 'His experiments with the cunnelwort herb were a success. He entered the spirit plane and made contact with beings possessed of unimaginable powers. He invited them to join his cause. These spirits see the material plane as no more than a playground and its creatures as no more than insects, to be toyed with as you and I might play with a small beetle. And, if their fancy takes them, to be crushed as easily as you could crush that beetle underfoot. But they are fascinated by worldly magic. Curious about Dire's magical powers, they listened to his story and some even entered the material plane with him. But a battle with the Ganjees drove them all back to the spirit plane. When he realized the extent of their power, Balthus Dire resolved to return to the spirit plane and open the gateway once more. With the spirit creatures at his side, he would have been invincible.'

'*Would* have been . . . ?'

'Yes.' Zagor nodded. 'Dire's plans were foiled by another intruder into the spirit plane.'

Darkmane sat up in his seat. He remembered the image of Lissamina in the Moon Crystal.

'Your friend the sorceress,' the warlock continued. 'She entered the spirit plane and confronted Dire. But his magic was far stronger than hers. She could neither hope to defeat him nor prevent the spirits entering the material plane if they so wished. So she did the next best thing: she sealed off the gateway, trapping the spirits and Balthus Dire and herself in the spirit plane. She is there now. I cannot guess at her fate.'

Darkmane's throat went dry. He had seen her only

a few times, yet she was the first magic-user he had ever felt he could trust. It was her advice that had sent him off to seek out Zagor, and now she had sacrificed herself. He was silent, staring at his fingers knotted tightly together on the table.

Eventually he spoke. 'Is there anything we can do?'

Zagor shook his head. 'Nothing you or I can do. I cannot send you into the spirit plane, nor enter myself. Her fate rests with the gods.'

Darkmane's jaw tightened. He forced his mind to return to his mission. The news about Balthus Dire was a mixed blessing. With him trapped in the spirit plane, it would simply be a matter of time before Zharradan Marr's forces were victorious. Without a leader, the creatures of chaos would return to their holes in the Craggen Heights. And what had Zagor said to him? The *Galleykeep* is nearing Craggen Rock? The Black Tower!

'What of Zharradan Marr?' he asked.

'Now, *that* is why we must act quickly,' said Zagor. 'His *Galleykeep* is sailing towards the Black Tower. We must catch him before he reaches the citadel, or he will entrench himself within it and we shall lose him for ever. We must tackle him on the *Galleykeep* itself.' Zagor leaned forward. 'I say "we" . . . But it must be *you*, Chadda Darkmane. I cannot both make this journey with you *and* cast the spell. The risks are great. I may do no more than transport you to the *Galleykeep*. Once on the deck of the *Galleykeep*, the rest is up to you.'

Darkmane considered the warlock's words. He was ready to face Zharradan Marr. But he wanted advice from Zagor. 'I will not fail you, Zagor. But first, tell me what you know of Marr's weaknesses. I have been told that you know him well. I have risked my life seeking you out. Tell me how I may defeat him.'

'You cannot hope to beat him in a fight. He is as strong as you, and he will use all his powers of sorcery against you. His weakness is his mirror.'

'What mirror?'

'Zharradan Marr is not human. He is an undead demi-spirit who draws his power from a mirror which is always either in his quarters or closely guarded by his slaves. It is no ordinary mirror but a gateway to Marr's own world, which is not the spirit plane, nor the heavenly plane, but a kind of limbo. The truth is, no one knows for certain where the mirror gateway leads to. Destroy the mirror and you destroy his power, however. If he is inside at the time, then he will never escape back into our own world. If he is outside, then he will be no more powerful than an ordinary mortal.'

The task was not an easy one. Once on the *Galley-keep*, he would have to avoid the guards, find his way to Marr's chambers and destroy the mirror without giving himself away.

'How do I destroy it?'

'It will shatter, like any other mirror. Simply strike it with your sword.' The warrior waited apprehensively for further help. Zagor sat staring past Dark-mane at the wall, deep in thought.

Finally he got up and crossed the room to a cupboard. He took out a small package and brought it to the table. 'Here,' he said. 'You should take this with you.'

'I will not touch sorcery. I do not trust magic trickery. I place my trust in my sword.'

267

'Yes of course,' said Zagor sarcastically. 'I would not offer you sorcery. If Marr were to capture you, he would know where it had come from. But this is no magical device. Inside this package is *firepowder*. It will explode like a fireball. Look. Do you see this string here? It is the fuse. Light the string with this tinder-box. It will glow when it catches. There will be a delay while the string burns. But when it burns down to the package, a great fireball will burst out of the package and destroy anything within range.'

'And of what use is this to me?'

'You are a soldier, Darkmane. And you know that wars must be won at all costs. The lives of troops are the currency of victory.'

'Speak plainly. What are you saying?'

'Marr must be defeated at all costs. Even your own life is expendable in this regard.'

'Aye.'

'Your mission is dangerous. But should you fail to smash the mirror, this opportunity to set Marr's plans back must not be wasted. When you locate the mirror and lay your plans, first hide this package of firepowder and light the fuse. Then go after the mirror. If you destroy it, return and snuff out the fuse. But if you are prevented, then this package will ensure that your attempt will not be entirely in vain. For when the fuse burns down, the fireball will destroy the *Galleykeep* and, with luck, the mirror too. But Darkmane, if the powder lights, your own life will be lost with the ship. Do you agree?'

Darkmane considered for a moment. There was no real choice: if he failed in his mission, then his life would be forfeit anyway. He could see the sense in taking the *Galleykeep* with him if that happened.

But there was another possibility. What if he destroyed the mirror but failed to get back to the firepowder in time?

He turned to Zagor. 'How long do I have?'

'Count like this: *One* cabbanat; *two* cabbanat; *three* cabbanat . . . at that speed. When you reach *one hundred* cabbanat, the fireball will spark. Try it.'

Darkmane counted: 'One cabbanat, two cabbanat, three cabbanat . . .'

'A little slower.'

'*One* cabbanat, *two* cabbanat, *three* cabbanat, *four* . . .'

'That's better. Remember, as soon as you light the string, you must start counting. And *never* stop. If you lose count, it may cost you your life.'

'And then . . . ?'

'As soon as you have broken the mirror, find the package and snuff out the fuse. Get back on the deck. Tell the legionaries that their master is dead. Force them to fly the ship to Salamonis and let you off.'

'And if they refuse?'

'Then you light the string again. But do not worry. If Zharradan Marr is dead, they will do as you say. Do you agree?'

Darkmane shifted on his seat. He ran his hand through his hair and stared deep into Zagor's eyes. 'Aye. I will do it.'

'Good. Then let's get started.'

Zagor opened his book again and began to read the pages intently. Darkmane stood up and paced the room. This was a dangerous mission – the most dangerous of his life. What if he was captured before he could light the fuse? What if the fuse burned out?

What if the firepowder was discovered before the fuse burned down?

He stopped beside Mantrapper's body, still lying on the ground. The Orukk dagger lay next to it, covered in the mercenary's blood. He knelt down and picked it up, turning it over in his hand.

'I am ready,' Zagor announced. 'The time has come. It will still be dark; you must go now. If we wait for the light, you will be observed on deck.'

The wizard lifted a rug. Underneath, two crescent-shaped symbols had been drawn on the floor. Zagor took two vials of liquid from a cupboard and sprinkled them on the ground in the centre of the crescents. Smoke began to rise in the air. The warlock raised his hands and turned the palms to face the smoke. He chanted words which Darkmane could not understand. The more he chanted, the more smoke rose into the air. It turned from grey to dirty blue to deep red to yellow.

Darkmane looked up at the ceiling above the symbols. A patch of light appeared and began to glow. It too changed colour along with the smoke – blue, then red, then yellow. Finally it turned pure white and an image began to form. The smoke rising from the floor curled upwards and disappeared into the image on the ceiling. Darkmane's eyes widened as the image took shape. Brown and black patches moved and merged. As they grew more substantial, he could make out the image more clearly: it was a ship, a large ship with black sails. The symbol of a cowled skull was painted on the central sail.

The *Galleykeep*!

'Hurry, Chadda Darkmane.' The warlock's words echoed round the room.

Darkmane stood up. His stomach was knotted. Moisture dampened his hairline, his palms. He stepped towards the tower of smoke, cursing under his breath: sorcery! Yet again he was at its mercy. He stopped before the smoke and took one last look at Zagor, who was watching him intently. He glanced down at the Orukk dagger, still in his hand, then back at the smoke. His chest swelled as he took a deep breath.

Then, in a single movement, he stuffed the dagger into his belt and stepped into the smoke.

21

The Final Struggle

The wind hit him with an icy blast, causing him to stagger back against the railings. His hair strained at its roots as if the wind was trying to pull it out of his scalp. He could hear the rhythmical creaking of the three gigantic masts taking the strain and the occasional flap and snap of the sails as they billowed and heaved. The *Galleykeep* was rocking from side to side as it made its way above the jagged peaks of the Craggen Heights. And the great winged Tooki sailed alongside the ship, each bobbing up and down as they escorted the *Galleykeep* on its journey. All was dark but for some flickering lanterns dotted about the deck.

Darkmane grabbed the hilt of his sword and glanced around sharply. Had he been spotted?

No.

Zagor's spell had placed him at the rear of the *Galleykeep*, well aft of the ship's wheel. Quickly, he crouched down by the rail and took stock of his surroundings.

The deck was empty except for three figures. A few paces in front of him, at the wheel, was a thick-set, armoured figure with a horned snout. A Rhino-Man, steering the ship. He could hear the creature's snorts clearly but the wind was carrying any sound he might make away from the Rhino-Man. He should be able to ambush the creature without much difficulty. But what would happen to the ship then? If no one was present to attend to the wheel, surely it would swing away from its course? Any sudden lurch would also doubtless alert the rest of the crew. His eyes fell on a broken spindle from the ship's rail. Perhaps that would do the trick.

Steps led down from the bridge to the middle of the deck. It was difficult for Darkmane to see down to this lower level, but he could just make out a human figure, sprawled over a pile of rigging. The warrior hoped fervently that he was asleep.

Towards the bow of the ship he could make out another human shape; this one was definitely not asleep. The tall man was grossly overweight; he was leaning against the forward mast, staring into the distance and watching the ship's progress. Darkmane recognized the huge round profile and untidy clothes. His thoughts returned to the night in the Fatted Pig. *Vallaska Roue!*

This could pose a problem. He should be able to dispose of the Rhino-Man quickly. No doubt he could then climb down to the half-deck and deal with the crewman lying on the rigging. But could he count on Vallaska Roue continuing to peer into the distance while he climbed up on to the foredeck? If he were to turn around, surely he would notice the missing Rhino-Man! Perhaps he could leave him and head straight for Zharradan Marr's chambers. And what of the Tooki? No – they were too far away to see anything happening in the darkness.

The Final Struggle

He formulated his plan.

A thin smear of red light spread across the horizon. Dawn was approaching. Soon the rest of the crew would be waking up and Darkmane would be faced by many more adversaries. He must act quickly.

He pulled his sword carefully from its scabbard. Half crouching, he crept stealthily towards the figure at the wheel, trying his best to keep his footing as the *Galleykeep* pitched. He rose slowly to his feet behind the Rhino-Man and aimed the point of his sword at the middle of its back. His hands tightened their grip on the hilt, holding the weapon like a huge dagger. He waited for the ship to steady itself.

Then he struck!

'Hhuunnnnngh!'

Darkmane froze.

His blow had been strong enough to fell a Fire Demon. Instead of falling, however, the Rhino-Man wheeled around to face him, the sword sticking out from between his shoulder-blades like a knife thrown into a tree. *Damn!* The Rhino-Man's skin was so tough that the sword had lodged itself in its back without piercing its heart!

And now Darkmane was unarmed!

He gathered his wits and reacted instantly. He leapt at the creature, feet first, and landed a two-footed kick squarely on its chest. The weakened Rhino-Man gave a loud snort and stumbled. Darkmane dropped heavily on to the deck. The ship's wheel spun and the *Galleykeep* lurched to starboard. The Rhino-Man lost his balance and toppled over backwards. His snortings were cut off abruptly. The creature's own weight had forced the sword through its skin and into its heart. It lay, dead, on the deck.

Darkmane picked himself up. Had the sounds of the struggle spread across the ship? His glance flashed to the figure on the rigging, then ahead to Vallaska Roue. Neither had noticed the Rhino-Man's death-cries.

Quickly he grabbed the broken spindle and wedged it tightly under the wheel. At least this would prevent the ship from losing its bearings. He tested it; the wheel was firmly fixed. Then he turned the Rhino-Man's body over to retrieve his sword.

A new idea occurred to him. He dragged the body across the deck and, with a superhuman effort, managed to haul it to its feet. Then he propped it up against the wheel. At least that would give him a little more leeway with Vallaska Roue.

Catching his breath, he turned his attention to the sleeping figure on the deck below. He climbed silently down the stair-way.

The rigging provided a bed of sorts for the sleeping crewman, who lay sprawled awkwardly across it; his mouth was gaping open and he was snoring loudly, an empty bottle in one hand.

A shame to disturb him, thought Darkmane, as he placed the tip of his sword against the man's windpipe and etched a short red line across his throat. The cut was not deep. Darkmane had a use for this fellow.

'Who? What . . .?' The man awoke abruptly. Darkmane pressed a little harder with his sword and raised his finger to his lips. The man took his meaning; he fell silent and gulped heavily.

'Your life is mine for the taking,' said Darkmane. 'Do you agree?' The man nodded as best he could. The sweat was now streaming down his

face. 'One twist of this blade and you will never again enjoy whatever it is you drink from that bottle. Tell me what I want to know and I may spare your life.'

'W-what is . . . ?'

'*Silence!*' Darkmane glowered. The red line on the man's neck lengthened. '*I* will tell you when to speak! Just tell me this: how do I find your Lord Zharradan's chambers below?'

'S-sir. I-I cannot tell. My life would be lost.'

'If you do not tell,' hissed Darkmane, 'then your life is lost *now*. Which would you prefer?' The point of his sword dug deeper into the man's neck.

'Aaahh! All right. I will tell you! P-please. Take your sword away!' Darkmane did not move. The man spluttered: 'T-take *that* stairway down into the ship. You will find yourself in a circular hallway with five doors: each has a symbol on it. Take the doorway with a water jug on it; that is Lord Zharradan's room. Now, *please*. Spare me!'

'*What is all this?*'

An angry voice sounded from the deck above. The words startled Darkmane. He turned his head, to see the huge bulk of Vallaska Roue peering down at him!

The crewman chose that moment to attempt an escape. He pushed Darkmane's sword to one side and tried to struggle to his feet.

The warrior's well-trained reactions were immediate. His sword slashed sideways and again found the crewman's throat. But this time its bite was not so delicate. The razor-sharp blade cut deep into his neck and his body slumped back on the rigging, his blood soaking into the ropes.

With the same motion, Darkmane drew the Orukk dagger from his belt and flung it at Vallaska Roue.

The Final Struggle

Before the man had time to shift his bulk, the dagger had found his heart. He staggered, swayed on the edge of the deck and finally toppled. The whole of the *Galleykeep* shook as he crashed down on to the lower deck.

Darkmane's mind raced. The crash would surely bring a horde of guards on to the decks – he must act quickly. He spotted a small wooden box containing a handful of belaying pins. Hastily he pulled out Zagor's firepowder, put it in the box and lit the fuse with his tinder-box. It frizzled and sputtered, then finally caught. The red glow at the end of the fuse spurred him into action. He picked up the pins and arranged them over the bundle of firepowder.

'*One* cabbanat, *two* cabbanat, *three* . . .' He realized he was speaking aloud. The counting continued, but now in his mind only.

He rushed to the staircase and flung open the hatch.

Sounds were coming from below decks . . .voices. No doubt Vallaska Roue's fall had woken the entire ship. But there seemed to be no immediate danger from this staircase. He took the stairs two at a time, using the handrail as a support so as to keep silent.

Ten cabbanat, eleven cabbanat . . .

The crewman had told the truth – at least, about the hallway at the bottom of the stairs. Five doors led from the hallway and Darkmane's eyes leapt from door to door. One bore the sign of fire; another the sign of a crown; another the sign of a snowflake; another two crossed swords; and the last bore the sign of a water jug.

Fourteen cabbanat, fifteen cabbanat . . .

He listened at the door. No sound came from within. He tried the handle. The door was *locked*!

Darkmane cursed. He would have to charge it down.
More noise. His heart was thumping.

Twenty cabbanat . . .

There was no time for hesitation. He stepped back
across the hallway, readied his shoulder, and charged.

The door splintered round its hinges; it was heavier
than he had thought, and a stab of pain shot through
his shoulder. He tumbled forward as the door burst
open but regained his balance inside the cabin. The
rush of air blew at a candle mounted on the wall; it
flickered and dimmed but just managed to stay alight.
The yellow glow finally steadied and Darkmane surveyed the cabin.

On first impression, he thought he was in the wrong
place, for these were hardly the stately quarters of a
sorcerer-lord. The room was dusty and untidy. The
wall to his left formed part of the hull of the ship.
Two portholes and a larger viewing-window had dirty
curtains drawn across them. A candle was mounted
on the wall next to the large window. And standing
before the viewing-window was a brass viewing-
scope, like a smaller version of the one at the top of
Yaztromo's tower. An unmade bunk ran along the
wall to his right. Next to this stood a battered
wardrobe . . .

Darkmane's heart stopped!

Standing at an angle to the wardrobe was a *figure*,
facing him!

His hand reached for his sword. As he moved, the
figure matched his gesture perfectly . . . too perfectly.
Darkmane stopped. So did the figure. His hand released the sword-hilt. The figure did likewise. He was
looking at a reflection of himself in a mirror.

A mirror? THE mirror!

The Final Struggle

He sighed. Had he reached his goal? Would it be as easy as this for him simply to step over and smash the glass?

It would not.

Plop! *Sssssssschh!* Plop!

The low-pitched sound came from the far end of the room. His eyes darted in the direction of the sound. They picked out a spiral staircase leading upwards. Next to the staircase was a desk littered with papers. But there was a shape writhing behind the desk. *Something* was there – something he had not seen before.

His jaw dropped. Seated in the chair behind the desk was a seething mass of living matter. In fact it could hardly be described as being 'seated' at all. The formless shape was like a gigantic blob of jelly that had dropped from the ceiling on to the chair. Snake-like tentacles grew from the middle of the glistening mass and then contracted back into its body. Inflamed blisters grew and erupted on its surface. As the creature seethed and spread over the chair and across the desk, it was as if it were pulsating with scores of worm-like creatures squirming around within it.

Darkmane took a step back and stumbled over the fallen door. *What was this?* The sight had given him such a shock that he almost forgot to count. Quickly, he concentrated his mind. *Thirty-two cabbanat, thirty-three cabbanat* . . .

The creature oozed off the chair on to the floor and landed with a soft plop, drawing pseudopods of slime with it as it fell. It reappeared beneath the desk and slithered forward.

A slimy tentacle grew from the fore-end of the mass and reached out across the floor towards Darkmane.

He saw it just in time and dodged to one side as the tentacle tried to wrap itself round his leg. It stayed where it lay, fastened itself to the floor and pulled, dragging the rest of its body along behind it.

Darkmane drew out his sword and hacked down at the glistening tentacle. The blow chopped it in two – but as soon as he drew his sword away, the worm-like things inside squirmed from the two severed ends and drew the two pieces together, joining them up again. Avoiding the creature, he sidestepped towards the viewing-scope, then raised his sword again, aiming for the main body of the squirming mass.

'Put your weapon away, human. It will do no good against this creature!'

The voice stopped Darkmane in his tracks. It was a deep, powerful voice resonating with an otherworldly tone. The words were spoken with such authority that he could not help but obey and he lowered his sword. His eyes searched the room for their source. No one was there. Then he saw the mirror: two glaring red eyes were looking directly at him and a shape was forming within it. He stared, watching it form.

Suddenly, he felt something cold and clammy on his foot!

Another slimy tentacle had grown from the oozing creature and had climbed up his leg and down inside his boot. His foot began to feel cold. Freezing! Darkmane yelped and drew his foot away. His boot came off. But he could not free himself from the rubbery tentacle which pulled and gave like a length of elastic. He hacked at it with his sword. Again his blow cut the tentacle in two and his foot came free, but the end of the tentacle was still wrapped firmly round it and was tightening its grip. His foot was numb. He shook it about and plunged both hands into the seething blob, frantically trying to scrape it off.

Finally he managed to wipe the blob from his foot and it dropped to the floor. Again the worm-like things inside oozed from the wound. Another tentacle grew out from the main body and the two merged. Darkmane could feel nothing in his foot and his hands were growing numb. The creature advanced.

'Fool! You will obey me! Lay down your weapon. Now!'

The voice was louder. Darkmane's attention returned to the mirror. A face had now grown round the eyes: a dark-skinned face with a high forehead. A pointed crest of wiry hair crowned the top of the head of the man's image that had taken shape in the mirror.

But Darkmane knew that this was no man. He recognized the stern lines across its forehead, the large, jagged ears on either side of the face, and the long, bony fingers which ended in sharp, talon-like nails. The creature's thin lips were moving in a curiously rhythmical way that bore no relation to the words coming from its mouth. The lips curled back into a sneer and the expression on the reflection's face took on a look of *fury*. This was no man.

This was Zharradan Marr.

For a moment Darkmane was awestruck as he stared into the deep red eyes of the ghostly reflection. Again he broke out of it by keeping up the rhythmical counting: *Fifty-five cabbanat, fifty-six cabbanat.*

He had forgotten about the formless mass which was now surging around both his feet. Plopping, gurgling and hissing, the creature formed a thick circle at a distance which made it impossible for him to take a step in any direction without stepping into it. It was waiting for its orders from Zharradan Marr.

'Lay down your sword. Tell me who has sent you. NOW! Or else your death will be painful, as my creature slowly freezes you!'

Darkmane took a deep breath. What could he do? One step into the squirming mass would mean both his feet becoming numbed and useless. If he did not do as Marr ordered, he would not possibly be able to escape when the creature tightened its ring. Perhaps his cause was lost – but if he played for time, then his mission *could* be salvaged, even though it would cost him his own life. How could he smash the mirror?

He relaxed his sword-arm in obedience to Marr's orders. His weapon hung limply in his fingers.

'Drop it. On the ground.'

Darkmane lowered his head and let his shoulders drop.

A hint of a smile appeared on Zharradan Marr's quivering lips. The human was beginning to see sense. Now he must discover who had sent him into his *Galleykeep*.

But Darkmane's submission was an act, part of the warrior's plan. In a single motion, he grasped the sword tightly and swung his arm back to throw it! He was laying down his weapon all right – but not at his feet. Instead he was aiming it at the mirror! His hand whipped forward to fling it . . .

And stopped.

He was unable to release it! Marr's sorcery held him motionless!

The Final Struggle

'Idiot!' hissed Zharradan Marr. *'If this is your choice, then you must suffer the consequences!'*

The slithering creature on the floor moved in quickly. The circle tightened, and Darkmane felt the slimy substance round his legs and feet, rooting him to the spot. The creature's touch was icy! He screamed with pain and dropped his sword to the floor. It landed in the gelatinous mass and was engulfed.

'Aaaaaagh!' Darkmane shrieked. His legs were freezing and the pain was spreading. 'Call your creature off, Marr. I will tell you what you want to know!'

Silently, Darkmane was counting: *Seventy-six cabbanat, seventy-seven . . .*

He was stalling for time. Just twenty-three more 'cabbanats' and his mission would succeed.

The gelatinous creature shrank away from him and resumed its position in a circle round him. Darkmane bent down and rubbed his legs, trying to restore the circulation and get some feeling back into his feet.

'Tell me who sent you.'

'I come from Salamonis. It is my home. And a fair city. One where . . .'

'SILENCE!' Zharradan Marr's thundering voice cut him short. His image quivered in the mirror, his anger all too obvious. *'WHO sent you?'*

'My Lord is . . .' Darkmane feigned his reluctance, then stammered: ' . . . is King Salamon.'

In his mind he was counting: *Eighty-nine cabbanat, ninety cabbanat . . .*

Zharradan Marr's lips twitched. *'So you are not one of Balthus Dire's warriors. Tell me why you have come here. Tell me how much you are being paid.'*

Darkmane could not concentrate his mind on answering the question. He was sweating with anxiety – but this had helped restore some of the feeling to his legs and feet. He shifted nervously and a rush of blood to his head made him feel faint. He tried to concentrate and a few meaningless sounds came from his mouth. All he could hear was the sound of his own heartbeats getting louder and louder, and his only thought was of the impending explosion.

He opened his mouth to speak again but the words that came out were uttered involuntarily: 'Ninety-eight cabbanat, ninety-nine cabbanat, ONE HUNDRED CABBANAT!'

Nothing.

Darkmane stared incredulously at the image in the mirror. Though he was staring straight at Zharradan Marr, he was not even seeing him. What had happened?

'What? One hundred cabbanat? Explain yourself!'

Darkmane was struck dumb. Something had gone wrong. Zagor! The fool! Had his firepowder been faulty? Or had this been part of his plan? Before Darkmane had time to think of an answer, however, a figure appeared in the doorway and a burly Half-Troll stepped into the room holding a wooden box.

'Lord Zharradan!' Thugruff panted. 'We found this on deck. Next to the body of Vallaska Roue. Look! Firepowder!'

He pulled out the bundle of firepowder, its fuse extinguished just seconds away from ignition.

Darkmane's heart sank. His plan had been discovered. And he had been captured. What on earth was he to do now?

'So we see what our visitor was up to!' Zharradan Marr snarled. *'His plan has failed. And his life shall end now.*

The Final Struggle

Over the side with him and his package. And we shall watch to see which death takes him first. See to it, Thugruff.'

The Half-Troll smiled. He uncoiled a length of rope from his waist and stepped carefully towards Darkmane. On deck this would amuse the crew. First he would light the fuse and then push Darkmane over the side. No doubt the crew would enjoy wagering on whether he would be blown to bits before or after he hit the ground.

Darkmane was in a state of shock. This would be his last chance face to face with Zharradan Marr. His mission had taken too long for it to fail. And the lives of the people of Salamonis depended on him. *What could he do?* It was time to risk all.

As Thugruff stepped forward, he leapt into action. His right hand grasped the candle, mounted on the wall behind him, and he dropped it into the glistening blob surrounding him. As he expected, the creature shrank away from the candle and allowed him passage. He sprang painfully across the room on his numb feet and tore the mirror from its mounting on the wall. The weight was considerable, but he was fired with a superhuman burst of energy. Then he swung around, facing the large viewing-window.

Thugruff stepped forward to intercept him but arrived, just as Darkmane and the mirror were smashing through the glass window and diving out into mid-air. The Half-Troll teetered on the brink but just prevented himself following them into space.

'You FOOL! What have you done!' Zharradan Marr's voice, screaming from the mirror in Darkmane's hands, was frantic. He was trapped: if he left his mirror, he would plunge to his death. Inside the mirror he was safe – though he could not prevent the

mirror shattering when it hit the ground – but his gateway to the material world would be destroyed.

Darkmane, plunging to his own death, looked down at the Cragrock peaks, looming closer and closer below him. He managed a smile. The smile became a grin. And the grin burst into a laugh.

'Ha-ha-haaaaaa . . .'

22

The Judgement

The calm silence of the Celestial Court was disturbed as the debate grew more heated.

Three figures, seated round a low table, were arguing bitterly. A fourth stood, deep in thought, stroking his chin and staring down intently at the miniature landscape before him.

The landscape – a small but perfect likeness of that part of Allansia round Trolltooth Pass – was colourful and meticulously detailed. Small puffs of cloud hovered in the air round the Moonstone Hills. A dusty haze hung over the desert oasis town of Shazâar. And close inspection showed signs of life and movement. The waters of the great Whitewater River shimmered as the current took them out to sea. Within the towns of Salamonis and Shazâar scores of miniature black dots milled in the streets like so many tiny ants.

Logaan's eyes surveyed the battleground. The charred remains of the village of Coven were a black scar on the landscape. Balthus Dire's citadel rose proudly from the Craggen Heights. And a tiny sailing vessel could be made out clearly, hanging in the air over the Cragrocks. It had black sails.

The Judgement

'What say you, Logaan? What is your judgement? As Balthus Dire is the only survivor, I claim the victory!'

The trickster god broke out of his trance and turned to face Hashak the creator.

Before he could speak, however, Slangg preempted his thoughts. 'Ha! *Survivor?* You cannot call a mortal locked in the spirit plane a *survivor*! Look! Here is my *Galleykeep*, mere hours away from the Black Tower.' Slangg, god of malice, reached out across the landscape on the table and pointed to the miniature sky-galleon hovering over the tiny mountains. 'My forces are strong and the *Galleykeep* is intact. When they reach the Black Tower, the Half-Troll will take command and snatch the prize. Victory will be mine!'

'But your necromancer is gone,' Hashak mocked. 'His mirror was destroyed. Can you expect a Half-Troll to rule over half of Allansia? *No* – of course not! The creature is too dim-witted. Remember the rules of the contest: victory may only be claimed by a *surviving* champion. All I need to do is release Balthus Dire by opening the gateway from the spirit plane . . .'

'NO!' Libra, goddess of justice, rose to her feet. 'You may *not* interfere. We agreed. Only *I* may assist my champion, since he had no magical powers. Or are you intent on winning this contest by trickery?'

The two gods looked away. It was true; they had agreed at the outset: since both Zharradan Marr and Balthus Dire had powers of sorcery, Chadda Darkmane was granted Libra's aid . . . But with certain restrictions, and on one condition: the others could plant a traitor in his party. And Jamut Mantrapper had failed them.

Libra continued: 'The victory, I believe, is mine.

The Trolltooth Wars

Both your champions have been removed from Allansia. Thus the Trolltooth Wars are over. And my champion has saved Salamonis from the threat of further wars against the dark forces. His plan has succeeded.'

Logaan had listened to all the arguments. He looked down at the table in front of him. The *Galleykeep* had strayed off course and was now sailing north towards the remains of the village of Coven. He turned to Libra. 'I agree that your achievements are closest to the victory conditions of our contest,' he began, 'but remember, we also agreed that a victory could not be claimed if your champion died. Chadda Darkmane performed admirably for you. But his body now lies broken in the Craggen Heights . . .'

'Not so,' smiled Libra. 'As you will see . . .'

At that moment, two figures appeared and approached the table. The shorter figure was leading the other, a tall, broad-shouldered man with a mop of black hair, who was evidently bewildered by his surroundings.

The smaller of the two was Telak, god of courage – though his appearance suggested anything but such a grand title. Telak was still in his earthly guise: dark-skinned, with wide eyes and two large ears, one sitting at either side of his bald head. His role in the contest had brought great pleasure to him and even – for this was a new experience for him – *excitement*. In choosing to unite with the Chervah rather than with a man, he had found his thoughts and his outlook very different from those of a human. The Chervah, of course, had had no idea that he was playing host to a guest of such importance; he felt no different. Nor was the god permitted to help him – the contest rules forbade it. Telak had merely been an observer, his mission simply to report his observations back to Libra.

Telak now felt a strange affinity for the creature, and therefore he had chosen not to resume his celestial body yet. It was as if he had grown fond of a favourite – but threadbare – set of clothes. Though the Chervah had died, Telak took great delight in imitating his mannerisms. To the others, his spindly limbs made him almost comical to watch, as he eagerly pulled the awestruck warrior across to them.

Libra beamed at her opponents. 'If you will remember, the contest rules allowed me one remaining opportunity to aid Chadda Darkmane,' she announced. 'They forbade me to change his fate on Titan itself. So I have used this last opportunity to pluck him from the sky and bring him here!'

At the mention of his name, Darkmane turned to face the goddess of justice. He recognized the face: soft, fair skin; cascading golden locks of hair falling down round her shoulders; and two deep green, emerald eyes. He opened his mouth to speak: 'Lissami – '

Libra held a finger to her lips and cut him short. 'Do not worry, Chadda Darkmane,' she smiled. 'I will explain everything to you in good time. Now, Telak, take our champion away. Let him rest. He has earned it.'

The little creature tugged at Darkmane's hand, and the two retraced their steps away from the table.

'Ah, what an adventure!' Telak chattered as he led the warrior away. 'Remember our times in Shazâar? And the mercenary? I *did* want to warn you of him – but it was forbidden. Tell me what happened in Zagor's study after those death demons took me . . .'

*

Libra turned to the others.

'Well, Logaan? My champion is still alive. The contest has ended. Is not the victory mine?'

Logaan nodded. 'Aye. Victory is yours.'

Also in Puffin

Steve Jackson's
SORCERY!

1: THE SHAMUTANTI HILLS

Your search for the legendary Crown of Kings takes you to the Shamutanti Hills. Alive with evil creatures, lawless wanderers and bloodthirsty monsters, the land is riddled with tricks and traps waiting for the unwary traveller. Will you be able to cross the hills safely and proceed to the second part of the adventure – or will you perish in the attempt?

2: KHARÉ – CITYPORT OF TRAPS

As a warrior relying on force of arms, or a wizard trained in magic, you must brave the terror of a city built to trap the unwary. You will need all your wits about you to survive the unimaginable horrors ahead and to make sense of the clues which may lead to your success – or to your doom!

3: THE SEVEN SERPENTS

Seven deadly and magical serpents speed ahead of you to warn the evil Archmage of your coming. Will you be able to catch them before they get there?

4: THE CROWN OF KINGS

At the end of your long trek, you face the unknown terrors of the Mampang Fortress. Hidden inside the keep is the Crown of Kings – the ultimate goal of the *Sorcery!* epic. But beware! For if you have not defeated the Seven Serpents, your arrival has been anticipated . . .

Complete with all the magical spells you will need, each book can be played either on its own or as part of the whole epic.

THE CRETAN CHRONICLES

BLOODFEUD OF ALTHEUS
AT THE COURT OF KING MINOS
RETURN OF THE WANDERER

John Butterfield, David Honigmann, Philip Parker

Set in the mythological world of Ancient Greece, this 3-book epic brings an exciting historical dimension to Adventure Gamebooks. YOU are Altheus, sent to avenge the death of Theseus, your elder brother, whose body lies trapped in the labyrinth of King Minos. The combat system has been extended to incorporate the concepts of honour and shame.

OUT OF THE PIT
Fighting Fantasy Monsters

Steve Jackson and Ian Livingstone

From the darkest corners, from the deepest pools and from the dungeons thought only to exist in nightmares come the Fighting Fantasy monsters – the downfall of many a brave warrior. Two hundred and fifty of these loathsome creatures from the wild and dangerous worlds of Fighting Fantasy are collected here – some are old adversaries, many you have yet to meet – each of them described in minute detail. An indispensable guide for Fighting Fantasy adventurers!

FIGHTING FANTASY

Steve Jackson

The world of Fighting Fantasy, peopled by Orcs, dragons, zombies and vampires, has captured the imagination of millions of readers world-wide. Thrilling adventures of sword and sorcery come to life in the Fighting Fantasy Gamebooks, where the reader is the hero, dicing with death and demons in search of villains, treasure or freedom.

Now YOU can create your own Fighting Fantasy adventures and send your friends off on dangerous missions! In this clearly written handbook, Steve Jackson has put together everything you need to become a successful GamesMaster. There are hints on devising challenging combats, monsters to use, tricks and tactics, as well as two mini-adventures complete with GamesMaster's notes for you to start with. The ideal introduction to the fast-growing world of role-playing games, and literally countless adventures.

THE AMAZING SPIDER-MAN
in CITY IN DARKNESS
Jeff Grubb

YOU are the Amazing Spider-Man! Something – or someone – has plunged Manhattan into a blackout in order to send YOU a warning. And it's clear that they want YOU out of the picture! It could be any one of your old foes – all dastardly villains using their powers to further their own evil aims. But your super-human abilities are used in the fight *against* crime . . .

CAPTAIN AMERICA
in ROCKET'S RED GLARE
Kate Novak

YOU are Captain America, defender of liberty and champion of justice. Viper is a vicious adversary – her scheme to shatter world peace and replace it with anarchy propels you into action! Can you outmanoevre this venomous vixen and save your country from annihilation?

Fantasy titles in Penguins, for older readers

THE DRAGONLANCE CHRONICLES
Margaret Weis and Tracy Hickman

From the creators of *Dungeons and Dragons* now comes *Dragonlance*, an exciting new fantasy trilogy about the creatures of legend who threaten the destruction of the world of Krynn.

A group of long-time friends – knight and barbarian, warrior and half-elf, dwarf and kender and dark-souled mage – are given the power to save the world. Join their exciting adventures in a quest to find the True Gods and save Krynn from endless night.

1. *Dragons of Autumn Twilight*

A small band of unlikely heroes set out on their quest to save Krynn from the dragons' evil grasp. They have hope – a blue crystal staff in the hands of a beautiful woman – and they have courage. But the forces of evil are strong . . .

2. *Dragons of Winter Night*

The darkness deepens and the companions begin a dangerous search for the Dragon Orbs and the legendary Dragonlance, ancient weapons of the True Gods.

3. *Dragons of Spring Dawning*

The dread enemy, Takhisis, the Queen of Darkness, poisons all with her evil. Only Tanis, the leader of the band of heroes, has the will to destroy it. He must summon all his strength, courage and faith for the ordeal which lies ahead . . .